I0679058

Wicked Games

Kerrie DuBrock

Wicked Games

Copyright © 2013 by Kerrie DuBrock

All rights reserved. No part of this book may be reproduced or transmitted in any form or by any means without written permission of the author.

ISBN-10: 0615870899
ISBN-13: 978-0615870892

Authors Note

This is a work of fiction. Names, characters and incidents either are the product of the author's imagination or are used fictitiously, and any resemblance to actual persons, living or dead, business establishments, events or locales is entirely coincidental.

Dedicated to Beverly Raines

Acknowledgments

I'd like to thank the readers for following me on my adventure! Without you, I'd have no reason to write!

My sister, Kim Courtright, who has supported my writing every step of the way!

My brother-in-law, Steve Courtright, who gave me the name of my last book (Merchants with Evil Intent). I ashamedly forgot to mention in him in those credits! But to make up for it, I created a character who represents him in this book!

My friend, Susan Rakis, for offering to read the unfinished product and encouraging me all the way.

Kathy Royce, once my mentor but forever my friend, for reading rough drafts, finding errors and being a pain-in-the-ass for the rest of the manuscript!

My brother, Wayne Gray, for the inside drawing. I really wanted this to be the cover, but, unfortunately, it didn't work the way I planned.

And last but not least, I'd also like to thank my nephew, Allen Gray, for not only coloring in the drawing, but for also creating the final cover!

Prologue

Ten year old Chase Storm dribbled a basketball as he headed home. Nearing his house he spied a limo in the circular driveway.

Is dad going on another business trip?

The chauffer loaded several suitcases into the trunk, causing Chase to frown. Dad never took more than one suitcase.

His mom, Andrea, climbed into the backseat, holding a tissue to her eyes, while his dad stood stoically on the cement steps leading to the house.

Chase clutched the basketball and ran as the limo began to pull away.

Reaching his dad he panted, "Where's mom going?"

Preston Storm placed a trembling hand on his son's shoulder. "I'm not sure."

Chase's bottom lip began to quiver. "I don't understand."

"Neither do I," Preston sighed, shaking his head.

Tears pricked the back of Chase's eyes and when he glanced up he noticed unshed tears pooling in his dads eyes.

"Come along, son," he gently murmured.

"When's she coming back?" Chase whimpered, wiping the escaped tears from his flushed face.

"She isn't, son."

Five year old Emily Waters tugged at the life jacket with a frown. "I don't wanna wear this mama!"

A worried look crossed Martha Waters face. Gripping Emily's shoulders she replied, "I know sweetie, but keep it on."

Waves pounded against the fishing boat while the sky overhead crackled with lightening.

"Marty! Help me!" yelled Dorothy Waters, from the cabin. Marty turned, giving Emily a firm look.

"Stay with your cousin and don't move," she warned.

Emily's bottom lip trembled as she watched the adults scramble to ready the boat for departure. She glanced at her older cousin and scowled. *He's not wearing a stupid life jacket!*

The outboard motor roared to life and pulled away from the beach.

Gusts of wind rocked the boat side to side, up and down. It felt like the carnival ride she rode with her dad, but not as fun. She gripped the straps of the jacket and pulled them apart, ridding herself of the garment.

"Big wave! Everyone hold on!" Uncle Gary shouted.

Emily placed her tiny hands on the metal railing, but her grip wasn't strong enough. The boat pitched to the side tossing her into the lake.

She tried to scream, but water filled her mouth and lungs. As she sank deeper into the water she felt a gentle tug on her hand.

"I'll take care of you, baby," rasped the flesh-eaten man.

*   *   *

The Grey One lurked in the murky depths of the lake, shaking angrily. "Checkmate," chuckled Shekinah, hovering in the clouds.

Chapter One

20 years later

"I've got to go, baby," he murmured, pulling away from the luscious red-head beneath him.

"Chase, it's only two in the afternoon. Stay with me," she breathily pleaded.

Pulling on his khaki slacks he looked over his shoulder and grinned, exposing deep dimples. "You've had me an hour longer than we agreed upon. Remember? Seven days of heaven? Baby, your time was up an hour ago."

Denise sat up with a jolt. "I thought that was a joke. You only wanted a week with me?" she pouted.

He tugged his dark blue polo shirt over his head. "Yep," he replied matter-of-factly.

"You're an asshole!" she screamed, lunging for him.

"Whoa, baby, watch the talons!" he smirked, backing away.

Denise wrapped the pink bed sheet around her. "You used me," she whispered.

Chase shoved his feet into brown loafers. Shaking his head he snorted, "We used each other. I told you when we met I'm not the dating kind. You said you understood. Clearly, you didn't," he shrugged. "Not my problem."

*   *   *

"Em! Come here!" Freddie shouted through the back door of Play it Again Sam.

Emily bid goodbye to the last customer of the day, promptly locking the front door, before heading into the back room of her antique shop.

Freddie leaned against his pick-up truck, arms crossed over his chest, beaming.

She tucked an errant strand of hair from her ponytail behind her ear and raised a thin eyebrow. "Well?"

"Come here," he urged, taking her hand.

He opened the tailgate of the truck and lifted the window of the cap. "Ta-da!"

Emily peered inside and grinned. "Where didja get it?" she asked.

He shrugged, "On the side of the road. Not a thing wrong with it, either. Come on; let's get it in the shop."

Together they wrestled the antique maple armoire from the truck and carried into the storeroom.

Emily walked around the new acquisition, eyeing it curiously after removing the nylon rope that held the doors closed.

Freddie returned with a skeleton key. Wiggling his eyebrows he grinned, "Let's see if there's anything inside."

A soft click was heard with the turn of the key causing the doors to open slowly.

"Whew! Did someone pour a whole bottle of perfume in this thing?" he asked covering his nose.

Emily frowned. "No, not perfume."

Freddie's eyes widened at her expression. "Crap! Again?"

2

"Yep," she mumbled, smiling at the transparent woman in front of her.

*   *   *

"My gift arrived safely, I hope," Chase murmured into his cell phone.

"Yeah! Can't you ever do anything on a small scale?" complained his brother-in-law, Neil.

From the eighty-sixth floor of his condo, Chase took a deep breath. The skyline of Chicago was always something to be marveled. "Small scale isn't in my vocabulary."

Neil glowered at the phone. "Are you coming for the unveiling?"

"I wouldn't miss Candace's birthday for the world. See you at five," Chase replied ending the call.

He checked his watch. He had a few minutes before leaving for the suburbs.

Christ, how could people live there? Still, he supposed someone had to.

After all, he did help design some of those homes. He shuddered at the thought.

He much preferred designing buildings. Not just buildings, but huge fucking skyscrapers. Yep, that's where the money was.

Dad preferred cookie cutter homes, said they were the bread and butter of life.

And, after all these years, dad hadn't changed his tune.

*   *   *

"She didn't follow us home, did she?" asked Freddie as he and Emily walked into their house.

"No, she's at the shop. She's attached to the armoire. Said the owner of it was a jackass and didn't deserve such finery," Emily laughed.

"Did she say how it ended up alongside the road?"

"Lilly slammed the doors to show her displeasure with the owner and she spooked him enough that he dumped it."

"Great. It's haunted by a psycho ghost," he snorted, flopping onto the hunter green couch.

"It'll be fine. She'll pick the right person to purchase it and then she'll go away," Emily offered. "Now I have a birthday party to get ready for."

"Are you going to make the show tonight?" Freddie frowned.

She ruffled his light brown hair. "I'll always be there to see you play, you know that."

He shot her a lop-sided grin as she climbed the steps to the bedroom.

*   *   *

Climbing into his Porsche 911, Chases cell phone vibrated; an incoming text message from Denise.

ASSHOLE!

He shook his head disgustedly, then quickly brightened. Thank God he only gave her his cell number and not his address!

*   *   *

Emily arrived at the party, maneuvering to the back yard.

It was a beautiful day. The sun nestled between white fluffy clouds, a gentle breeze kept away the bugs and the scent of peonies enveloped the air.

Instantly she was greeted by Neil.

"Em! So glad you could make it!" he grinned, hugging her.

"Sorry I'm late," she murmured into his shoulder.

4

"No problem. Come on, let's get you something to drink," he replied, tugging her hand.

Beth Storm-Lane squeaked when she saw Emily and ran across the lawn to pull her into a tight embrace.

The way the Lane's acted, a bystander would be led to believe that the three people had been friends forever. That wasn't the case, however.

A cursory stop at Emily's store caused the friendship to happen.

Beth had an overwhelming urge to stop in front of Play it Again Sam, not knowing why, only knowing she had to.

Upon entering the store she was greeted by Emily who instantly led her towards the avionic book section of her shop.

Beth snorted. She had no interest in flying, let alone reading about it, until she saw a book, written by her deceased Grandfather.

Her throat constricted as she ran her hand over the brown leather cover.

Emily backed away, nodding to the iridescent man standing next to his granddaughter.

With a blink of an eye, he was gone.

* * *

Neil walked past his brothers-in-law Chase and Jason to put Emily's present for Candace onto the gift table.

"Hey Neil, who's the babe talking with Beth?" Chase asked.

Neil looked over his shoulder. "Her name is Off-Limits."

Chase cocked his head, "Funny name for such a pretty thing."

"She's not your type," Neil scowled.

Chase smirked, "Why Neil, they're *all* my type. In fact, it's been a while since I've had a honey-blonde."

"I mean it. She's a nice girl," Neil hissed, tired of Chase's cavalier attitude towards women.

"Nice girls can be naughty, too," Chase sneered.

Neil shook his head in disgust. "Are you ever gonna settle down?"

"Nope. Why should I? Variety is the spice of life, my friend."

"Boys, can't we just get along?" Jason interrupted.

"Sure. All Neil has to do is introduce me," Chase offered.

"I said to forget her," Neil replied through clenched teeth.

* * *

Emily glanced around, sipping punch. A huge wrapped gift sat at the edge of the large yard.

Funny, Beth didn't mention Neil had built a playhouse for Candace.

Her attention was diverted when the roaring sound of motorcycles approached and shortly afterward three men entered the backyard.

"Chaser!" a bald man, with a long red beard, yelled across the yard.

'Chaser' moved towards him, hand extended.

'Chaser' was a looker; definite eye candy with tousled collar length sandy blonde hair.

He wore form fitting blue jeans with a white oxford shirt, unbuttoned low enough to see chest hair.

Emily took a gulp of punch and fanned herself.

* * *

"Danny! Lookin' good!" Chase said, pumping Dan Martin's hand.

"He looks like shit," teased Rick O'Shea, clapping Chase on the back.

"Where's the Harley?" frowned Denny Marsh.

Chase shrugged, "Drove the 911 today. Poker run tomorrow, right?"

Jason and Neil joined the small crowd and an animated conversation began about the next day's activities. Chase's gaze shifted, ignoring the men huddled around him, focusing only on the beauty in the brown sundress.

Her hair cascaded to her slim shoulders. Legs looked a mile long. He caught himself licking his lips.

"Earth to Chase," teased Rick.

"Huh?" Chase muttered, distracted.

"Tomorrow. We'll meet here?" Rick laughed.

"Yeah. Sounds great. Excuse me, won't you?" he mumbled, walking towards the beauty.

After all, she was ogling him as much as he was ogling her.

Nice girl, my ass.

*   *   *

"Oh-oh, Mr. Playboy is headed our way," mumbled Sarah, Jason's wife, to Emily.

"Mr. Playboy?" questioned Emily.

Sarah laughed. "Surely Beth has told you about her uber-rich brother, Chase?"

"Um, no."

"Well, he has a saying. 'Seven days of heaven'."

Emily smiled at the chestnut haired woman, shrugging. "Huh?"

Sarah laughed, "He only dates a woman for a week."

Emily cocked her head to the side. "I still don't understand."

"Sarah, you're looking beautiful, as usual," Chase crooned, kissing his sister-in-law lightly on the cheek.

"Chase. It's good to see you, too," she smiled.

He lifted his Ray-Bans and took Emily's hand into his. "Chase Storm and I'm *very* pleased to meet you."

All the spirits Emily encountered never left her feeling as she did now…unsteady.

"Chase, this is Emily Waters. Emily, Chase," Sarah replied, rolling her eyes.

"A beautiful name for a beautiful girl," Chase murmured, still clutching her hand.

When she finally found her voice Emily smiled, "Mr. Storm."

He smirked, exposing deep dimples, "Chase, please."

"Chase, behave yourself," Sarah warned before walking away.

Emily's hazel eyes matched the color of her sundress, he mused. And her perfume? It smelled like nectar from the god's.

Her throat went dry and to her dismay she was out of punch. But, it gave her good reason to move away from him. His cologne had an alluring effect on her. She could bury her face in his neck and breathe it in all day.

Her eyes widened. She needed to put some distance between them.

"Well, Chase, it was very nice to meet you," she smiled coyly.

"Are you leaving already?" he asked, grasping her elbow.

"Um, no, I'm going to get more punch."

"Oh, I'll walk with you," he offered, relieved she wasn't leaving.

He threw his beer bottle into the trash, taking the cup from her hands

8

he ladled Beth's homemade punch into it, sweeping a gaze over her quickly and thoroughly.

His gaze intimidated her. He reminded her of a lion ready for the kill.

"Emmy!" Candace screeched, clutching Emily's legs.

The force of Candace against the back of her legs threw her off balance. Chase caught her from falling.

"Candace!" Chase admonished.

Emily flushed, gripping onto Chase's upper arms for support. *Wow. His biceps are huge.*

"I'm sowwy, Emmy," Candace pouted.

Emily righted herself and smiled at Chase. "That's okay, Candace. Happy birthday, sweetie," she murmured, hugging the little red haired girl.

Chase caught a glimpse of cleavage when she bent to pick Candace up.

Nice, he grinned.

"Didja see the big pwesent Uncle Chase got me?"

Emily turned her head and caught him admiring her chest.

When he looked up at her, his face reddened. He wasn't a blusher, so it took him off guard.

"Um…the…um…big wrapped present is from me," he choked out.

Emily lifted an eyebrow and pasted a false smile on her lips. "What do you think it is?"

Candace squirmed to be put down, "A playhouse! 'Cause that's what I want!"

Emily purposely turned to face Chase when she bent to put Candace down, this time giving him a full show of what he'd never get to enjoy.

He choked on his beer at the sight.

Choked so much that it damn near came out his nose!

*   *   *

The cake had been served, presents unwrapped and the sun settled low in the sky, casting red, purple and gold along the horizon.

Emily was saying her goodbyes when Chase approached.

"Hey," he said huskily. "You weren't going to leave without saying goodbye, were you?"

She shrugged, "I didn't think you'd be offended."

His chin jutted out smugly. "Well, frankly I am."

She extended her right hand, warily. "It was nice to meet you, Mr. Storm."

He took her hand, a huge grin on his face. "Chase. I'll walk you to your car."

She started to protest, but he lifted an eyebrow daring her.

"So, do you visit Beth often?" he asked, holding the white wooden gate open for her.

She shrugged, "Yeah. She's become a good friend."

Chase scanned the cars lined along the street. He spotted a blue Chevy sedan and walked towards it.

She pulled away from his grasp. "Where are you going?"

"To your car, of course," he mumbled.

She tilted her head. "My car is that way," she motioned.

"Oh, my mistake," he murmured, curious now as to what vehicle she drove.

She stepped in front of a red Dodge Challenger and fished keys from her purse.

10

His mouth dropped. *A muscle car?*

"Is something wrong, Mr. Storm?" she grinned.

"You're kidding, right?"

She grinned, pulling the door open. "Thanks for walking me to my car."

With that, she closed the door and put the key in the ignition.

Expecting to hear the loud rumble of the car's engine, she frowned when it didn't even make a clucking sound. She steeled herself and tried the ignition again. Nothing.

Chase tapped on the window, a grin on his face. "Something wrong?" he asked when she opened the door.

She snapped, "Clearly, if the engine isn't turning over."

"Pop the hood," he offered.

She climbed out of the car and looked at the engine with him.

She parked under a street light, but he couldn't see any noticeable problems. Resting his hands on the edge of the car he looked at her. "I can jump you."

She narrowed her eyes and crossed her arms over her chest.

"I mean your car. Maybe the battery is dead," he clarified.

"Oh," she mumbled, embarrassed.

Neither of them saw the blonde woman hiding behind the elm tree, giggling.

*   *   *

She appreciatively glanced around the inside of his 911. It was an ostentatious show of money, but man, what a nice, smooth ride.

"Thanks for driving me," she said softly.

11

Chase shrugged, "No problem. I'll have a tow truck take your car to my mechanic, since the jump didn't work."

"Your offer is very kind, but Freddie can look at it tomorrow."

"Freddie?"

"Yeah. That's who I'm going to see tonight," she replied pressing a button on the door to roll down the window.

"Are you hot?" he asked seductively.

A smile formed on her lips, causing her to look away. "A little."

He was a bit rattled she had a 'Freddie'. It nagged him, actually. After several moments of silence he questioned her. "Freddie your boyfriend?"

She shrugged, "Well, he is a boy, a man actually, and a friend."

He tore his gaze away from the road and looked at her. Her face belied nothing.

"You're being evasive," he commented.

"And you're being nosey," she countered.

He pulled his car over and stopped abruptly, causing her to grip the dashboard.

"Look, obviously I'm interested in you and I think you're interested in me. Having said that I'd like for you to tell me if you're dating this Freddie person," he ground out.

A small laugh escaped her lips when she noticed a vein pulsing in the side of his head when he raked his fingers through his hair.

"Are you laughing at me?" he asked with a lop-sided grin.

"Yep!" she nodded and began a full out giggle.

Her laugh was contagious, causing him to laugh as well.

She was beguiling! And still didn't answer his question.

12

"Well..." he prompted.

She rolled her eyes. "We're friends who live together. Satisfied?"

His eyebrows knitted together, "Friends with benefits?"

"Ew! Gross! No! Jeesh! That's wrong on so many levels!" she snipped.

He raised his hands in the air and slammed them onto the steering wheel, exasperated. "You're giving me nothing here."

"What difference does it make? I'm not going to join your 'seven days of heaven club' or whatever it is you have," she snapped.

Blanching at her comment he pulled onto the street.

*   *   *

The remaining ride to The Razz was quiet.

Who the fuck told her about seven days of heaven? He wondered.

He pulled up to the doors and eyed her thoughtfully as she got out.

"Thank you, again, for the ride, Mr. Storm."

"You're very welcome, Miss Waters. Enjoy the rest of your evening," he coolly replied.

She nodded and closed the door. She watched him pull onto the street, not sure why she felt a sudden pang.

*   *   *

"What the fuck did you tell her Neil?" Chase yelled into the phone.

"What are you talking about?"

"Emily. She knew about seven days of heaven and I want to know exactly what you told her!"

"I didn't tell her anything but if you're so concerned what women think maybe you ought to stop acting like a juvenile!" Neil ground out.

"Put Beth on!"

"Chase? What's wrong?" Beth said into the phone.

Parked in a grocery store parking lot he ran his hand over his face. "Someone told Emily about seven days of heaven."

Beth laughed, "So?"

"So? So, I kind of like her," Chase admitted.

"For more than seven days?" she pushed.

Chase rolled his eyes and snorted, "Maybe."

But he really meant hardly.

*   *   *

Emily sat at the bar and gazed at Freddie in rapt attention. She could listen to him sing all day, his voice was melodious.

Plus, it helped to get her mind off Chase.

The nerve of him to assume she'd put time into a useless relationship.

She already did that with Joe.

A years' worth and she didn't plan on making the same mistake twice.

She sipped a Margarita and tapped her foot to the beat of *Black Magic Woman*.

*   *   *

After getting the full run-down on Emily Waters, Chase drove back to The Razz.

He couldn't understand it.

Women were never a challenge.

He supposed it had a lot to do with his money and less to do with his

14

personality.

It didn't matter. He used them as much as they used him.

So why, was he chasing after Emily Waters?

The reason escaped him.

* * *

Emily maneuvered her way to a table near the stage.

"I thought you weren't gonna make it," pouted Freddie.

"Sorry, but my car wouldn't start. Someone had to drive me here."

"You missed a kick-ass set, " he teased. "Who brought you?"

She shrugged and blushed, "Some guy."

Freddie leaned in. "Do tell."

She waved her hand dismissively. "Chase Storm. He's Beth's brother."

"Chase *fucking* Storm?" he asked with wide eyes.

She laughed, "I'm not sure if *fucking* is his middle name. Do you know him?"

Freddie eyed her incredulously. "Duh! He's one of the most eligible bachelors in Chicago *and* he's rich. His picture was in the paper yesterday, his company bought tons of farm land to put in tract housing."

She lifted a narrow shoulder. "Don't know, don't care."

Freddie grinned, "You like him."

"I do not! He's arrogant and pretentious," she scoffed.

"He's also here," Freddie smiled, motioning towards the bar.

* * *

She took a long pull on her straw and acted like she didn't see him.

He sauntered towards her, holding a bottle of Corona.

"Miss Waters," he winked.

"Mr. Storm," she nodded.

Freddie jumped up and took Chase's free hand. "Nice to meet you, Mr. Storm. I'm Freddie."

A smirk formed on Chase's face as he shook Freddie's hand firmly.

He measured Freddie for a long moment. Not a bad looking guy. His brown hair was kind of long, but then again so was his, he mused. Chase wondered what ol' Freddie would think if he knew he was interested in his woman.

A man and a woman don't live together platonically. Not possible. *Ever.*

"Do you mind if I join you and Emily?"

"Nah, besides I have to start my next set." He kissed Emily chastely on the cheek. "I'll play your favorite, 'kay?"

When Chase took Freddie's seat, his knee brushed against Emily's, causing her to fidget.

The rest of the band took the stage and Freddie began plucking the strings of his Fender Stratocaster. "This song is for my cousin Emily."

Chase lifted an eyebrow when Freddie began to sing *Wicked Game.*

Her cousin! Chase had a hard time stifling his grin.

When the song ended, Emily jumped up and clapped, Chase joined her.

"Favorite song, eh?" he said into her ear.

His breath fanned her face seductively, causing her to shiver slightly.

They didn't talk during the rest of Freddie's set. He'd wait to talk to her when he drove her home, if she allowed him the pleasure.

*   *   *

Emily would rather be anywhere at the moment except for Chase Storm's Porsche 911.

He chuckled, pulling away from the bar. "Am I really that abhorrent?"

"No, not really," she frowned.

"Then why do you look like you'd rather be somewhere else?"

"Because I don't know what your intentions are and it makes me uneasy," she said softly.

He ran a hand through his thick hair. "Look, I'm not as bad as you may have heard. I mean, yes, there is a thing I call seven days of heaven, but really, it can be enjoyable."

"How?" she snorted.

"Well, I take measures to be with a woman, you perhaps, for seven full days. Dinners, little trips, sex, whatever and then when the time is up, we go our separate ways. No strings attached," he stated, matter-of-factly.

She shuddered. "That sounds cold. Do many women agree to that?"

"There's been a few who haven't," he mumbled. "Look, I'm not looking for a serious relationship. I don't do the dating thing. I more-or-less do the *fucking* thing, which the woman also benefits from."

She shot him a glare. "That's crude, Mr. Storm."

"Chase. The name is Chase, okay?" he sighed. "Look, I'm not good at relationships. Been there, done that. I know my limitations."

"So, you just give up? Stop looking for Miss Right and screw anything in sight?"

"I don't screw just anything, Emily. I'm very selective in the women I choose," he clarified.

17

"This is my house," she pointed towards an old Victorian.

He pulled into the driveway and turned off the ignition, resting his head against the headrest.

"Look, Emily, I feel something between us," he confessed.

She lifted her chin. "It's called lust on your part and disgust on mine. Good evening, Mr. Storm."

* * *

It was three in the morning and Emily couldn't fall asleep.

Stupid Chase Storm.

What kind of name was that anyway?

She rolled over and punched her pillow. After a while she fell asleep and dreamt of a woman with short blonde hair and blue eyes.

* * *

Chase rolled into the parking garage a little after two in morning. He tried to drown his thoughts of Emily away by listening to heavy metal on the expressway.

It didn't work.

In fact, after a few shots of whiskey, he still thought of her.

Why?

'Cause she's not interested in you, ya dumb ass!

He lifted his chin.

It'd been a long time since he'd been snubbed by a woman. That was the beauty of seven days of heaven.

He got to be the snubber.

* * *

Freddie dropped Emily off at the Lane's home around seven in the morning. She brushed a bead of sweat from her brow, the humidity already stifling.

Beth came outside when she saw Emily standing by her car.

"Hey Emily."

"Hi Beth. I'm waiting for the tow truck," she frowned, looking at her watch. "He should've been here by now."

"Why don't you come in and have coffee while you wait," Beth offered.

"I don't want to impose. I know it's early." Emily's eyes narrowed when she heard the loud motor of the tow truck.

"Wow, he's a good looking guy," Beth remarked when the driver stepped out of the truck.

Emily lifted an eyebrow.

Yep, Joe was good looking. Jet black hair, baby blue eyes and a well muscled body. His white t-shirt hugged his body while tight faded blue jeans cupped his back-side in a very pleasing way.

Too bad he was an asshole.

He sauntered over, showing his pearly whites. Planting a kiss on Emily's cheek he crooned, "Hey baby."

The atmosphere went from muggy to glacial in nanoseconds. "Joe," she replied coolly.

"Ma'am," he nodded to Beth.

Emily made brief introductions and handed Joe her keys. "Please hurry. I need to get to the shop."

"Don't worry, baby, if I can't fix it now I'll drop you off and bring this beast back to my shop."

She rolled her eyes at Beth when he walked away.

Beth giggled, "I wish my mechanic looked that great and kissed me."

"Trust me, his looks are his *only* redeeming factor," Emily sighed.

Beth nudged Emily with her elbow. "Hey! What happened between you and Chase last night?"

Emily shrugged, "Nothing. He dropped me off at the bar and came back for some reason. Later, he took me home."

"So…" Beth prodded.

"So…nothing."

"He likes you," Beth smiled.

"Please! He just wants me to be part of his demented seven day scheme. Does he really do that?" Emily shuddered.

"Sadly, yeah. I've never understood why," Beth replied wistfully.

They were interrupted by the roar of rolling thunder as five motorcycles descended upon the Lane home.

Beth shook her head, looking up at the sky. "My neighbors are gonna shit!" She ran to the riders, yelling at them to keep the noise level down.

Emily's eyes widened when she noticed one of the riders was Chase.

He wore faded blue jeans that were ripped at the knees and a blue t-shirt. No helmet, just his Ray-Bans.

He acted as if he didn't notice her, purposely turning his back to her.

The slight stung her.

The sound of her car's engine coming to life startled her from her reverie.

Joe got out of the car and grinned. "Nothing wrong with the car," he murmured, putting his hand on her waist, pulling her close.

She pulled away, but he held her still. "What did you do?"

He snorted, "I put the key in the ignition and turned it." She lifted her eyebrow to him. "You just wanted to see me, didn't you?" he smiled.

* * *

"Who's the guy groping Emily?" Chase growled.

Beth smirked, "Her mechanic."

He turned away. *What the fuck is wrong with me? Why do I care?*

He tried to make casual conversation with his riding buddies, but when he heard Emily yell, he rolled his head towards his back and cursed.

* * *

"Get your hands off me," Emily said through gritted teeth.

"C'mon, baby, there's nothing wrong with your car. You wanted to see me, didn't you?" Joe murmured, wrapping a strand of her hair around his finger.

"I believe the lady said to take your hands off of her," Chase said menacingly low.

Joe's eyes blinked and he stepped hesitantly away from her. "This is none of your business," he growled, fists at his sides.

Chase took his sunglasses off and peered into Emily's eyes. His eyes were dark, not the light blue color they were yesterday, she noticed.

"Emily, are you okay?" he softly asked. She shook her head slowly. "Do you want this guy to leave?" She nodded, chewing her bottom lip.

Chase narrowed his eyes at the mechanic. "Beat it," he uttered in a clipped tone.

Joe snorted, "Fine, I'm outta here. I'll send you a bill Em."

"For what? You only started her car," Chase scoffed.

21

Joe pointed at Emily, not taking his eyes from the man next to her. "She's haunted, dude."

Chase wrapped a protective arm around her shoulders, replying icily, "We're all haunted. *Dude*."

*　　*　　*

The tow truck started noisily, screeching its tires in its departure.

"Hey, you okay?" Chase asked, running his hand up and down her arm.

She nodded. She'd never have a normal life and Joe was always so eager to point that out.

Chase hesitated. She *wasn't* okay and that jag-off really upset her. He wanted to pull her into his arms, but wasn't sure how she'd react.

He didn't deal well with rejection.

"Come on, Chaser! We gotta roll," the red bearded man yelled.

"I gotta go. Poker run," he explained.

"Um, thanks," she said softly.

He nodded, put his Ray Bans on and strode towards his motorcycle.

"My, he's handsome," a feminine voice said next to her.

Emily turned. It wasn't unusual for her to not see spirits. Sometimes she only heard them.

"You should've kissed him goodbye. You know you want to," the voice murmured. "He's got that bad boy look today. Mussed hair, jeans that hang low on his hips, and you've already felt how muscular he is."

Emily narrowed her eyes at the annoying voice.

She leaned against her car and watched as the riders pulled away from the curb; Chase followed the pack.

"You may never get another chance, Emily! You've brushed him away before. He won't make another move until you do," the voice urged.

She held up her hand to stop him. Quizzically he stopped in front of her. The rumbling from the bike made her skin vibrate and her pulse quicken. Without thinking, she took his chin firmly in her hand and kissed him chastely.

Chase smiled beneath her lips. Steadying the bike between his legs he brought his palms up to her face and kissed her deeply.

The sensation of his warm, minty tongue against hers and the vibration of the bike caused a soft moan to escape from her lips.

Satisfied he just rocked her world, Chase pulled back and grinned smugly at her. "Gotta roll, baby."

She watched him race to catch up with his friends, breathless.

"Ahem."

Emily turned and blushed when she saw Beth's expression. "That was some kiss," Beth commented.

Emily brought her hand to her moist lips and blushed again.

Beth took her gently by the upper arm. "Please don't tell me you're going to do the 'heaven' thing, Em. You're too good for that."

Emily looked at her, offended. "Of course not. I don't even know why I kissed him." Beth lifted an eyebrow. "I mean, yeah, I thought about it, but a voice told me to do it," she stammered.

Beth whipped her head around. She'd always wanted to see a ghost.

"She goaded me into doing it," Emily sighed.

"Yeah, but did you like it?" Beth prodded.

Emily rolled her eyes. "Yeah. Your brother knows how to kiss."

*　　　*　　　*

She kissed him! Chase still reeled about that four hours later and the smile hadn't left his face, either.

Maybe she *was* interested in the 'heaven' thing. He scoffed. Of course she was interested!

Chapter Two

Emily took a steadying breath. "Lilly, are you sure you weren't with me earlier?"

"Now sweetheart, you know I'm bound by my armoire," the blonde haired spirit replied. "It must've been some other ghost."

"Ya can't pin it on me!" Phyllis roared, appearing from behind a large oval mirror.

Emily smiled at her warmly. Filly was a flapper from the 1920's and still dressed the part with a short black fringed dress, black sequined head-band and black boa wrapped around her neck.

Emily hastily turned on the lights around the shop preparing to open.

"Em, ya look like hell!" Filly noticed as she applied bright red lipstick to her full lips.

"Yeah, I didn't get much sleep last night," Emily sighed. Thoughts of Chase Storm kept her from slumbering.

Filly's eyes brightened and she followed Emily into the storage room. "Spill it!"

Blushing, Emily rolled her eyes. "It's nothing. I met a cute guy and let's just say he's not my type."

"He's livin' and breathin' ain't he?"

"Um, yeah," Emily laughed.

Filly shrugged, "So, what's the problem?"

"He only dates women for a week and then moves on," Emily lifted a shoulder.

"I've never!" Lilly gasped, putting her hand over her mouth.

Filly rolled her eyes and muttered, "That's obvious." She tossed her boa around her neck and sighed. "In my day men like that were called lounge lizards."

"Lounge lizards?" both Emily and Lilly asked.

"Yep. It meant that they liked to have sex," Filly shrugged. "Don't fall for him, Em. He'll only break your heart." She smiled wistfully and disappeared.

"She seems sad," Lilly noticed, frowning.

"Yeah, she's never told me much about her life," Emily replied as she counted the money in the register.

"Has she been around here long?" Lilly wondered.

Emily closed the cash drawer and smiled. "Yeah, I met her when I was in high school. Jeesh, that's been eight years now. In fact, she came in with a piece of jewelry, a brooch. C'mon, I'll show ya."

There were three glass jewelry cases in the front of the shop and the light from the sun showed how dusty and finger smudged they were.

Emily rolled her eyes. "I'll look for it while I clean."

Lilly wrung her hand. "I wish I could help."

"Me too!" Emily laughed. "I'll tell ya what. I'll tell you about myself and then if you'd like, you can tell me about yourself."

"I'd like that," Lilly smiled, following Emily to the storage room.

"I took over this store after I graduated from college with a degree in marketing. My parents retired to Florida and knowing how much I love the store, they gave it to me as my graduation present. But then, with money being tight, my cousin Jenny offered to be my partner so you'll be seeing her around here often."

Lilly sat in an armless rocker, gently rocking listening to Emily. The conversation seemed so normal to her-despite the fact she was dead and had been for many, many years.

"So you can see spirits and talk to them?"

Em chuckled, "Yep. I've been able to communicate with spirits since I was very young." She shrugged and blew a strand of hair away. "While I've been able to deal with it, others can't."

Lilly's eyebrows knitted together. "Like who?"

Emily sprayed glass cleaner on the jewelry case and wiped in a circular motion, snorting. "Well, Joe, my ex-boyfriend, for one." She continued, "I don't tell many people of my ability. I've lost a lot of friends because of it."

Lilly sniffed, "It seems to me they must not have been very good friends to begin with."

Emily cocked her head. No one, alive or dead had ever said that before.

"Anyway, that's pretty much it, in a nutshell," Emily murmured.

Lilly lifted a thin eyebrow. "No husband?"

"Helllllllooooo darlin'!" Frankie crooned ala the Big Bopper, minus the baby part; he knew Em didn't like to be called 'baby'.

Emily grinned when he appeared. "This is Frankie, Lilly."

Frankie smoothed his hand over his greased hair and wiggled his eyebrow at Lilly. "Ma'am," he said deeply with a nod.

Lilly gaped at Frankie. He was dressed in blue pants that were cuffed at the bottom, a white short-sleeved t-shirt that had a small box rolled up in the sleeve, black shoes and a black coat draped over his thick arm.

Emily watched the two of them survey each other. "Um, Lilly, Frankie is from the 1950's. Back then the young guys dressed this way," she explained.

"What about the way she's dressed?" Frankie snorted, looking over her very prim white ruffled dress that barely showed any skin.

"Frankie!" Emily admonished. "Mind your manners! Lilly is from the 1800's and they dressed conservatively then."

"I'll say," he murmured, looking away from Lillie's stink eye. "Where's Filly?" *At least she's fun*, he thought.

Emily started to answer him when the bell over the front door chimed.

She smiled at her first customer of the day. "Good afternoon. Can I help you find anything?"

"That rocker," the blonde haired woman pointed at the rocker Lilly was seated in. "I want that."

Emily carefully picked up the antique rocker. It was always one of her favorites with the pink and red rose needle pointed cushions.

After the lady paid for her purchase, Emily carried the rocker out to her car and bade her a good day.

She reentered the shop, frowning. Lilly and Frankie were gone.

Frankie always left when a customer came in. He said he didn't want to give them the heebie-jeebies.

Emily sighed, wistfully. It'd be a long day without them to talk to. She picked up the cotton dust rag and began cleaning.

*   *   *

"Ricochet, another beer," barked Chase.

Rick O'Shea filled the mug to the top, frothy foam spilled over the sides. "So, what's the deal with that chick this morning? Didja get some last night?"

Chase's upper lip curled. It sounded crass when Ricochet put it that way. "No," he glared.

Ricochet choked on his beer. "No? Have you lost your touch?"

Chase shrugged nonchalantly, "Look, if I really wanted her, I could have her. I might make this one beg."

Ricochet let out a hardy laugh and downed his beer.

Chase sipped his slowly. He'd never had to lie about a woman before.

What was she doing to him?

*   *   *

Emily went around the shop turning off lights after locking the front door. While closing the cash register for the day she felt a presence. Standing on the other side of the counter was Lilly, with a puzzled expression.

"Lilly? Are you okay?"

She nodded slowly, her eyes distant. "No spirits left with your customers," she whispered.

Emily chuckled. "Not everything in my shop has a spirit attached."

"How many are here?" questioned Lilly.

Emily tucked a loose strand of hair behind her ear. "Well, right now it's you, Phyllis and Frankie. Frankie's been with me for three years and you're the newest addition."

Lilly's lip trembled. "And you don't mind that we're here?"

Emily reached out and placed her palm where Lilly's shoulder was. "Heavens, no. I consider Phyllis and Frankie part of my family and now you are too."

"Geez, Em, I didn't know you felt that way," Frankie suddenly

29

reappeared, skimming his black loafers against the carpeted floor.

"Of course I do, ya silly spook. I just wish Freddie and Jenny could see you so they'd know how wonderful you are," Emily frowned.

Frankie slid his palm against his greased hair and grinned. *Damn, if only he was alive*, Emily thought. He reminded her of Tony Curtis in his younger days. Jet black hair and killer blue eyes

Emily didn't notice Chase gazing at her through the large display window.

*   *   *

Chase's eyebrows furrowed. She was looking straight at him and her mouth was moving, but when he tried to pull the door open it was locked.

So, he pointed towards the door and saw her smile. "That's right, baby, let me in and I'll really give ya a smile," he muttered to himself.

He heard her laughing inside, but the door was still locked. He peered inside the small window on the door and frowned.

She stood behind the counter, making no move to open the door. Maybe that's why she was laughing.

His face burned. Then, he became indignant. No one laughed at him!

He furiously banged on the door.

*   *   *

The loud knocking on the door caused the three of them to jump. Emily rolled her eyes. Six customers all day and *now* someone wanted to shop?

"I'm sorry, but we're closed," she yelled through the door.

Chase's face filled the small window.

She placed her back against the door and closed her eyes.

"Want me to get rid of the problem, darlin'?" Frankie offered.

30

Blowing out a long breath she whispered, "No, I'll do it, but don't leave, okay?"

Chase glanced at her briefly before striding into the shop, like he owned the place. It didn't smell musty like he thought it would. In fact, it smelled like perfume, but not Emily's.

Frankie circled him, a scowl on his face while Lilly blushed.

Thinking Emily snuck up behind him, Chase turned and frowned when he saw her standing against the door.

"Is someone else here?" Chase asked.

"No. Just us."

Chase arched a brow and his eyes narrowed. "I saw you talking to someone."

Emily laughed it off. "Oh, I'm practicing for a play." It was her standard line when she got busted talking to thin air.

Chase grinned slightly. "Really? You like to act?" He stuffed his hands into his faded blue jean pockets.

She walked a wide arc to avoid walking into Frankie since he was practically nose to nose with Chase. She hid her grin. It amazed her that he didn't feel something with Frankie standing so close. Static electricity, goose bumps or at the very least a temperature drop.

"Who's the dream-boat?" Phyllis sighed breathily, inching closer to Chase.

Frankie rolled his eyes and snorted, "It's me, Frankie!"

Chase whipped his head around, positive someone stood behind him.

Emily half-coughed, half-laughed, "Mr. Storm is something wrong?"

He shook his head. "After that kiss earlier you're still calling me Mr. Storm?"

31

"You *kissed* him?" Frankie grimaced.

"Oh! My, my! This is the problem from this morning. The only problem he'd pose would be to *not* kiss him all day," Filly murmured, licking her red lips.

Emily cleared her throat. "Actually, you kissed me."

"Yeah, after you kissed me," he clarified. "If I recall correctly, you didn't resist."

"He's wearing an earring!" Frankie gasped.

"Big deal! It's a small gold hoop. I like it," cooed Phyllis. "Look at the arms on him! Hubba-hubba! And the five o'clock shadow? Emily, for all that's holy please, please go out with him!"

Chase returned her gaze. It almost seemed as if she didn't know how to respond. "Emily?"

"Well, it won't happen again. It was a moment of weakness," Emily stumbled.

A slow, sexy grin slid across his face. "That's unfortunate. I was hoping to get to know you better."

"But only for a week, right?" Emily spat.

"Hey, a lot can happen in a week," he murmured, running his fingers lightly on her forearm.

She snatched her arm away and walked into the storage room. "You can show yourself out," she snippily replied, over her shoulder.

"Or I can show him out," growled Frankie. "With the end of my loafer!"

"Actually, I was hoping to take you to dinner tonight," Chase replied, following her.

Emily turned around quickly, causing Chase to bump into her. He gripped her elbows to stop her from falling.

Damn, he smells good, she grumpily thought.

"Obviously I affect you in some small way," he grinned. "I mean, you have one helluva blush going right now."

She hastily pulled away, rolling her eyes. "I'm not dead, ya know."

"Hey! I'm dead and I think this guy's the bees-knees!" Filly giggled.

"What I mean to say, is that I can control my hormonal urges," Emily snipped, both at Chase and Filly.

Chase sighed, "It's just dinner. I'm not going to jump your bones." *At least not yet,* he thought.

"You're not my type," she replied, lifting a thin brow.

Chase snorted, indigently, "Not your type?"

Emily grabbed her purse and brushed past him. "Not my type. I like to date and you like to fuck. Hasn't anyone ever said that to you before?"

A collective gasp filled the air.

"Frankly, no and I'm offended by your lack of filtering," he groused.

"Sorry, no filters here. I say what I mean and I mean what I say. So see, I'm not your type, either. Problem solved," she grinned, walking towards the door.

Frankie, Lilly and Filly hovered nearby, not wanting to miss a thing.

"Now can I toss him out?" Frankie complained.

"Shh! This is getting good!" Lilly giggled.

Filly wrapped an arm around her. "Hey, we may get to be good friends after all."

Chase placed his hands on hips in a patient manner, noticing Emily must be having conflicting emotions since she made no move to open the door to leave.

33

"So? Dinner then?" he asked.

"You're a masochist, aren't you? I've already told you no," Emily reminded, opening the door and waving him through.

His eyes narrowed as he walked past her. "Fine, baby, your loss," he said through clenched teeth.

She locked the door to the store and heard the engine of his Porsche spring to life, then the peeling of tires against the hot pavement.

She smiled wistfully. Apparently Mr. Storm wasn't used to rejection.

Well, too bad. She didn't need another heartache.

*   *   *

Not her type? Of course I'm her type! I'm every woman's type!

He had money, was the president of Storm Design Group and lived in a luxury condo that overlooked the city of Chicago.

Dammit! Her ex-boyfriend looked like white trash!

Christ! He hated driving in the suburbs and he was practically begging her to go out with him.

He pulled over, to collect his thoughts and to soothe his damaged ego. He banged his hands against the steering wheel in frustration.

Rejection didn't set well with him.

It never had.

Fuck it! And her!

So why did he pull behind her car when she drove past?

*   *   *

Emily fumbled with the buttons on the radio looking for something loud and obnoxious to drown him from her mind.

A short while later she pulled into the grocery store lot and slipped her car next to a blue sedan.

She frowned. Why would Chase think she owned something like that?

She frowned again. Why did she care what Chase thought at all?

*   *   *

"Beth, what's Emily's phone number?" Chase asked as he parked several slots away from Emily's car.

"Aw, Chase, I don't know if I should give it to you," Beth sighed.

"Why? You saw her kiss me this morning. You know she digs me."

"She's become a good friend and I don't need you ruining my friendship because you can't control your libido!"

"Look, I just want to text her, okay? Ask her out for a date," he sighed. *What is it with women?*

*   *   *

Emily shopped in the produce section to make a chef salad when her cell phone chimed.

She dug it from her purse and frowned when she saw Chase's name.

Please have dinner with me.

She rolled her eyes and shook her head, putting the phone back into her purse.

She pushed her cart towards the tomato bins, lifting an eyebrow.

She pulled the phone out of her purse and responded to his text.

How did you get my number?

Doesn't matter. Dinner? Tonight?

She quickly responded. **No!**

His response was just as immediate. **Do I need to beg?**

She giggled, causing a nearby shopper to purse her lips. **Maybe...** she replied and waited for a response.

After five minutes of standing near the tomatoes she threw her phone back into her purse and absently picked out three tomatoes.

"Tsk, tsk. Do you always purchase tomatoes with bruises?"

She turned quickly, bumping into Chase.

After finding her voice she shakily asked, "What are you doing here?"

"Why, Miss Waters, I'm here to beg," he replied, getting onto his knees.

A small group of shoppers gaped around them causing color to form onto Emily's cheeks.

He took her very soft and small hand into his.

"Emily, please have dinner with me tonight," he asked loudly.

"I'll go with ya," some middle-aged overweight woman snorted as she passed.

Chase ignored her and looked into Emily's eyes. If she said no, he'd cut his losses and call it a day.

I'm on my fucking knees for chrissakes!

Emily looked around nervously. He was certainly causing a scene in the frickin' produce department!

She pleaded, "Chase, get up!"

He tilted his head to the side and lifted a hand to his ear. "I'm sorry. What did you say?" He loved to hear her say his name.

"You heard me! Get up!" she flushed.

He lifted his eyebrow to her and a small grin lifted his cheek.

Damn him for looking so vulnerable and sexy at the same time!

Every molecule in her body told her to say no.

"Okay," she said breathily.

*   *   *

"How romantic!" one woman swooned.

Chase smiled and took Emily by the elbow.

"I can't just leave my cart!" she squeaked.

Chase sighed and began putting her meager items back, but not in the right bins. It didn't matter. Produce was produce.

She covered her mouth with her hand to stifle a grin. No one had ever pursued her. She kind of liked it, but she was also wary.

There was no way in hell she was going to be one of the 'seven days of heaven' girls!

*   *   *

"I'm *not* leaving my car!" she protested. Just because she agreed to have dinner with him didn't mean she'd leave her prized possession in a grocery store parking lot!

"Christ! Do you always have to be so challenging?" he growled, running a hand through his sandy-blonde hair.

She crossed her arms over her chest. "I'm. Not. Leaving. My. Car!"

"Fine! I'll follow you to your house and you can drop it off," he acquiesced.

She lifted her chin defiantly. "Why don't you leave your car?"

"Are you crazy? My car is worth three times as much as yours!" he snorted.

"Not my problem if you spent too much money," she sneered.

Chase looked up at the sky, looking for divine intervention or at the very least a bolt of lightning to strike him.

She watched with mild amusement as he leaned against the trunk of her car, folding his arms over his chest in the process.

He stood for a few minutes, not saying anything. He reminded her of a spoiled child who was in her shop earlier in the week.

"Fine!" she hissed. "I'll drop my car off at my house. Keep up with me or dinner is off," she called over her shoulder.

He snorted, "No problems there, baby."

She opened her car door, stopped and strode towards him.

"Don't call me that again," she warned.

"What? Baby?" he grinned, exposing those damn dimples.

She shivered. "Yeah. I don't like to be called that!"

*　　　*　　　*

Keep up with her, he laughed to himself. She was funny. And adorable.

He couldn't wait to have her alone. Maybe he wouldn't find her as appealing.

Then he gulped.

Maybe he'd find her more appealing.

*　　　*　　　*

Emily blared heavy metal music as she wove between traffic. She knew she wouldn't lose him, but it was fun to try.

Besides, by having dinner with him she might find out what made Chase Storm tick.

And why he felt compelled to do the seven day thing.

*　　*　　*

Chase laughed as he watched her weave through traffic. Surely she didn't really think she'd lose him?

He turned up the volume on the radio. It was a classical station. He thought it might be Pachelbel, but wasn't sure. He only knew what he liked when he heard it.

He wondered what kind of music she listened to.

He wondered a lot about her.

More than he ever had about Cassie and definitely more than the seven day women.

With that startling thought, he eased up on the gas pedal.

*　　*　　*

She pulled into her driveway and frowned when he didn't pull in behind her.

In fact, she didn't see his red car in the rear-view mirror for quite a length of time.

Maybe she did lose him, she sulked.

After ten minutes she scowled, removed the key from the ignition and slammed the car door closed.

She walked to the edge of the driveway and looked down the street for any sign of him.

Then she checked her phone for messages. Finding none she sighed and let her fingers do the walking.

Did you get lost?

When he didn't respond, she growled and stomped to the front door.

*　　*　　*

39

Chase parked along a tree-line street two blocks from Emily's house.

"Get a grip, Storm!" he admonished himself.

His phone vibrated indicating an incoming text.

Glancing at the phone he lifted an eyebrow.

He looked both ways before making a u-turn in the street.

*   *   *

Emily sat in the house for a while before going out to her car.

She eased out of the driveway and drove the way she came home, worrying he'd been in an accident. She even went as far to drive back to the grocery store.

After slipping her car into a slot she pulled out her phone and dialed his number.

After four rings, it went to voicemail.

"Storm. Leave a message."

She rolled her eyes. Even his voice message was curt.

"Hi, it's Emily. I'm not sure if you got lost or if something…well, I just wanted to make sure you're okay."

Her face burning, she quickly disconnected the call.

As she dialed Beth's number she shook her head.

"Hello?"

"Hi Beth, it's Emily."

"Hey Em! What's up?"

"I ran into Chase earlier and he was following me home, but never made it to my house," Emily said hurriedly.

"Have you called him?" Beth asked.

"Yeah and I've texted him, but he's not responding."

Beth laughed, "Don't tell me he's gotten to you!"

Emily's chin lifted. "The man got on his knees in the store and begged me to have dinner with him. I'm concerned something happened."

"I'll call and see if he answers. I'll call you back," Beth promised.

* * *

Chase pulled into the parking garage when his phone rang. He glanced at the caller ID and answered. "What's up, sister dear?"

"Thank God you're okay. Poor Emily's worried you've wrapped your Porsche around a tree," Beth teased.

Chase flinched as he got out of the car. "I'm fine," he replied stiffly.

"Ya beg the girl to have dinner and then pull a disappearing act?"

"Christ! She told you?" he growled.

Nothing like feeling totally emasculated! It was bad enough he did it in front of a produce section full of people. Did anyone recognize him?

Beth laughed, "It sounded sweet. I didn't think you had a romantic bone in your body!"

Chase rolled his eyes. "I'm fine so you can quit worrying about me."

He pressed the button on the elevator. He'd be glad to get inside his condo and have a stiff drink or two.

"I wasn't worried. Emily was. Did you change your mind about having dinner with her?" Beth snorted.

"Yep. Simple as that. It that all?" he snipped.

Beth gasped, appalled. "You're such an asshole sometimes! Do that shit to your bimbo's, not Emily!"

41

He pulled his phone away from his ear. It was the first time his sister hung up on him.

He frowned, not knowing if he should be shocked or angry. In any case, it didn't matter.

A bottle of bourbon was just a few feet away.

*　　　*　　　*

Emily perused the produce section, picking up items she'd picked up before Chase interrupted her, when her phone rang.

"Hello?"

"Hi Em," Beth paused and continued. "First I want to apologize for my idiot brother. You're too good for him."

Emily swallowed hard. "I take it he's okay and just decided to blow me off."

"Em, I'm so sorry," Beth whispered.

"So'kay. I mean, I never would've gone for the seven day thing and hell, he's outta my league anyway," Emily murmured, emptying her green shopping basket. She no longer felt like eating.

"Hey, are you okay?"

Emily walked out of the air-conditioned store, into the sweltering heat, towards her car. "Yeah. He's a jerk," she said with a catch in her voice.

*　　　*　　　*

Chase stripped down to his dark blue briefs and grabbed a shot glass with a gold etched capital 'S' from behind the bar. He poured a copious amount of whiskey; a small puddle formed on the highly polished wood.

How did she manage to wheedle herself under his skin? He couldn't even pour a decent shot! He slowly brought the glass to his lips and threw back his head.

The liquid amber warmed his throat and his stomach. Before he got too wasted, he grabbed a cloth and hastily wiped the bar.

Taking the bottle only, he went into the entertainment room and powered up the 58 inch HDTV. He took a long pull from the bottle as he scanned the channels.

He settled for a sports show which recapped the day's events. Not that he paid it much attention.

After several shots he had an epiphany.

Emily Waters scared the hell out of him.

*   *   *

Nothing like a half-pint of chocolate brownie ice cream to soothe one's damaged ego, Emily thought as she tossed the empty container into the trash can and the spoon into the sink.

The house felt warm even though she wore a pair of shorts and a tank top.

Maybe it wasn't the house.

Maybe it was her blood pressure.

She adjusted the ceiling fan to high and crawled into the cool crisp sheets of her bed.

Chase Storm could bite her ass.

*   *   *

"Chasey…" the gentle voice murmured into his ear.

A frown formed on his lips. He hadn't been called that in years.

A stab of pain filled his chest.

His mom called him that.

He shifted on the couch and felt something cool and hard between his

43

legs.

His eyes suddenly darted open.

Fuckin' whiskey bottle. He rolled his eyes upward and felt a throbbing pain. Fuckin' whiskey period.

He switched off the television and stumbled to bed.

He wrapped his arm around the pillow next to him, wishing it was a blonde.

Not just any blonde.

"Fuck!" He growled into the blue satin sheets.

It took him a while to fall asleep and when he did, she appeared.

She gazed down at him lovingly. He'd grown into such a handsome man. With issues.

She caused those issues. She frowned, pushing a strand of hair from his eyes.

She'd make it right and Emily Waters would help her.

Chapter Three

"You haven't said much about the hot guy lately," Filly said nonchalantly, adjusting her boa.

Emily stiffened as she picked a box up from the floor.

She walked past Filly and put the cardboard box on the large maple table in the storage room.

Filly hated the table and shivered every time she stood near it.

Emily got it free from a funeral home and used it to hold her flea market or auction finds until they were ready for sale. Frankie and Phyllis officially dubbed it the 'mortician table'.

She took out each newspaper wrapped piece of glassware and laid them carefully on the table, ignoring Filly's remark.

It'd been two weeks since she heard from Chase. She now slept peacefully at night and didn't have disturbing dreams of him.

"What gives? Cat got your tongue?" Filly chided. Em hadn't been this quiet since that jerk Joe.

Emily stuck her tongue out, indicating all was as it should be.

"Real mature, Em. He really got to you, huh?" Filly prodded.

"Hardly!" Emily snorted. "I knew him for a minute!"

"Maybe, but you liked him? He was a tasty morsel, as you would say."

"Filly, I'm fine. It just stung, ya know? First Joe then some guy I hardly know? It's not easy to be rejected and it seems to happen to me on a regular basis."

Emily tucked a strand of hair behind her ear and bit her lip. "He didn't even get a chance to know me. He knew nothing about my ability and yet, he ran." She paused and said the words she'd been thinking for so many years. "Maybe it's not my gift that turns guys away. Maybe it's just me."

"That's a load of shit!" growled Frankie, entering through the light pink plaster wall. He crossed his beefy arms over his chest. "I'm offended you'd think that!"

"Come on, you both know I can't keep a man interested very long. The only logical solution is that it's my personality," Emily shrugged. "Anyway, who cares? I've got you two to keep me company. In fact, I should bring your things home so you can always be with me."

Filly and Frankie eyed each other warily before Filly spoke up. "Look, Em, we love ya, but you don't want to hang out with ghosts all the time."

"Hey, you're the most interesting people I know!" Emily admonished.

"Thanks a lot!" came a voice from the doorway.

The two spirits and Emily looked up and saw Jenny leaned against the door jamb, arms crossed over her chest.

Emily shrugged, "Sorry, nothing personal."

Jenny tossed her long red hair over her shoulder and frowned. "Tonight we're going to the city to a great bar and hang out with live people."

Filly nodded, "I agree with her. Ya need to get out. Go to some ritzy joint, drink some giggle water and dance!"

"Yeah! Make the scene, Emily!" Frankie interjected.

A slow smile spread across Emily's face, causing a puzzled expression to form on Jenny's. "What are they saying?"

"That I should go and have a good time."

Jenny lifted her hands. "Finally! They agree with me!"

*　　*　　*

"Look, I don't give a rat's ass! This project was supposed to be completed a month ago and here we are with our dicks in our hands!" Chase yelled at his brother Jason.

Jason stonily looked out the window, down eighty stories. It made him woozy. "Shit happens, Chase. You know how contractors are."

Chase pushed his chair away from the cherry desk and strode to Jason, jabbing his finger into his chest. "Get. The. Fucking. Job. Done!"

Jason lifted a black eyebrow while pushing his brother's finger away. "We're working on the aesthetics. Don't worry big brother, I won't embarrass you," he replied sardonically over his shoulder.

"You already have," growled Chase watching his brother walk out the office door.

As far as Chase was concerned, he did the hardest part by designing the fucking retro-movie theater! It was Jason's company, Storm LLC, which had the easy shit to do!

A disembodied voice interrupted his thoughts. "Mr. Storm? Your father is on line two for you," Darcy, his personal assistant, purred into the phone.

"I'm busy!" Chase snapped.

"I'm sorry, but he said you'd say that and to patch him through anyway," she shuddered.

Chase ran his hand over his face and sat on his Italian desk chair in a huff. "Fine!"

He picked up the receiver before the second ring. "Storm," he said gruffly.

47

"How formal of you, " Preston Storm teased.

Chase sighed, "Sorry dad. Havin' a bad day. What can I do for you?"

"You can get your ass out of your office and play golf with your old man."

"Dad, I'm still working on the final paperwork for the farm acreage we bought. Have you decided on the style of the houses you want to build?" Chase asked, knowing they'd be cookie cutter homes, again.

"Actually I was hoping to work on those with you. Maybe come up with something unique this time," Preston murmured into the phone.

Chase's eyebrows shot up. His dad wanted to do something different? "You're the house guy and I'm the skyscraper guy," Chase laughed.

"Expand your horizon's my boy! I'm sure you can think of something interesting."

Chase rolled his eyes. This was a project he didn't plan on taking on, only overseeing. "I don't think I'll have time to come up with designs since I'm still working on the Paris project."

"That's right. When are you scheduled to fly there?"

"As of now, August, unless they want to see my sketches sooner."

"That's two months away. I'm sure you can come up with some wonderful designs in that time," his dad replied.

"Sure dad, I'll just live in my office."

"It's not like you have a steady girlfriend," scoffed his dad.

"Nope. Sure don't and that's the way I like it. Seven days dad!" Chase sneered. "Speaking of which, I have a gorgeous blonde waiting to see me, so I'll talk to you later."

"Before you go, do me a favor and get off Jason's ass. He's doing the best he can since he's shorthanded."

"This theater job was supposed to be finished a month ago! My ass is getting chewed out because we're behind schedule," Chase growled into the phone.

"I understand your frustration, Chasey, but ease up a little. Jason told me that you've been calling him several times a day to bitch at him. I'm asking that you limit those calls to two a day, capiche?"

He lost Chase after he called him 'Chasey'.

"Chase? Did you hear me?" asked his dad.

"Why did you call me that?" he squeaked out past the lump in his throat.

"What? Chasey?"

"Yeah," Chase frowned.

"I'm not sure. I guess I've been thinking about your mom lately," Preston replied softly.

"Well, don't call me that again. That woman's been dead to me since she walked out on us!" Chase spat, before hanging up the receiver.

*   *   *

"Jared, Keith and I will be at your house around seven," Jenny called over her shoulder, heading toward her small pick-up truck.

"Wait!" Emily yelled as she locked the door to Play It Again Sam. "Who's Jared?"

Jenny grinned, "Keith's friend. He's adorable, single and he's interested in meeting you."

"Ew! A blind date? Jennyyyyy!"

*   *   *

Freddie and Ian, the drummer in the band, sat in the living room going over a song set for their next gig.

When Emily came downstairs they both looked up and whistled.

"For not wanting to go on a blind date, you look pretty fantastic," Freddie teased.

Emily looked at the dress that took her a half-hour to decide to wear. It was nothing special, just a strapless indigo blue dress that came down to the tops of her knees. She opted to let her hair hang in loose curls instead of putting it up into a chignon.

"If you wanted a date, I'd have gone out with you," Ian muttered.

She grinned at the spiky blonde haired man, with four days stubble on his face and laughed. "I don't think Katie, *your wife*, would appreciate it."

He winked a blue eye at her. "We just wouldn't tell her!"

Freddie rolled his eyes at Ian. "So, this Storm guy is gone for good?"

"He was never here, Freddie," she scowled.

"Are you talking about Chase Storm?" Ian asked, tapping his drumsticks against a pillow.

"Why? You know him?" Freddie asked.

Ian shrugged. "Not personally, but Katie's sister, Margo, just started dating him. I guess he's got something he calls 'seven days of heaven'."

Emily stopped him. "Yeah, yeah. I know all about it. I can't believe a woman would actually agree to something like that."

Freddie beamed. "I think the man's a genius! Date a chick for seven days, have your way with her and move on to the next chick! He really ought to patent the idea."

"You're just as demented as he is!" Emily snidely replied. "It'd be a cold day in hell when I'd agree to those terms!"

Ian nudged Freddie's arm. "Is that why he dumped her?"

Emily spun around, glaring. "He. Did. Not. Dump. Me!" She was about to verbally abuse him when the doorbell rang.

She heard Freddie mutter as she closed the door. "You, my friend, were literally saved by the bell!"

*   *   *

Emily was fuming when she walked into her date on the porch. He extended his hand to her. "Hi Emily, I'm Jared."

Her icy demeanor quickly dissipated. "Hi Jared, it's nice to meet you."

He flashed a wide grin and gently took her elbow, leading her to Keith's Cadillac.

On the drive to Chicago the conversation flowed easily between the foursome. Emily quickly learned that Jared worked for a very prestigious advertising firm with Keith.

"Keith tells me that you own an antique shop with Jenny," Jared said when there was a short lull in conversation.

"Yeah. It's a great little shop," she smiled.

He was actually quite attractive. His brown eyes seemed sincere and he kept them locked on hers when she spoke and not on her boobs.

Maybe this blind date wouldn't be so bad after all.

*   *   *

Chase picked up Margo, his latest conquest, at seven. She was quite the vixen. She made him forget about *her.*

Well, almost.

"Hey baby," he crooned when she settled in the passenger seat.

"Hey lover," she purred, stretching over the gear shift to shove her tongue down his throat.

Usually an action such as that and the not-so-subtle brush of a

51

woman's breasts against his arm caused a reaction in his lower region to occur.

Not so much lately.

It had Chase a little worried. Okay, *a lot* worried.

Especially after last night when he only got hard fantasizing that it was Emily on top of him and not Margie. Margo, whatever the fuck her name was.

*   *   *

"Emily have you ever been to Club 70?" Jared asked.

She smiled. "I don't come to the city much."

"Keith and Jenny told me you like to dance," he lifted an eyebrow.

"Only after a few drinks," she confessed. "I'm not much of a dancer otherwise."

Jared grinned and patted her bare knee. "Don't worry; I'm a pretty good dancer. I can teach you."

She half-grinned and turned her head to look out the window.

He wouldn't last a month with her.

Guys like him believed in straight lines and black and white.

Not ghosts, let alone people who communicated with them.

*   *   *

"What's your pleasure tonight, Margo?" Chase asked, easing the Porsche into Saturday night traffic.

"You. Let's go back to your place," she said breathily.

"Remember the rules, baby. Your place or a hotel, but never my place."

"Fine! Then I want a nice juicy steak and then I want to go dancing. Maybe later, if you're lucky, we can fuck," she hissed.

Two margaritas into it, Emily sidled closer to Jared in the circular booth.

"Hey, there's something you should know about me," she whispered in his ear.

He pulled away, a slow grin spread across his face. "I'm all ears."

"I talk to dead people," she stated matter-of-factly. She was giddy to see how fast he'd jet from the booth.

He tucked a strand of hair behind her ear. "I know. Keith told me. That's why he set us up."

She lifted her chin and narrowed her eyes. "So you just wanted to see the freak-is that it?"

Jared's dark brown eyebrows knitted together and he shook his head. "No Emily. I can see ghosts, too."

"Okay, now you're just fucking with me," she hissed and scooted out of the booth.

Jared grabbed her wrist. "Emily, wait. Please, sit down."

When she made no move to sit he continued. "I lived above a funeral home. My dad's a mortician. I've seen my share of ghosts, believe me."

She cocked her head. He seemed sincere so she sat next to him. "Go on," she murmured.

He ran his hand through his short spiky brown hair and laugh lines formed around his mouth. "For so long I felt like a freak; growing up and seeing people no one else could see. My parents took me to see shrinks."

Emily patted his arm. "My parents never questioned me."

"It's amazing that you can communicate with them. I can only see them. I'm actually kind of jealous," he grinned.

Emily called the waitress over and ordered another margarita.

The night just got interesting.

*   *   *

A waiting line formed outside of Club 70.

Chase tucked Margo's arm firmly under his and strode to the door, past the schmucks in line and nodded politely at the bouncer, Ed.

"Evenin' Mr. Storm," Ed said, opening the door. "Have a good time."

"Thanks Ed," Chase smiled over his shoulder.

Being somewhat famous had massive advantages; except the table he usually occupied was already taken.

It was just as well. He didn't want to be secluded with Margo tonight.

Instead, they were seated at a smaller table in the upper level which overlooked the dance floor.

She ordered a Sex on the Beach and raised an eyebrow to him. He shook his head and ordered a Corona.

He wouldn't last another hour with this chick. She annoyed the fuck out of him.

"Let's dance!" she yelled over the loud techno thump of the music.

He shook his head. "I'm waiting for my beer."

He hated this kind of fucking music!

The lights dimmed when the waitress brought their drinks. He pulled the lime out, threw it on the table and took a long pull. As the waitress walked by again, he grabbed her arm and ordered another Corona.

Margo pouted while he looked out at the dancers. The music was slow and less annoying.

Suddenly he felt her toes digging into his crotch.

"What are you doing?" he hissed, grabbing her foot.

"Let's go find a private table and I'll show you a thing or two," she rasped, leaning over the table.

He pushed her foot towards the floor. "There aren't any available," he growled.

Angrily he picked up his beer and took another long pull as he watched the dancers.

He wondered what Emily was doing. He wondered a lot about her lately. He finished off his first beer and picked up the second bottle.

His gaze shifted towards the dancers again. They were more interesting than his date.

He lifted the bottle to his lips and choked when he saw Emily with a guy wrapped around her.

*   *   *

Jared was a lovely dancer and held her tightly against him, like she would fly away.

Three or was it four margarita's could do that to a girl.

She leaned her head against his chest and breathed deeply. His cologne wasn't as appealing as Chase's. She reached for his bicep and frowned when she realized that it wasn't as muscular as Chase's, either.

No matter. He's nice looking, isn't a prick and didn't run away when he found out she talked to ghosts.

*   *   *

Jared was in heaven. He held a beautiful woman in his arms and she didn't run when he told her he could see ghosts. He felt an instant connection with her and hoped she felt the same way.

He grinned when she snuggled closer to him.

Yeah, she felt it, too.

He felt a tap on his shoulder and ignored it until the tapping got firmer, testier.

He slowly spun the two of them around and frowned when he saw an imposing man glaring at him.

"Can I help you?" Jared asked.

"Yeah, you can get your hands off her," Chase growled.

Jared frowned. "Excuse me?"

"I said get lost," Chase snapped.

*   *   *

Emily shook her head. She was thinking of Chase and now heard his voice in her head. She lifted her head from Jared's chest and frowned when she noticed the scowl on his face.

Then she heard Chase's voice again, this time behind her.

She slowly turned and gasped.

Chase Storm looked pissed off and damn sexy. Her eyes raked his body seductively. She even caught herself licking her lips.

He wore a white shirt with the sleeves rolled up, revealing a very nice tan. The colored lights from the ceiling made his sandy blonde hair look red, blue, yellow and green at varied intervals.

"Emily? Do you know this guy?" Jared asked, confused.

"Chase Storm, Jared…Jared…well, this is Jared," she slurred.

Chase gaped at her. "Are you drunk?"

She giggled. "Well, duh!"

He glared at the asshole holding Emily. "Did you just meet Jared Jared?" he asked her.

56

"Kinda. Blind date," she giggled again. "You called him Jared Jared. You're funny."

Chase's blue eyes smoldered. "Did this asshole get you drunk?"

"No, no," she laughed, pointing a thumb to her chest. "*I'm* the asshole who got me drunk!"

Chase pulled Emily away from Jared and hissed. "She's coming home with me. Fuck off."

He wrapped his arm protectively around her waist and wrestled his way through the dancers. When he found a less populated area he stopped and searched her eyes.

Her beautiful brown eyes were glazed, but alert. "Emily, can you walk or shall I carry you?"

"Why are you here?" she said so softly that he had to lean closer to hear her.

"I was on a date," he muttered.

She looked down at the floor and lifted her chin. "Then I suggest you continue your date and let me get back to mine."

"Do you always have to be so difficult?" he scowled.

"Me? Difficult? *I* didn't tell *your* date to fuck off!" she countered.

He rolled his eyes. "I told her to fuck off for you."

"I don't understand," she mumbled.

"I'll tell you in the car."

"I'm not going anywhere with you until you tell me what this is all about!" she yelled, gripping his forearms to keep herself from falling.

"Christ! I didn't like seeing some guy hanging all over you, okay?"

"It's none of your business who hangs on me," she replied haughtily.

He felt helpless looking into her eyes. He hadn't felt this helpless since...

He tucked the thought away and put his hands on both sides of her head, pulling her to him.

She didn't flinch or pull away. If anything, she closed the gap.

He kissed her gently, then the past two weeks of wanting her consumed him. He deepened the kiss, pulling her body closer to his. His right hand cradled her head, his left hand pressed against her lower back.

She needed air. She needed to think.

She pushed away from him, panting. Damn, he was a fine kisser. But it wasn't enough.

"I need to know why Chase."

"Why what?" he asked, breathless.

"Why you pulled me away from Jared."

He ran his hand through his hair. She wasn't going to make this easy on him.

"Because you're all I've thought about since we met! I've lost sleep thinking about you! Is that what you want to hear?" he said, exasperated.

"Only if you mean it," she replied haughtily.

He took a strand of her hair and tucked it behind her ear. "God help me, I mean it."

Chapter Four

Emily felt something along her arm and awoke to brush it away. She stopped in mid-flick when she felt fingers that weren't hers.

Bolting upright she looked around. Chase smiled lazily at her and turned his head to the road ahead.

"Ya feel okay?" he asked.

She shook her head. "Are you taking me home?"

Her phone rang in her purse and she struggled to free it from her shoulder.

"Hullo?" she asked, groggily.

"Emily! Where the hell are you?" Jenny ground out.

"Um, I'm with Chase," she sighed happily.

Jenny snipped, "What about Jared?"

Emily palmed her forehead. "Can you tell him I'll call him tomorrow?"

"I don't know if he'll want to see you again," Jenny huffed.

"Oh, he'll see me again. He totally digs me. Bye!" she giggled.

Chase's jaw clenched. Over his dead body would she see Jared Jared again.

He carried her to his bedroom.

It was a shame she passed out on the ride to his condo.

Maybe it was for the best. He might've blabbed more than he already had.

He removed her shoes and slid his palm along her silky legs. The thought of that asshole touching her caused him to scowl.

He should've punched the bastard in the face.

Emily stirred, rolling onto her back. Chase pulled his hand away and watched her for a few moments. Afterwards he covered her with a blanket.

He strode to the floor length window and looked out at the city.

It was the first time he'd ever brought a woman to his condo.

He removed his shirt, tossing it onto the blue overstuffed chair next to the window and sat to take his shoes off when she moaned.

"Bed's spinnin'!" She bolted upright, covering her mouth. When she saw Chase she mumbled through her hand, "Bathroom!"

He jumped from the chair and led her to the master bathroom.

She lifted the toilet lid and waved him off. "Go!"

Her body convulsed and then a horrible retching sound escaped from her lips as well as several margaritas.

He pulled her hair away from her face while she emptied the contents of her stomach.

Between retches Emily whimpered, "Go, please! This is embarrassing with you watching me!"

Chase frowned. "Trust me sweetheart, I'm not watching."

Her body convulsed again. The sound and smell made him want to vomit himself, but he was made of tougher stuff. At least, he hoped he was.

"Can you get me a glass of water?" she pleaded. *Anything...just go away!*

"I don't want to leave you," he murmured, rubbing her back with his free hand.

"I'm not going anywhere for a while," she replied, spitting into the toilet.

He hesitated, unsure what to do.

"Water? Please?" she mumbled.

"Okay, I'll be right back," he replied begrudgingly.

As soon as he left the room, she crawled to the door and locked it. She'd be damned if he'd watch her humiliate herself anymore.

She sat with her back against the bathroom door and blinked her eyes a few times. His bathroom was bigger than her bedroom!

She crawled towards the bathtub. It was encased in marble and stood about three feet high. Upon further inspection she gasped. It looked like a small frickin' pool!

Chase banged on the door. "Come on Emily! Let me in!"

She closed her eyes briefly and cursed under her breath. What difference did it make now? She didn't think she had anything else to yack up.

"Emily?" he shouted. When she didn't respond he began to jiggle the door. "Fuck! Emily? Are you okay?"

Suddenly she didn't feel well. Not pukey, but weak. She slid slowly down the white tiled wall and slumped to the floor. The cool tiles felt soothing against her warm skin.

Moments later Chase entered, picking her up from the floor. "You almost gave me a heart attack!" When she didn't respond he sat down on the floor with her in his arms and brushed the hair from her face. "Em?"

Her eyelids flickered. "I'm still alive."

He pulled her against his chest and held her.

His chest hairs tickled her nose and he smelled good, so she snuggled closer to him.

"You really like me," she murmured, a smile playing at her lips.

He pulled away slowly and when her eyes met his, he smiled. "I'd say so if I'm holding you and you smell like vomit."

"Why Chase Storm you say the most romantic things," she replied in her best southern drawl.

He laughed and pulled her closer, kissing her forehead. It was the most singular act of affection he'd ever shown to a woman. It startled him.

Nope, it scared the fuck out of him.

*   *   *

One minute she sat on his lap, his arms around her and the next she sat on the tiled floor, alone.

"I think a shower is in order," he mumbled, running a hand through his hair. She lifted a brow and he continued, "By yourself, of course."

She scowled and stood up slowly. "I prefer to shower at my house."

"It's late and we're both tired," he replied, taking a towel and washcloth from the cabinet.

She lifted her chin. "I'll call a cab."

He stopped gathering items and chuckled. "Do you know what it'd cost to take a cab to the suburbs? No. You'll stay the night here."

"I'm not sleeping with you," she hissed.

"Babe, I don't take advantage of drunken women, unlike Jared Jared," he said coolly.

62

She put her hands on her hips and narrowed her eyes. "He wasn't getting me drunk! *I* was getting *me* drunk! Besides, he's a nice guy."

Chase snorted and turned towards the door. "Yeah, I'll bet he's a real peach."

A smirk played across her lips. "You're jealous!" she accused.

He spun around and glared, "You're goddamn right I am!"

*   *   *

Well, the fucking cat's out of the bag now, he scolded himself.

Grinning, she sauntered past him, stepping into the bedroom. He tucked his hands into the front pockets of his jeans, leaned against the door jamb and watched her.

She fell to her knees and looked under the bed, stood up and picked the blanket up from the bed.

"Looking for something?" he asked with a bemused grin.

"My purse," she muttered, tucking her hair behind her ears.

"It's on the kitchen counter, but you're not going anywhere tonight."

She grinned, "Not planning to. I want to brush my teeth."

His eyebrows knitted together. "With your purse?"

She rolled her eyes as she walked out of the bedroom. She spun around slowly, taking in his condo. One entire wall was glass with a spectacular view of the city.

Vomit breath forgotten, she padded softly towards the view. His condo had a view of the lake. It took her breath away.

"Pretty, isn't it?" he murmured next to her.

She shook her head. "I think the word would be 'breath-taking'."

"Breath-taking it is then," he smiled down at her.

"I'm sure Margo was equally impressed with the view," she muttered.

"Nah, she didn't last seven days," he snorted.

Emily crossed her arms over her chest. "Her choice or yours?"

He shrugged. "Mine."

"Why?" she asked, cocking her head.

Stepping closer he ran his hands slowly from her shoulders to her elbows. "Because she's not you."

His expression caused a lump to form in her throat. "The others?"

Chase blew out a long breath. "No, none of them were allowed here."

"Why?"

"Because none of them were special enough."

"I'm listening," she grinned.

He sighed. "Don't you have to brush your teeth?"

He wasn't ready for this conversation.

"Sure, if you want to evade my questions," she muttered, walking towards the kitchen in search of her purse.

While she brushed her teeth she walked around the condo, marveling at the size. His condo had more square footage than her house. It was an open concept design that seemed to fit his personality.

He sat on the leather couch and watched in amusement. She was like a kid in a candy store, touching everything with wide eyes.

Emily quickly ran into the bathroom and rinsed the toothpaste from her mouth and looked at herself in the mirror. She looked like hell.

"Feel better?" he asked, leaning against the door jamb.

She wiped her mouth with a piece of toilet paper and tossed it into the trash. "Yeah. Much better."

He grinned, "Do you always carry a toothbrush and toothpaste?"

She brushed past him, nodding. "Yep. My parents paid good money for these teeth."

He found her in the kitchen, putting her dental items away. She sighed heavily and turned to look at him.

"What are your intentions, Chase?"

He lifted an eyebrow and smirked. "For?"

"Me."

"No beating around the bush with you is there?" he chuckled.

She waved her hand around. "Chase, you're out of my league. I'm Wal-Mart and you're...not. I use coupons, you don't. I live in the suburbs in an old Victorian that I've been repairing since time began and you live in the city, probably in a penthouse, judging from the view."

"Is that how you see me?" he asked softly. "Above you? Because that's not how I see things."

She bit her lower lip. "How can you not?"

He cupped her chin and lifted it. "I only see you. Your stubbornness, your beauty, the easy way you carry yourself and I like what I see."

He bent to kiss her and she pulled away.

She waved a hand between them. "This won't work. We're too different."

"And Jared is more your style?" he asked through gritted teeth.

"Well, I don't know, but we have a lot in common," she confessed.

"Like?" he prodded, visibly angry.

"I don't want to discuss him with you," she muttered, not sure exactly

65

what she and Jared had in common, other than ghosts.

He rolled his head onto his shoulders. He could do this. He could have a conversation with a woman that didn't lead to sex and in fact, he wanted to talk to her. Shit, he'd wanted to talk to her for two weeks, except he'd been too stubborn.

"Why don't we shower and then we can talk about what *we* have in common," he offered. "Hey, don't give me the stink eye! I wasn't implying that we shower together."

"I don't happen to have an extra set of clothes in my purse ya know," she sneered. "Besides, why do I need to shower?"

His nose wrinkled, "Because you have vomit in your hair and on your dress. Really, Emily, ya kind of smell."

She shot him a scowl and brushed past him towards the bedroom.

"I'll put something out for you to wear," he offered with a small laugh.

*   *   *

The warm water felt good, she thought as she wetted her hair in the large, clear acrylic shower. She stifled a giggle. At least they had shower tastes in common.

She grabbed a bottle from the built in shelf of the shower. Some fancy French shampoo. She rolled her eyes and applied a dollop onto her palm and lathered up her hair.

Why couldn't he see how different they were? Her parents were middle-class who managed to just eke by. By the looks of Chase's house and Beth's, they always had money.

She rinsed her hair and looked at the other bottles on the shelf. No conditioner, only two bottles of body wash. She lifted the cap from one bottle and sniffed it. Too manly. She closed it and grabbed the other bottle. It had a hint of cologne to it. Her eyes flew open. This is what he smelled like.

She applied a generous amount to the washcloth and lathered up.

She wouldn't have sex with him, but she'd smell like him.

*   *   *

He didn't know how to handle her reaction to his wealth. It actually offended him that she was so put off by it.

Hell, he worked hard for his money! It wasn't like it was just handed to him on a silver platter.

The other women he dated didn't have a problem with it. In fact, they couldn't get enough of it.

Chase rubbed his jaw in contemplation.

That was the problem.

They used him for money and he used them for sex.

It seemed like a fair exchange and it worked for him. It was all he wanted. No commitments, no false promises.

Then he met Emily.

And all that flew out the friggin' window.

*   *   *

She wrapped herself in a thick blue towel and poked her head out the bathroom door.

A Cubs baseball jersey sat on the bed. She wrinkled her nose. "Chase?"

He stood in the doorway, admiring the view. A ripple of heat seared through his stomach. "Yeah?" he asked huskily.

She pointed towards the jersey. "Is that for me?"

He shrugged, "It's the only thing I have." He laughed when she scowled. "What? You a Sox fan?"

She frowned. "Not a baseball fan period. I don't suppose you have any hockey jerseys?"

His eyes widened. "Really? You're into hockey?"

"Uh-huh," she grinned.

"Baseball's the great American sport! It's like saying you don't like apple pie," he teased.

"I like apple pie and tank tops. Do you have one?"

His eyebrow lifted. "Um, yeah, but…"

"No buts, just give it to me."

"Emily, it won't cover…" he stammered.

She held out her hand. "Tank top. Now."

"Okay, but I can't be held responsible for my actions," he muttered.

He begrudgingly pulled the shirt from his dresser drawer and handed it to her. She smiled, "I'll be out in a jiff," she replied over her shoulder.

Rolling his eyes he headed for the wet bar. He'd need a drink or two to quell the insatiable thoughts when he saw her in that fucking shirt.

*   *   *

She appraised herself in the mirror. *Maybe the jersey would be better.*

The tank top was blue and somewhat sheer and left almost nothing to the imagination. She rifled through his dresser and pulled out a pair of cotton boxer briefs and slid them on.

It was *his* idea for her to stay. He'd have to suck it up and deal with it!

*   *   *

Chase leaned against the bar, sipping Jameson from the crystal cut glass. He turned when he heard her enter the room.

He took one look at her and chugged the remaining amber liquid.

68

Holy hell! Her breasts nearly spilled from the tank top!

Little Chase began to awaken from his slumber.

"I borrowed a pair of your underwear," she grinned.

He slammed the glass on the bar and growled as he walked past her. "Gotta shower."

*   *   *

A cold shower was definitely in order. Maybe a twenty minute cold shower.

Was she purposely trying to fluster him?

He shuddered when the cold water hit his chest. He momentarily forgot about her outfit.

He took a long shower hoping she'd be asleep before he got out.

If she was still awake…gah! He didn't want to think about that!

*   *   *

She was thirsty, but didn't want alcohol. She'd met her quota for the month. She peeked into the stainless steel refrigerator and opted for bottled water.

She ran her hand over the cherry wood kitchen cabinets and then over the dark beige ceramic counters.

She tried to remember what Freddie said Chase did for a living. Was he a realtor? Surely they didn't make this kind of money?

She frowned when she realized she knew very little about him.

She knew more about Jared.

"What's that look for?" Chase laughed.

She turned and nearly choked on her water. His hair was slicked back and he wore cutoff jean shorts. She swallowed hard. How did she miss the six-

69

pack abs before?

She turned her eyes away, blushing.

His eyebrow lifted wickedly. Two could play this game.

"Aren't you going to put a shirt on?" she asked shakily.

"Why? I'm actually wearing more now than I normally do to bed," he grinned.

"Well, it's very distracting," she murmured, peeking again at him.

"I could say the same about you," he countered, edging closer to her. He pulled her hand and led her to the couch. "Let's talk about what *we* have in common. I'm sure there are lots of things."

She rolled her eyes and sat, pulling a red pillow to her chest.

"Okaaaay, I'll start," he offered, tucking his right leg under his bottom to face her. "We both like fast cars."

A small grin formed on her lips, encouraging him to continue.

"I like to read, how about you?" he asked.

She snorted, "Yeah." Small lines formed between her eyebrows. "What do you do for a living? Are you a realtor?"

He laughed heartily. "No. I'm an architect. What made you think I was a realtor?"

She lifted a narrow shoulder. "Something Freddie told me a while ago about your company buying or selling farm land."

"It's my dad's thing, building cookie cutter houses for people in the 'burbs." He wrinkled his nose.

She smiled, "But not your thing…"

"Nah. Skyscrapers are where the money is." He lowered his head to meet her gaze. "You really don't know much about me, do you?"

She shook her head.

"After I graduated from Cornell I studied abroad for a few years. When I came back I became president of Storm Design Group where my dad is CEO," he offered.

"Your parents must be very proud of you," she murmured.

He shrugged, "I guess my dad is."

"What about your mom?"

His jaw clenched. "I don't know. She left when I was ten."

She touched his arm. "I'm sorry."

He drew away. "Don't be. She's been dead to me for years."

Way to go, Storm, nothing like adding levity like that. Say something upbeat for fuck's sake!

"Anyway, I like to shoot hoops to work off tension, draw, just for the sake of drawing and flustering pretty women such as yourself," he grinned.

She lowered her lashes and poked him in the stomach. "What do you do to get your six-pack abs?"

He shrugged, "I work out three times a week, again, to work off tension."

"Why are you so tense?" she asked with wide eyes.

"Because it's my job to design phenomenal buildings and to make sure they're erected correctly. I have oafs who can't complete a project in the promised time frame so my ass gets chewed out. Stress. Just. Happens."

"Are you stressed now?" she shyly asked.

"A little. I don't like to talk about myself much. Tell me a little bit about you."

She laughed, "Not much to tell really. I'm an open book and have nothing to hide."

He raised his eyebrow wickedly. "If that's true tell me what your first impression of me was."

"Not fair!" she protested, tucking both of her legs under her to face him.

"Wow, that good huh?" he grinned. "Must be! You're blushing all over!"

She rolled her eyes. "Of course I thought you were hot as hell." She waved her hand dismissively. "I'm sure you get that all the time. Your ego must be huge."

He shrugged, "It's just a face, besides I could say the same thing about you."

She snorted. "Um, not really. In fact, having two guys tell me tonight that I'm beautiful is way outside my norm."

He lifted his arm to the back of the couch and rested his head in his hand, frowning slightly. "Are you going to see him again?"

She mimicked his actions and rested her head against her hand. "Maybe," she said quietly.

Another lump formed in his throat. He swallowed hard and lifted her chin with his thumb and forefinger. "I really wish you wouldn't." When she started to pull away he held her chin firmly in place and leaned into her.

At first he kissed her softly, gently. She tossed the pillow she'd been clutching to the floor and scooted closer to him. He pulled her onto his lap, deepening his kiss.

She ran her fingers through his hair, pulling gently. This *so* wasn't like her, but she couldn't help herself.

Then she remembered the 'seven day' thing.

She stopped kissing him abruptly, causing him to moan slightly.

"What? What's wrong?" he rasped, his lips covering her jaw and neck.

"I can't do this. I'm sorry," she mumbled, scrambling to get off his lap.

"Kiss? I'd say you kiss damn good," he panted.

She wrung her hands. "Chase. Listen to me," she scolded. She paced in the living room until the grin faded from his lips. "I refuse to be just another bimbo. Call me silly, but I want more."

He sighed heavily and walked to her. "Look at me Emily."

She eyed him warily and a small grin formed on his lips. "If I only wanted you for seven days I sure as hell wouldn't have brought you to my home. I'm actually surprised you haven't asked me why I blew off our dinner date after I begged you in the middle of the produce section."

"Yeah, what happened?" She pushed his chest and glared. "I thought you were in an accident! Imagine the embarrassment I felt after talking to Beth and finding out you just ditched me!"

He grabbed her wrists and pulled her closer. "I did that because frankly Miss Waters, you scared the hell outta me. Fuck! You still do."

She suddenly paled. "Did Beth tell you something about me?"

He released her wrists and placed his hands on her tiny shoulders. "No," he snorted. "Why? Is there something nefarious in your past?"

"Hardly," she muttered. "So, why do I scare you?" she asked, steering the conversation back to him.

He tugged her hand and led her back to the couch. "Like I said when we first met, I don't do relationships, but after meeting you I'm finding that seven days wouldn't be enough for me." She shot him a tilted glance and he continued, "I'm not talking about sex, either. Em, I wasn't kidding when I said that you're all I've thought about in the past two weeks."

She eyed him suspiciously, causing him to laugh. "Don't believe me, eh? Okay. Fair enough. Come with me," he reached for her hand.

"Where are you taking me?"

"Come on, I promise not to bite, unless you want me to," he teased.

He led her into an office off the rec room. A drawing table faced the city. On top of it were various colored charcoal pencils, erasers and large sheets of white drawing paper.

She gasped when she noticed the drawing in the center of the table. She looked up at him, unsure what to say.

He looked back at her in much the same manner.

He shrugged. "I took a picture of you with my phone when you were shopping. I wanted something more permanent, so I drew you. So, as you can see, I *have* been thinking about you."

Her fingers traced lightly over the drawing. No one had ever drawn her before. Well, there was that caricature artist, but he made her head look four sizes too big.

"I don't know what to say," she said hoarsely. She didn't want him to see her watery eyes so she kept her eyes glued on the drawing.

He placed his palm on her cheek, but she resisted. "Em?"

She shook her head. "I can't look at you now."

"Why?" he asked softly.

She sniffled, "Because!" She shuffled away and paced in front of the window. "That is absolutely the sweetest thing anyone has ever said to me and then for you to draw a picture of me? I'm having a female moment. Gimme a minute."

He gave her a few minutes to compose herself. He still had shit to say before he lost his nerve and the moment.

"Em. I'm not gonna lie, I can be a major asshole sometimes. I'm not perfect and I make mistakes just as much as the next guy." He moved closer, brushing his fingers against her shoulder. "I haven't been in a monogamous relationship in eleven years. I forgot how to be a boyfriend."

She raised a skeptical eyebrow and he continued. "I'm not sure how

74

this will work because I'm a selfish person. I like to be alone and don't like having to explain my actions to anyone."

Her bottom lip trembled. "What about the seven day thing?"

He shook his head. "I've already told you that seven days wouldn't be enough for me."

When she didn't respond right away he sighed. "Talk to me, Em."

"You scare the hell out of me, too," she admitted.

He pulled her tightly against his chest and murmured into her hair. "We'll be scared together."

Chapter Five

"So…we totally got off track of the things we have in common," Chase reminded her.

"Yeah, but this feels nice," Emily murmured into his chest.

Her breasts rubbed against his stomach. "You're killin' me girl," he moaned. "Come on; let's head back to the couch."

With his arm placed firmly around her waist he led her towards the rec room. "Hey! I just thought of something we both enjoy!" he grinned.

"Cuddling?" she offered.

He wiggled his eyebrows. "Well, there is that, but I was referring to the arts. You like to act and I play the guitar and piano."

"Really?"

"Yeah, when I was sixteen I had a little garage band," he shrugged. "I'm interested in hearing about this play you were practicing for though."

She glanced away and quickly came up with a make believe play. "Um, it's about a girl who can see and talk to ghosts."

She turned her head in time to catch his reaction and wished she wouldn't have.

"Aw c'mon, I'm sure it's a good play," he replied half-heartedly. "Who wrote it?"

"Some local guy," she sniffed. " Don't you believe in ghosts?"

He snorted, "Nope. When you die, that's it."

*   *   *

The dark blue velour sectional couch in the rec room was quite comfortable, for doing just about anything, she noted.

He sat in the corner of the couch, patting the space next to him.

She arched an eyebrow and sat on the other side, pulling her legs under herself.

He rolled his eyes. "As much as I'd like to, I'm not going to attack you, Emily."

"Just removing temptation, Mr. Storm," she grinned slyly.

He stared at her, well, actually gaped at her. The tank top stretched perfectly in all the right places. He lifted a gray throw pillow and placed it over his lap.

Little Chase wanted to come out and play at all the wrong times.

"Why, Mr. Storm, I do believe I see color staining your cheeks," she drawled.

Yeah, and my dick is straining my shorts, he thought morbidly.

"So when did you get into the acting thing?" he asked, to take his mind from his delicate condition.

"A while ago. It's no big deal, really. I never get a part."

Lying is a great way to start off a relationship, dipshit, she admonished herself.

"Why don't you tell me about your garage band?"

He rolled his head onto the back of the couch and laughed. "Well, we did get a few gigs at local high schools, but nothing more than that. It was hard

78

to fit in practice time when I was on the basketball team, so eventually we disbanded."

"I bet you had a lot of groupies," she teased.

He ran a hand over his face. She needed to sit still because every time she moved, her tits jiggled. It was very distracting.

His voice cracked, "Um, no, not really."

"I find that hard to believe. I can't tell you how many women swarm to Freddie after a show. It's kind of disgusting," she scowled.

Chase shrugged. He needed a drink to subdue his carnal urges, but was afraid to get up because he'd look pretty damn silly walking with a pillow over his crotch.

She frowned. "For someone wanting to talk so much, you're awfully quiet."

He pointed his index finger at her. "It's your fault!"

"How?" she laughed.

"Look at the way you're dressed!" he scowled, waving a hand.

She laughed, "Well, I'm wearing more than you are!"

His mouth opened into a big circle. "You think this is funny, do ya?"

She placed a hand over her mouth to stifle a giggle.

He tossed the pillow to the floor and crawled towards her. "Stop right there Chase!" she warned, giggling.

He crept closer causing her to jump from the couch. He chased in full pursuit.

She felt silly trying to run away. So she stopped in mid-flight, allowing him to catch her.

Her back was to his front and she felt his hardness in her lower back.

His arms encircled her waist. Panting, he whispered in her ear. "I want you, but I won't do anything you don't want me to."

He slid his tongue seductively around her ear and lower to her neck.

She leaned into him, giving him full access to her neck. This was so not like her! A first date? Shit! It wasn't even a first date! *Jared* would've been a first date. Chase was a *first date interruptus*!

"Chase," she moaned. When he didn't stop she turned around him. He warily gazed at her.

He was a creature of habit. He liked to fuck! But, for her, he'd lasso a rope around his urges. He extended his arms out, putting distance between them. "Sorry," he muttered. "I got caught up in the moment."

"It's just that…I usually date someone for a while before I go that far," she mumbled.

"How long is 'a while'?" he asked.

Shrugging, she replied, "I don't know. Six months?"

Six months! Holy fuck! No way he'd be able to wait that long! *Christ!*

She giggled nervously at his expression. Oh what the hell!

Reaching up she grabbed the back of his neck and pulled his face down to hers. She chastely kissed him on the lips, expecting him to reciprocate. When he didn't, she gently pushed his lips apart with her tongue.

He grabbed her around the waist and lifted her up, his hands holding her bottom. She wrapped her legs around him and drove her tongue deeper into his mouth.

A loud moan escaped from his lips and he released her, but she clung to him. "Emily, I can only maintain my composure for so long. Let's stop before we do something you'll regret later."

She ran a hand through his hair and gazed into his eyes. "I don't want to stop."

His head jerked back. "Em, don't tease," he replied sternly.

She ran her tongue around his throat and bit him gently on the side of his neck. "I'm not teasing," she purred, planting hot wet kisses along his jaw.

His breath caught in his throat. She was a nice girl and *he* corrupted her! He squeezed his eyes shut and rested his forehead against hers.

"Not tonight, Em," he said huskily. Some things are worth waiting for and he didn't want her to think it was all about sex to him.

Nope, somehow, Emily Waters managed to touch something deep inside of him and he wasn't going to blow it.

*   *   *

She slid down his body and wrapped her arms around herself, self-consciously.

Chase ran his thumb over her cheek softly. "Em, it's not that I don't want to, because clearly, I do," he paused and gestured to the tent forming in his shorts. "But I want to start our relationship off right."

"It's fine," she replied, waving a hand dismissively. "I'm not upset."

But she was.

Chase Storm didn't get to where he was by being a stupid man. "Em," he said softly, walking towards her.

When she wouldn't respond or turn around he gathered her in his arms and carried her to his bedroom.

A trill of excitement roiled in her belly. Well, that and nerves.

Suddenly she didn't want to have sex with him. She writhed in his arms, protesting.

"Sh-h-h," he murmured, placing her gently on the bed.

"But," she cried against his lips.

"Goodnight Miss Waters. Sleep well," he whispered, pulling the blanket over her.

She sat up on her elbows and watched him close the bedroom door.

She laid her head against the pillow, not sure if she should feel relieved or pissed off that Chase Storm found his morals.

*   *   *

Chase picked up the television remote and climbed onto the velour couch with a sigh.

A beautiful, half-naked woman, who wanted him, was lying in his bed.

He snorted at the irony of it all.

When the fuck did he get all ethical?

Aggravated, he ran a hand over his face and begged for sleep to come.

*   *   *

Chase rolled onto the remote causing the volume to rise at ear-deafening levels. "Fuck!" he growled groping around his stomach.

Finding the remote he switched off the television and rolled onto his back.

"Oh! Excuse me, Mr. Storm. I didn't realize you were in here," Nicole, his maid flustered.

Chase lifted a gritty eyelid. "What time is it?" he snapped.

"It's eleven, sir. Would you like some coffee?" she offered, smoothing her green apron nervously.

He closed his eye and groaned. "A glass of water and ibuprofen would be better."

"Yes, sir." Her footsteps padded quickly across the wood floor.

She returned shortly and cleared her throat. Chase sat up and took the proffered items and glanced at her.

Nicole had been with him a year and he didn't see much of her. Usually he was at the office. He swallowed two pills and looked at her with eyebrows raised.

"Nicole? It's Sunday. Why are you here?"

"Sir, I left a note for you on the kitchen counter the other day. I couldn't be here on Friday and offered to come in today to clean. Didn't you get it?" she asked, fumbling with her hands.

He eyed the young raven haired woman and shook his head. "Sorry, I must've missed that. Is Miss Waters awake?" he asked.

"Sir?" she questioned.

"Um, Miss Waters...never mind, I'll check on her," he mumbled.

Nicole turned to leave, glad to be on her way.

"Nicole?"

She stopped and hesitantly turned around. "Sir?"

He wiggled the glass and bottle of pills in his hands. "Thanks for bringing these to me."

Color stained her alabaster skin. "You're welcome." She turned to leave again, this time with a small smile on her lips.

"Oh Nicole?" he grinned.

She wiped the grin from her face and turned. "Sir?"

"Why don't you call it a day?"

She fumbled with her hands again. "I just arrived."

Chase shrugged, "And my dust will be here tomorrow. Go on. Enjoy your day."

"Thank you Mr. Storm!" she beamed.

She was quite a looker, but Chase never mixed business with pleasure.

He placed the glass in the sink and put the pills on the kitchen island. Surely Emily was going to have one hell of a hang-over.

He frowned momentarily. Why wasn't she awake yet?

Padding across the floor to his room he opened the door and heard faint snoring.

She lay on her side with her right arm and leg wrapped around one of his pillows.

He swallowed hard while little Chase woke up. *Lucky damn pillow*, he thought.

Quietly he walked to the closet and then to the dresser. He stopped to look at her again and smiled in amazement.

He was the perfect gentleman last night. Who would've thunk it?

*　　　*　　　*

After Chase dressed he hastily scribbled a note to Emily, in case she awoke while he was gone, leaving it on the breakfast nook. Then jotted down a few things for himself, slipping the paper into his pants pocket.

Traveling down the elevator to the first floor, plans formed in his head.

The beauty of living where he did was the fact that downstairs there was a mini-mall of sorts. One could easily never leave the building. It had just about everything; restaurants, clothing stores, a bank, two newspaper stands, a dry-cleaner and a pharmacy.

His first stop was the dry cleaners, to drop off Emily's soiled dress.

Next stop was the women's clothing store where he purchased a short sleeved white cotton blouse and a pair of short denim jeans. The sales girl called them 'Capri's'.

"Do you sell shoes here?" he asked as his eyes searched the shop.

The petite chestnut haired girl smiled, "Sure we do!" and promptly led him to a small section along the back wall. He chose a pair of comfortable looking white sandals.

"Will there be anything else?" she asked him sweetly.

Chase reddened as they walked past the lingerie section. He looked at the girl apologetically and pointed at the bras, mumbling about size.

Nodding she grinned and helped him to pick out a size and color, assuring him that if it didn't fit he could exchange it.

Panties were much easier to purchase.

After he paid for his selections he went on the hunt for breakfast.

*　　　*　　　*

Chase returned an hour later and hung the clothing bags on the coat rack and placed the breakfast items on the kitchen nook next to the ibuprofen.

His note was still there.

He kicked his shoes off and stepped into the bedroom. It didn't look like she'd moved an inch since he last checked on her.

He knelt next to the bed and lightly ran his fingers along her arm.

Her right eye flew open. Then she sat upright, clutching the pillow.

He smiled in amusement. "Good morning," he said softly.

She smoothed her hair down. "Morning," she croaked.

He pulled himself up and sat next to her. "How's your stomach feel?"

She shrugged and smiled. "I think it's still asleep. What time is it?"

"About one, but by my calculations it's breakfast time. Come on," he murmured, holding his hand out to her.

As he led her from the bedroom, she released his hand and put on the Cubs jersey lying on the bed.

She sat on a dark blue fabric stool at the kitchen nook while he set out plates and cutlery.

Something smelled good, causing her stomach to rumble.

"Did you sleep well?" he asked, pulling bagels and cream cheese from the bags.

"Surprisingly enough, yeah," she mused. Normally, at home, she'd awaken for one reason or another. Here she slept like a baby.

Must've been all the margarita's she'd had.

"Coffee?" he offered.

"Thank you."

He placed cream containers and sugar packets in front of her as well as a stirrer and continued slicing the bagels.

She scowled while watching him.

It wasn't fair.

He looked pretty freaking hot with messy hair, like he ran his fingers through it.

Sure she looked like death warmed over, caused her scowl to deepen.

"What's with the face?" he grinned.

She waved a hand at him. "You! How long have you been up?"

"A little over an hour, why?"

She sighed, "Never mind. You wouldn't understand."

He placed his hands on the ceramic counter. "What wouldn't I understand?"

"You look…well, perfect and I'm sure I look like shit, that's what!" she hissed, rolling her eyes.

"You look fine. Come on and eat. We'll have freshly baked bagels now and later when we're sure your stomach can handle it, we'll have lunch."

"I'd say it's lunchtime now," she muttered, slathering cream cheese on a bagel.

"Technically it is, but since we slept in, it's breakfast," he mumbled, sitting down next to her.

She chewed her bagel, thinking about what he'd said. "Lunch? Are you planning on holding me hostage?"

He licked a bit of cream cheese from his thumb. "Would you rather go home?"

She thought about it for a few minutes as she took a sip of coffee and shrugged. She had nothing planned for the day.

"Excellent!" he grinned. "Besides, I have some really cool things planned for us to do today."

Her eyebrow lifted, but she couldn't contain a smile. "Such as?"

"I'd like to take you to Navy Pier. Check out stuff there," he shrugged.

She looked down at her clothing. "Yeah, I can't really wear this and since my dress has seen better days…"

He jumped from the stool. "Not to worry! I have that under control."

She spun around and watched him walk toward the door. Her eyebrows knitted together when he handed her two packages.

"For you," he offered.

"I don't…what is this?"

"Well, open them," he urged.

She eyed him quizzically while pulling the garment bag from the hanger. A white cotton blouse with a rounded collar was the first item she saw and behind that was a pair of Capri's. Her lips tipped upward into a small grin.

She placed the garment bag over the back of the couch and peeked inside the other bag.

"Panties and a bra?" She pulled them out and lifted a questioningly eyebrow.

"Well, I didn't think you wore a bra last night…and the panties…well, I can't have you wearing the same panties," he stammered.

She eyed him warily and dug into the bag, pulling out a shoe box.

"Chase!" she admonished. "Sandals, too? How the hell did you even know my size?"

He pulled the sheet of paper from his pocket. "I got the sizes from your dress and your shoes. The salesgirl said that if the bra wasn't the right size we could exchange it."

He snapped his jaws shut. It felt like he was babbling and by the looks of her grin, he was.

She shook her head and held out her hand. He took it into his and kissed the palm.

"No, silly. Receipts. So I can pay you back," she replied.

He drew away stunned, or hurt. She couldn't tell.

"I don't want your money, Em. I bought those things for you because I wanted to."

Hurt, she mused. "Chase…"

His eyes darkened. "You don't like them?"

"It's not that. They're great, but we hardly know each other and you're buying me personal things," she frowned, dangling the bra and panties in front of him.

"I liked buying you those things and I'm not just talking the lingerie."

"I'll be right back," she sighed, taking the packages with her.

*   *   *

Chase cleaned up while he waited for Emily to dress. He didn't understand her hesitation with the clothes. All the other women he'd bought stuff for didn't have a problem accepting gifts from him. In fact, some of them looked deeper into the bags, expecting more.

Maybe that's what set her apart from them.

*   *   *

Emily mentally added up the cost of the clothes. Who the hell would pay three hundred dollars for a pair of jeans, a blouse, panties and a bra?

Chase *fucking* Storm that's who! The man had no money sense!

Rolling her eyes at each item she put on, she dressed slowly.

Afterwards she used his hairbrush and bent at the waist brushing her hair forward. She stood upright and brushed it back where it fanned softly around her face.

*   *   *

"Well, you have an eye for sizes," she teased entering the living room.

He jumped at the sound of her voice.

"Sorry, I didn't mean to startle you," she apologized.

He turned his back on the view of Chicago and nodded at her. "You look great."

She snorted, "I should, wearing a three hundred dollar outfit. Honestly, Chase! Don't you ever do anything cheap?"

He shrugged, "Are you ready to start our first official date?"

She cocked her head. "Is this the first of seven dates?"

He crossed the room to her, placing a palm on her cheek. "I've already told you, seven days wouldn't be enough for me."

89

*　　　*　　　*

In the car Chase put the air conditioner on. The temperature was steadily climbing and was expected to break records for the day.

"So, have you ever been to the Pier?" he asked, moving through traffic slowly.

She blushed. "I told you, I don't come to the city much."

He blinked in disbelief. "How long have you lived in the area?"

"My whole life. Jeesh! I don't like driving in the city! It scares the hell out of me with people weaving in and out of traffic," she confessed.

"There's always the train," he offered with a grin.

She rolled her eyes. "Don't get me started on the train. What if I got off at the wrong stop? I don't know my way around Chicago at all. I'd be screwed, which is why I don't come to the city."

He gripped her hand and squeezed it. "You're fuckin' adorable!"

"Why because I'm a moron when it comes to Chicago?" she snorted.

He laughed. "No, because you're so honest. It's very refreshing."

*　　　*　　　*

They spent the day playing mini-golf, eating fudge from a specialty shop along the way and talking.

"So, did you do this sort of stuff with the other girls?" she asked as they held hands on a bench.

"Do you mean did I bring them here?" She nodded, biting her lip. He brought her hand to his lips and kissed it. "No. This is a first. This sort of stuff wouldn't have interested them."

"Well, I happen to like it, so thank you," she grinned.

Maybe it was her grin or her honesty, Chase wasn't sure, but he felt a subtle shift in his chest causing his breath to hitch.

He pulled her against him and kissed her. She tasted like chocolate fudge. "Mmm…you taste mighty fine, Miss Waters," he murmured against her lips.

She laughed, "Well, I wasn't expecting you to kiss me when I still had fudge in my mouth." She wiped her mouth with a paper napkin and pointed towards the sky.

He turned his head and looked back at her with a puzzled expression. "What?"

She rolled her eyes. "The sun!"

He shrugged, "Um, yeah?"

Tugging on his hand she stood. "Let's go watch the sun set."

He threw out the remains of their watered down soda and wrapped an arm around her. "Are you getting cold?" he asked.

"A little," she shrugged.

"Come on."

"The sunset is the other way," she pouted.

"We won't miss it, I promise," he replied as he walked towards a sports shop.

Emily's eyes lit up when they entered the store. Jersey's from every Chicago sports team lined the walls. Chase pulled her towards the hockey jerseys.

He took one off the rack and held it up to her. She wrinkled her nose. The player wasn't one of her favorites. "Hm…how about this one?" he offered. It was Seth Brice, captain of the Chicago Wind's jersey that he held in his hand.

"Now that's more like it," she grinned.

She caught the price tag in her hand and gaped. "I can't afford that."

"I can," he grinned over his shoulder, taking the jersey to the counter.

"Chase! No!"

"Can you clip the tags for me?" Chase asked the cashier. "She's going to wear it now."

The teenaged cashier nodded and handed Chase back his credit card.

Emily rolled her eyes. "Chase! I can't accept that! Are you crazy?"

He pulled the jersey over her head, kissing her nose. "Yep. I'm crazy about you. Now come on, quit pouting and let's go watch that sunset."

*   *   *

They sat on a bench that edged Lake Michigan and watched the boaters skim across the water.

"Ever been on a boat, Em?"

She shivered slightly. "A few times. It's not my thing."

He wrapped his arm around her. "You're still cold," he mumbled in her ear.

She closed her eyes briefly and sighed. "No, not really." She turned to face him. "When I was five I went boating with my family. Anyway, the water got choppy and I fell overboard."

He gasped, "My God!"

"We weren't far from the shore, but I couldn't swim."

His eyebrows knitted together as he softly caressed her cheek, encouraging her to continue.

"No lifejacket," she said softly. "They figure I was clinically dead for five minutes."

"Holy shit!"

A corner of her mouth lifted slightly. "Yeah. So…I tend to avoid large bodies of water now." She turned and waved her hand towards the lake. "This is the closest I'll get."

He pulled her closely and planted a kiss on her forehead. She snorted, "Kind of ironic, don't ya think? I'm afraid of water and my last name is Waters."

He lifted the corner of his mouth slightly at her candidness.

"I don't tell too many people that story." She frowned, "I'm not even sure why I told you."

She spared him the stories of seeing the long past bloated victims of the lake.

To add levity Chase shifted so they could watch the sunset. "Now that…that's a sunset," he said softly.

The sun nestled over the water casting the sky with red, orange and purple hues.

"Wow!" Emily exclaimed breathily. "I've never seen such a magnificent sunset!"

Chase lifted a brow. He'd seen many sunsets from his condo, but he'd never appreciated them. Until now.

*   *   *

He'd been told many years ago the girl would return. He knew she had when he felt drawn towards the shore. He lurked in the shadows searching the faces of women that passed by. When he no longer felt a pull a curse passed his lips.

"There! On the bench," Mitch pointed.

The Grey One glanced at his underling and grinned. "Well done, Mitch."

"Shall I jump into her?" Marianna asked excitedly. She'd do anything to please Grey and move on from this realm.

93

"Not yet, my child. Let us follow her for a spell," Grey cackled.

*   *   *

"I had a wonderful day," Emily said softly when Chase pulled into her driveway.

He lifted her hand to his mouth and kissed it. "Me, too."

And he didn't want it to end. "Can I come in?" he asked, hopefully.

She grinned, "Of course, but I must warn you. My dwelling isn't as affluent as yours."

"Em stop that, okay?"

"I'll try," she smirked, getting out of the Porsche.

As she fished her keys from her purse she noticed Chase in the middle of the yard, staring at the house and then across the street.

"Something wrong?" she frowned.

"Your house is different from the other ones on the block."

"And?"

He shook his head. "I'm wondering why. It's very unusual."

"Well, from what I've heard, the land was purchased by a builder who designed this house especially for his wife. A home that was unique from the others and something she'd be proud of."

She didn't tell him that she heard it straight from the horses' mouth, sixty years after he died.

"I like it," he beamed under the porch light. She rolled her eyes and he laughed, "Seriously. I really like the turret."

"Thanks, but my ideal home is an old farmhouse," she grinned.

She pushed the door open and was greeted immediately by Freddie.

"Where the hell have you been and why aren't you answering your cell?" he yelled.

"Why hello, Freddie," she replied sarcastically.

He glared at Chase momentarily then turned his attention back to Emily. "Rule number one: if you're going to stay out the entire night, call the roommate to let them know. Your rule, remember?" he replied icily.

Chase held up a hand. "It's my fault. She wasn't well enough to bring home so I took her to my place."

"Not talking to you," Freddie growled.

"Lighten up, Fred. I'm sorry I didn't call, but I was super drunk and then later sick. I didn't think to call," Emily shrugged.

Freddie motioned his head towards Chase. "Is he the one who got you drunk?"

She spluttered, "No! I got me drunk! Back off, willya?" She cast a menacing look at Freddie. "I'll be right back. Play nice with Chase."

Freddie watched Emily go up the stairs. When he heard the bathroom door close he turned to Chase, jabbing his forefinger into his chest. "You! She's not doing the seven day thing so forget about it."

Chase smirked, pushing Freddie's finger away. "I don't expect her to. She's a nice girl, Freddie."

"You're damn right!" Freddie huffed, walking into the living room.

"You're very protective of her," Chase commented, following Freddie.

"She's my only cousin and my best friend. So, yeah, if anyone thinks of hurting her they'll have to deal with me."

A wrapped package sat on the pine coffee table, stirring Chase's curiosity. "Emily tells me you have a lot of female admirers. Is that a gift from one of them?"

Freddie snorted, "Chicks don't send guys flowers."

95

"Says who?" Emily laughed, bounding down the stairs.

"No guy wants a bouquet of flowers sent to them. It's emasculating," Freddie sneered. "Besides, they're for you."

Emily cocked her head at Chase and grinned.

He lifted an eyebrow and shrugged as she tore the paper from the bouquet.

The arrangement consisted of pink carnations, several red and white roses, purple statice and baby's breath.

"Oh! They're beautiful Chase!"

Chase frowned. "I think you should read the card, Em."

Her eyebrows knitted together as she pulled the card from the white envelope. Freddie grinned when he caught Chase glowering.

She read the card, frowning. "I assumed they were from you."

Chase clenched his jaw. "Apparently I have some competition."

She tore the paper away from the crystal vase to hide her uneasiness.

"So…who are they from?" Freddie prodded gleefully.

She shot him a glare, causing him to flash a smile at her.

"I'd like to know who sent my girlfriend flowers, too," Chase replied tightly.

Freddie sucked in a lungful of air. "Whoa! You two are dating now?"

"Um…I dunno," Emily blushed.

Chase pulled her down onto his lap. "I'd like for you to be my girlfriend, " he said softly, caressing her cheek.

The smoldering gaze he held her with made her insides turn to a mushy mess.

He pulled her closer, pressing his lips gently against hers.

"Ahem...I'm still sitting here," Freddie complained.

"Sit somewhere else if you don't like it," Emily mumbled.

Freddie shifted in the chair. "C'mon, who sent you the flowers?"

Emily pulled away from Chase long enough to shoot a look to Freddie, that implored him to shut up. When she returned her attention back to Chase he lifted an eyebrow.

"Who are they from?" he asked quizzically.

She rolled her eyes and huffed, "Jared."

"You must've made quite an impression on him, although I can't say I'm surprised," Chase grinned brightly at her, but inside he was beyond pissed off.

"Maybe, but I left with you," she gently reminded him.

Chase lifted her from his lap and stood. "Speaking of leaving, I need to go."

She frowned, "Because of the flowers?"

He gripped her hand and pulled her towards the front door. "No, because I've had an exhausting day with a beautiful lady and I need my beauty sleep."

Outside he pulled her against him and ran his hand over her hair. "I had a really good time today," he said softly.

"Me, too," she replied breathily. The way he looked at her made her feel woozy.

"Can I see you tomorrow night?"

"Actually, Freddie and his band have a concert in the park. You're welcome to come with me," she offered.

"I'd like that. I'll call you tomorrow to get the details." He chastely kissed her goodbye before getting into his car.

Her eyes followed his car until she could no longer see it.

When she turned towards the house Freddie stood in the doorway with his arms crossed.

"What?" she asked, brushing past him.

"What's the deal with that guy?"

She poured herself a glass of lemonade and told him the events that transpired the night before.

"I get that Storm is good looking and rich, but it sounds like Jared should be the guy you date. I'm not trying to be a dick, but Storm's kinda outta your league," Freddie commented.

She shot him a glare. "You think I don't know that? I even went so far to tell him that last night." She sighed and looked over her shoulder at him. "I'm going to shower and hit the sack."

As she climbed the stairs Freddie's words echoed in her mind.

Chase *was* out of her league.

*   *   *

Chase turned off the radio on his drive home. What was it about Emily? Certainly when he first met her all he thought about was making her a seven day girl.

But he realized she wasn't like those women. They never held his interest like she did.

He didn't want to know anything personal about them. When he took them out they'd drone on about their lives and he'd feign interest but it was different when he was with Emily.

He wanted to know everything about her, but why?

When he pulled into the parking garage he had another epiphany.

He felt comfortable with her.

*   *   *

The next day as soon as Emily unlocked the door to her shop she was hit with twenty questions from Phyllis.

"Tell me why Jenny stomped around here yesterday complaining about you and some guy!"

Emily shook her head, smiling. "Was she really pissed?"

"Helllloooo darlin'!" Frankie crooned, popping out from a wall.

"Hi Frankie!" Emily and Phyllis said in unison.

Frankie laughed, "Yeah, ol' red was hoppin' mad. She was so mad she yelled at us! Said you were a better friend to us than to her."

Emily rolled her eyes. "Jenny can be a drama queen." She began turning on lights and headed towards the storage room.

"Ahem…we're still waiting," Phyllis whined.

"Do you remember the guy who came in here and asked me out?" she smiled.

Phyllis nearly panted, "Oh yes!"

Frankie snorted, "That pip squeak?"

"Hush!" Phyllis admonished, slapping his arm.

As Emily readied the shop for opening she relayed the tale of the previous two evenings. Afterwards she sat down on a vintage stool behind the counter, still smiling.

"You're glowing!" Phyllis laughed. "I haven't seen you smile this big since…well, never. Just be careful sweetie."

"Yeah, watch out for Mr. Got Rocks. Em, men are only interested in

99

one thing and once we get it, we tend to move on," Frankie warned.

Emily rolled her eyes. "Look, I offered myself up to him Saturday night and he flatly refused."

They turned when they heard a squeak from the corner of the room.

Lilly blushed. "I don't mean to interrupt, but Emily, why would a man buy a cow if he can get the milk for free?"

*   *   *

At noon Chase put the finishing touches on a house design. The subdivision on the farm land would be different from anything Storm Design Group ever created. These houses would have personality and character, each would be vastly different than the others.

He found himself growing more excited about the houses as he scanned the internet looking at homes from the early 1900's, like Emily's.

He pushed his arms out and stretched. It'd been a long morning. He awoke at five and couldn't get back to sleep. Instead he started up a pot of coffee and went directly into his office and began sketching out designs.

The late morning sun glinted off a nearby building nearly blinding him. *Maybe shades wouldn't be a bad idea*, he thought as he stared out the ceiling to floor windows.

He heard Nicole in the living room and rose from his chair.

"Nicole? I'm home," he warned before walking out of his office.

She jumped at the sound of his voice. "I'm sorry to disturb you."

"Ya didn't. I'm working from home today. I just didn't want to frighten you," he grinned.

She eyed him warily. He never stayed home from work, even when he was sick with the flu last year. "Are you sick, sir? Would you like some soup?"

A knock at the door caused her to jump again. "I've got it, Nicole," he replied walking towards the door.

"Dad! You got my e-mail?"

Preston Storm gripped his son's shoulder and grinned. "I love it! I knew you'd come up with great designs. I came by to check-it out in person. I hope that's okay?"

Chase led him to his office, laughing. "Of course! You don't need an invitation!"

Preston noticed a subtle change in his son and smiled. He was going to ask what happened when he noticed the drawing of a very pretty woman on Chase's drawing table.

He studied the house plans, nodding and grunting. "I like where your head is at with this, Chase. People are looking for something unique, different." He tapped at the design with his forefinger. "Storm Designs will give it to them. Well done, Chase!"

Chase beamed at his dad's words. "Who's this charming creature?" Preston asked, pointing to the drawing of Emily.

"Emily. She's a friend of Beth's," Chase replied huskily causing Preston's eyebrows to lift.

"Oh, I thought perhaps she was your latest conquest," Preston joked.

Chase shook his head. "Um, actually, at first I did want her to be a seven day girl, but she's not like that."

"She told you no, huh?"

"Well, that and other things," Chase laughed, raking a hand through his hair. "Seven days wouldn't be enough for me anyway."

Preston rested his arm on the drawing table. It'd been a long time since Chase talked like this with him. "So, you like her?"

Chase shrugged, "Yeah. Go figure, huh? She's exasperating, befuddling, beautiful and did I say exasperating?"

"Twice," his dad smiled.

Chase stuffed his fists into his jean pockets and paced the room. "She's so different from the other women. I mean, I want to get to know her before we have sex. Can you believe it?"

The skin around Preston's eyes crinkled. "How long have you known her?"

"I met her at Candy's birthday party and haven't been able to get her out of my mind. Then Saturday night I saw her at a bar with some guy and nearly lost my fucking mind! Anyway, I brought her back here and…"

His dad cut him off. "You brought her here?"

Chase smirked, "Yeah. I know, completely out of character for me. But that's what she does to me! Makes me completely irrational! She's got me breaking my own damn rules!"

Preston laughed and patted his son's shoulder. "That's what love does to a man."

Chase's jaw clenched. "I'm not in love with her dad."

"If you say so," Preston winked. "Are you seeing her tonight?"

"Yeah. Her cousin's in a band and they have a show at a park in the 'burbs."

"You're driving to the suburbs?"

"Emily actually lives near Beth, so yeah. I'm becoming quite the suburbanite. See what I mean? She's making me do crazy shit!"

"Sounds like it could be a romantic evening with a picnic dinner, a bottle of wine…" Preston murmured.

Chase slapped his dad on the back. "You're such a romantic!"

Preston gazed at the drawing of Emily. "It seems to run in the family."

*　　　*　　　*

Emily had just finished with a customer when her phone rang. Her heart leapt when she read the caller ID.

"Good afternoon," she said breathily.

"Hello, beautiful," Chase replied. "What are your plans for dinner tonight?"

She tucked a strand of hair behind her ear and turned away from the three ghosts. "I haven't thought that far ahead, I've been pretty busy."

"I'll bring a picnic dinner and we'll eat at the park."

"Why Mr. Storm, you're going to make me swoon," she teased.

"Why Miss Waters, those are my intentions." She giggled, causing a grin to form on his face. "I love to hear you laugh," he said softly. "I'll pick you up at six."

"I look forward to it," she replied, smiling like an idiot when she hung up the phone.

"Don't be such a weak sister!" Phyllis chided.

"Huh?" Emily frowned.

"A push-over. Like Lilly says, ya need to play hard to get! Use your noodle, ya follow?"

"Yeah, that guy frosts me," Frankie added.

Emily shook her head. "I promise I'll be careful, okay?"

"We just don't want to see you get hurt is all," Phyllis said with a smile that didn't meet her eyes.

103

Chapter Six

Emily placed a blue blanket under a large oak tree. When she and Chase got settled she caught Freddie's eye and waved. He fumbled with his guitar, shaking his head at her.

"I get the impression Freddie doesn't like me," Chase muttered.

"He's just concerned. He'll get over it."

He blew out a hard breath. "I've told him that it wasn't a seven day thing with you."

She placed her hand on his knee. "Don't stress about it, okay?"

"Wine?" he sighed, opening the wicker basket.

Emily got on her knees and peered into the large basket, her eyes widening. "Wow! You went all out!"

The basket was lined with red checked fabric and on the inside lids two wine glasses and cutlery were held in place with elastic. Nestled inside were plates, napkins, a bottle of Pinot Grigio and a cold container which held the food.

Chase smirked as he opened the wine. "I hope you like turkey sandwiches."

She held the glasses as he filled them. Afterwards she handed him a glass. "A toast," he said softly. "To our second of many dates."

"Have you done this before?" she asked.

"Picnic?" he asked. She nodded and he laughed. "Nope. It's my first time."

"You're so prepared, I had to ask," she muttered.

He pushed the basket away to sit closer to her. "I went to a specialty shop and they put it together for me." He laughed and continued, "If I'd done this on my own we'd be eating peanut butter and jelly sandwiches."

She leaned in and kissed him. He brought his palm up to her cheek and kissed her deeply. After a few minutes he pulled away, resting his forehead against hers. "You taste mighty fine," he breathed heavily.

She blinked and laughed.

"You also look mighty fine," he murmured, his blue eyes raking over her. "Your blue checkered dress kinda reminds me of Dorothy's from *The Wizard of Oz*. Except, I don't think Dorothy's neck-line plunged so deeply," he gently scolded, running his index finger from her throat towards the top of her breasts.

A loud guitar twang came from the bandstand causing Chase to withdraw his finger quickly. He looked over his shoulder to see Freddie glaring at him.

Emily laughed, ignoring her cousin. She gently cleared her throat turning Chase's attention from the bandstand. "I'm getting a little light-headed from the wine."

Together they made their plates with turkey sandwiches and potato salad.

Chase gawked at the crowd forming around them as he chewed his sandwich. "Are these people fans or just here to make a night of it?"

Emily grinned. "A lot of them look familiar. You'd be surprised how many fans Double Exposure has."

His eyebrows knitted together. "That's the name of his band?"

106

"Yeah. They were called Four Dudes until they asked me to take a picture for a flyer and it came out as a double exposure." She shrugged and continued, "I told them they should change their name to Double Exposure. I thought it sounded better than Four Dudes."

"I have to agree with you. Four Dudes," he snorted.

"You can kiss me again," Emily whispered in his ear.

Chase grinned lazily. "I can?"

She pointed to the people standing in front of them, blocking Freddie's view. Chase wiggled an eyebrow and placed his empty plate behind him.

"Thank God for crowds," he murmured, pulling her chin gently towards him.

She playfully licked his lips causing little Chase to rise to the occasion.

Chase groaned the instant he heard his sisters voice. "Em? Is that you?"

Emily quickly pulled away from Chase and saw Beth standing next to her. She blushed, "Hey Beth, Neil. I didn't know you'd be here."

"Well, I didn't expect to see you here Chase," Beth laughed.

He rolled his eyes. "Small world, huh?"

"Mom and dad offered to watch the kids so we could get out," Beth replied placing a blanket next to Emily's. "I've heard Emily gush about her cousin's band so, here we are."

Chase shot his sister a grimace and she stuck her tongue out at him.

Neil sat next to his wife and held out his hand to Chase. "Hey Chaser, how's it going?"

Chase took his hand and replied snidely, "Awesome."

Emily looked at Chase quizzically. "Chaser?"

Neil laughed, "Yeah he got the nickname because he's a skirt chaser."

Chase scowled at him causing Beth to intercede. "They're starting!"

Emily put everything back in the basket except for the wine. She refilled her glass to the top.

Skirt chaser.

The words dredged up ugly images in her head. And made her bitchy.

"Hey! Down in front!" she yelled at the hippy foursome that blocked her view of the bandstand.

Chase looked at her quizzically. "Are you okay?"

She waved a hand at the hippies. "I can't see with the *Grateful Dead* wannabe's standing in front of us."

"Emily, no one is standing in front of us," Chase said slowly.

She glanced at Beth who shrugged and shook her head.

Emily momentarily closed her eyes and released a nervous laugh. "Must be the wine," she muttered, gaping at the hippies.

Chase frowned and emptied her glass on the grass next to him.

"Far out! The chick can see us!" a bewhiskered hippie whooped.

Chase leaned into her. "Em? Are you sure you're okay?"

She shook her head at the hippie. She *so* didn't need this right now!

"Hey, chick! Have the dudes play Hendrix!" the hippie begged.

Emily patted Chase's hand. "I'll be right back. I have to request a song."

He watched her dodge an open space of air on her way to the bandstand.

Emily grabbed a guy in a Double Exposure t-shirt and whispered something in his ear.

"How many of you follow us?" Freddie yelled out to the crowd.

A large applause erupted from the park. Freddie grinned, "Excellent! Then many of you are probably familiar with my cousin, Emily, who, when coerced, will come up and sing a few songs with us."

Emily shot Freddie a glare. She hated to get on stage! She only did it when she had enough drinks in her and two glasses of wine hardly constituted enough!

"A round of applause for the lovely Emily!" Freddie urged the crowd.

Her face grew hot when the band started chanting her name causing the crowd to follow.

Chase grabbed Beth's arm. "She can sing?"

Chase's eyes darted to the stage and when he didn't see her he got up and walked towards the stage.

He saw her shoot Freddie a glare as she wrapped her hands around the microphone.

A steady drum beat slowly began then her voice suddenly took over followed shortly by the guitars.

She kept her eyes closed, not wanting to see the crowd in front of her, let alone Chase.

Chase crossed his left arm over his chest, his right hand covered his mouth slightly as he watched her move her hips and belt out *I've Got the Music in Me.*

The woman had a voice on her!

He edged closer to the bandstand, the music vibrated in his chest from the large speakers placed on both sides of the stage.

He noticed the more she sang, the more relaxed she became. She saw him near the stage and shot him a wink.

Amazing wouldn't be a word he'd use when dating a woman, but dammit if she wasn't just that. She was full of surprises.

A lump formed in his throat as he watched her. She absolutely beguiled him. Not even his first love, Cassie Seton, had that affect on him.

The song ended and she bowed to the crowd and began to walk off the stage when someone yelled, "Encore!" urging her to sing another song.

"Any suggestions?" she said into the microphone.

A mix of songs were yelled, but Freddie opted for *Chain of Fools* in his attempt to be witty.

Ignoring his cheekiness, Emily strutted across the stage with the microphone firmly in hand and belted out the song with the same fervor Aretha Franklin was known for.

Watching her gyrate on stage put Chase on edge. If he was getting aroused looking at her, what effect was she having on the guys in the crowd? His jaw clenched along with his fists.

She attached the microphone to its stand and curtsied for the crowd when the song was over.

The crowd chanted her name but she begged off when Chase extended his hand in front of the stage. Grinning she leaned forward as he caught her in his arms. The crowd whooped and cheered when he twirled her in his arms with his lips firmly attached to hers.

He wanted *everyone*, including Freddie, to know that she was his.

*   *   *

With his arm firmly wrapped around her waist Chase led her back to their blanket. Emily noticed that the hippies moved closer to the stage to hear *Purple Haze*.

"Well, it seems as if I don't know very much about you," Chase breathed into her ear.

His warm breath against her neck made her shiver despite the warm

110

air temperature.

She shot him a lopsided grin. "Freddie says I have a good voice, but I think he's nuts."

Chase brushed his thumb along her cheek and gazed deeply into her hazel eyes. He realized in that moment how much he wanted her.

And not just for sex.

Nope, it went *way* the fuck deeper than that.

He quickly pulled away, muttering something about getting a bottle of water.

Emily watched him meander through the crowd wondering what caused the change in his demeanor. She leaned over to Beth and whispered, "Hey, do I smell?"

Beth edged closer to her wrapping her brown hair around her ears and sniffed the air. "Um, no, why?"

Frowning, Emily mumbled, "One minute he's looking, well, lovingly, into my eyes and the next minute he's running away."

Beth patted her friends' knee. "Just give him time, Em."

*   *   *

Chase stumbled around, not sure exactly where he was going but he had to put some distance between himself and Emily.

She was making him feel things that he hadn't felt in a long time, because he never allowed himself to.

After Cassie, he built a wall, no, a fuckin' fortress around his heart and damn if he didn't feel the mortar chipping away.

He stumbled past a mass of people until he found a restroom. There he splashed cold water on his face. As an afterthought he threw some water on his head to cool off and slicked it back.

111

He left the restroom and strolled to a small concession stand that had a long line of people. Ordinarily this would've annoyed him, but he wasn't in any hurry to get back to Emily.

A brunette wearing a flimsy tank-top turned around and smiled at him. He returned the smile which only encouraged her.

"Hi," she said huskily.

"Evening," he replied, casting a look over his shoulder.

She leaned into him, "Great band, huh?"

He turned and jerked when he realized just how close she'd gotten in nanoseconds. "Yeah. Have you seen them before?"

"Yeah. My girlfriend and I drove from the city to see them. How about you?"

He flinched as she jiggled and giggled her way closer to him. Now *she* could be a seven day girl, if he were so inclined, but oddly enough, he wasn't interested.

He shrugged. "My girlfriend is cousins with the leader of the group."

"Oh, how nice," she muttered, turning her back.

He chuckled, amazed the chick gave up so easily.

She turned and shoved a piece of paper into his hand. "My number, in case you lose interest in your girlfriend."

He glanced at the paper and sighed.

*   *   *

Emily grew agitated wondering where the hell Chase was.

Maybe he was skirt chasing.

The thought made her flinch.

"Emily?" a male voice said behind her.

112

She spun around. "Jared?"

"You were great up there," he grinned.

Color stained her cheeks. "Thanks. I'm sorry about the other night."

He shrugged, "I enjoyed it until we were rudely interrupted."

She touched his arm, "I'm sorry."

Jared looked down at his feet. "I didn't realize you already had a boyfriend."

"I didn't," she stammered.

"Did you like the flowers?" he asked.

"Yes, but you shouldn't have."

"Hey, I don't give up easily," he grinned, brushing a loose strand of hair from her face.

The intimate gesture caused her to stiffen in response.

She didn't have time to reply because Chase was suddenly next to her.

"Jared Jared," he said snidely, handing Emily a bottle of water.

Jared glared, "The last name is Buckley."

Chase wrapped an arm around Emily, staring angrily at him. "Like I give a fuck."

"Chase!" Emily admonished, flushing.

"It's okay Emily, I was leaving anyway. Enjoy the flowers," he smirked.

She watched Jared walk away then turned, narrowing her eyes at Chase. "You. Are. Rude!"

He feigned innocence. "What? The guy was panting for my girlfriend and I had a problem with it."

"Maybe he wouldn't have come over if you hadn't left me for a half hour. Where were you?" she snipped.

"I was getting water and the line was long," he shrugged, turning his attention towards the stage.

She crossed her arms over her chest when Chase wrapped his arm around her. When she didn't respond he nuzzled his nose to the area under her ear and kissed her. She almost forgot her anger until two women walked in front of them and ogled Chase. She heard the brunette whisper, "That's him."

"You seem to have an admirer," Emily said icily.

Chase lifted his head from her neck and followed her line of vision.

He nodded politely, causing the brunette to giggle.

"Is she a friend of yours?" Emily asked sarcastically.

"Nope," he replied nonchalantly.

The brunette walked towards them, purring "Hello, again," to Chase.

Emily didn't flinch, although she wanted to. In fact, she acted as if she didn't hear the woman and kept her attention on the stage and Freddie, who was wrapping up the evening.

"Wow Emily, your cousins' band is great!" Neil gushed, picking up their blanket from the ground.

"I'll tell him you said so. Although, it'll enlarge his over-inflated ego," Emily joked tensely.

When Chase bent to pick up the picnic basket a piece of paper fell from his shirt pocket. They grabbed for it at the same time, but Emily came up with it.

He held out his hand to her. "I believe that's mine."

His attitude didn't sit well with her. "Is it something I'm not supposed to see?

He released a hard breath. "Come on Em. Quit fucking around and give it to me."

Normally not a nosey person, she made an exception, opened her hand and saw the name Sherry along with a phone number.

"Em! It's not what you're thinking!" Chase uttered quickly.

She sadly nodded her head. "It's exactly what I'm thinking." She picked up the blanket and threw it over her shoulder.

"Em, the chick handed me her number and when I saw that douche bag talking to you I stuffed it in my pocket. I wasn't planning on calling her."

"It's not my business who you call or go out with Chase, but I really wish you'd quit sending me mixed signals," she replied over her shoulder.

She walked away, not daring to look back.

He rolled his eyes heavenward and went after her.

"Em, where ya goin'? My car is on the other side of the park."

"Freddie can take me home," she replied bitchily.

Chase gripped her wrist and spun her around. His blue eyes smoldered. "Look, there are three things you ought to know. Number one, I wasn't going to call her. Number two, I don't like to be walked away from. Number three, I brought you and I'm taking you home."

"News flash, Chase, I don't give a rat's ass about your three things!"

The corner of his mouth lifted, causing her to mirror his image.

She really wanted to walk away and forget she ever met him. But, she resolved to give him the benefit of the doubt.

This time.

*   *   *

Halfway to Emily's house Chase broke the silence. "Would it be easy

115

for you to walk away from me?"

She tore her attention from the window and gazed at him. The oncoming headlights showed his somber expression.

She sighed heavily. "Easy? No. Doable? Yes."

"Even with everything I have to offer you?" he asked shakily.

Her words were like a knife in his chest.

She rolled her eyes, "What are you talking about?"

He stopped at a red light and turned to her, snorting. "Damn near anything you want. Jewelry, clothes, vacations."

Sadly, she shook her head. "You don't get it Chase. I don't want *things*." She looked away from his penetrating stare. "Green light," she muttered.

He accelerated, render speechless by her comment.

When he pulled into her driveway she leapt from the car as soon as he stopped.

His expression was grim as he watched her climb the steps. He blew out a hard breath and opened his door. She was a hard chick to figure out.

Emily fumbled inside her purse looking for her keys. *So much for a smooth exit,* she thought bitterly.

She felt his warm hand against her back. "Em, talk to me, please." When she flinched he closed his eyes and rolled his head back onto his shoulders.

"Look, if you're still pissed about that chick's phone number..."

Narrowing her eyes she spun around. "It's not just that, it's you! You're confusing me with all the bimbo's you've been with! I don't want you to buy me things or take me on vacations!"

His face twisted in anger and he threw up his hands. "What the hell do you want then?"

She stammered, "I want to fall in love, get married and have babies. I just don't think you're the one who can give that to me."

"For fuck's sake Emily, this is only our second date!" he ground out.

Narrowing her eyes she snapped, "I get that. But I also get the fact that no matter if we date a week, a month or longer, your eyes will always be roving for someone else and I'm not willing to deal with that."

He ran a hand through his sandy blonde hair. "*She* came on to me! I didn't ask for her number."

"Are you going to tell me you didn't contemplate her?"

He partially rolled his eyes, shaking his head. "For a millisecond, but only as a seven day girl and then I dismissed it." Emily shook her head sadly at him. "I dismissed it because I want to be with you."

They stared at each other for a beat longer until she turned away, pulling keys from her purse.

"What? *Fuckley's* more your type?" he asked sarcastically.

She sucked in an outraged breath, opened the door and glared at him.

He waved a dismissive hand at her. "Fine, fine. I'm sure you two will have a great life together!"

*   *   *

Chase tore out of the driveway, squealing his tires in the process. *Fuckin' chick is crazy! Talking about marriage and babies! No doubt about it-she's certifiable!*

Fuck it. He'd go back to the seven day thing. Much safer that way.

He sped along the expressway indignantly, snorting at the outrageous things she'd said.

Then his thoughts turned to seeing her onstage. His heart swelled with pride watching her and knowing she was his.

He snorted again at his silliness. She wasn't his. She didn't want him.

*   *   *

Emily climbed into bed, feeling wistful.

The man had issues though and she wasn't a psychologist.

*   *   *

Jenny was dusting knick-knacks when Emily stumbled into the store at noon. She glanced at her watch, frowning at her cousin. "You look like shit, Em."

"Hey, good morning to you, too, sunshine," she replied snarkily.

Another sleepless night courtesy of Chase Storm, she thought bitterly.

"I take it the date didn't go so well?"

Emily stowed her purse in the back room and grabbed a cup of coffee, contemplating her answer.

"Hellloooo darlin'!"

"Hi Frankie," she grinned. No matter how shitty she felt, Frankie always made her feel better.

He sat on the maple table, swinging his legs. "What's your tale, nightingale?"

Jenny leaned up against the doorway and rolled her eyes. She was past tired of Emily talking to the ghosts more than she talked to her.

"Well the evening started out great," she muttered. She began explaining her evening when Phyllis and Lilly arrived.

The conversation took all of thirty minutes. For several long moments no one said anything.

"So? That's it then?" Jenny finally asked.

118

Emily shrugged, "I guess so."

"He doesn't have a lick of sense!" Lilly frowned.

"Yeah, Em. He's a real dope. You deserve much better," Phyllis chimed in, trying to wrap her ghostly arm around Emily.

Emily cocked her head. "I can feel you," she gasped.

"Huh?"

"Oh my gosh! I can feel your hand on my shoulder!"

Phyllis grinned and pulled Emily tighter, resting her head on her shoulder. "Can ya feel that?"

Emily frowned, "Yeah, but why? I mean after all these years?"

"Let me try!" Frankie bellowed. Lowering himself onto the floor he cautiously walked towards Emily with his arms extended and a big grin on his face. "Come here, doll."

She walked into his muscular arms with a lopsided grin on her face. She always wondered how his arms would feel around her.

At first she didn't feel anything except a cool spot. She looked up at him and noticed his penetrating gaze. Suddenly she felt his arms envelope her and even felt his hand against her hair, comforting her.

Jenny stood gaped mouth at the sight. Emily had her arms wrapped around well, nothing and grinned like an idiot! "Okaaaay…Em, I really think you need to hang out with some live people. No disrespect," she amended.

Emily pulled away from Frankie and brushed her palm against his cheek and sighed, "Oh Frankie, if only…"

He choked up a little and laughed, "You're too old for me doll. After all, I'm only nineteen!"

She rolled her eyes at him and laughed. "Yeah, but by my calculations you're really 72."

Frankie touched his chest. "You wound me."

*   *   *

A week passed and Emily hadn't called.

It drove Chase nuts.

Sitting at his Italian desk he rubbed a hand down his face and sighed.

He shuffled papers on his desk to tidy up and glanced out the window.

The sun was beginning to set.

A lump formed in his throat as he walked slowly towards the window.

Sunsets now reminded him of Emily.

He admired the palette of colors before him. Two different shades of purple, deep orange and pink settled over the lake.

Closing his eyes, he pinched the bridge of his nose with his forefinger and thumb.

He pulled his phone from his pocket and dialed her number.

Pressing the phone to his ear his heart thudded heavily in his chest.

It rang four times before he pressed end.

*   *   *

Emily ran to the kitchen and dug her phone from her purse. By the time she found it, it stopped ringing.

When she checked the missed calls her breath caught in her throat.

For an hour she toyed with the thought of calling him back before she finally got the nerve to actually do it.

He answered on the third ring.

"Storm," he answered, sounding very upbeat.

"Hi, it's Emily. I noticed that I missed your call," she replied breathily.

Chase laughed half-heartedly. "Really? I'm sorry, I must've pocket dialed you."

His eyebrows furrowed at his reply.

She wanted to kick her own ass for calling him, but instead she muttered, "Oh, I see. Um, take care then."

"Wait!" he said a little too loudly. "Don't hang up. How've ya been?"

She sat on her blue plaid comfy chair and pulled her legs under her bottom. "Fine and you?"

He paced his condo. "Ya know, same ol' same ol'. Working on sketches for the new housing tract. Late hours at the office and at home."

It felt good to hear his voice. "Yeah, I've been pretty busy at the shop myself. I'll be driving all day tomorrow checking out estate sales."

It was great to hear her voice. He wanted to keep her talking. "Are you driving locally?"

A soft laugh escaped her. "No actually I'll be driving downstate just outside the Peoria area."

Chase's jaw tightened. "You are bringing someone with you, right?" The thought of her driving alone made his insides clench.

"Nope, just me," she muttered, pulling an Illinois map onto her lap.

"Em, I don't think you should travel that far alone. It's not safe."

Her eyebrows knitted together. He almost sounded concerned. "I'll be fine."

"Can't Freddie or Jenny go with you?" he spluttered.

"Jenny has to man the shop and Freddie has to work. It's no big deal," she huffed.

121

He shook his head angrily. "I'll clear my schedule and go with you."

She jutted her chin out. "I seriously don't need you to go with. I'll be fine."

He ground out, "Christ! Do you always have to be so exasperating?"

She stood and stomped around the living room. "I'm not exasperating! I'm a grown woman and I sure as hell don't need to be told what to do!"

His voice softened. "Emily, I'll worry if you don't allow me to go with you."

She took a deep breath trying to organize herself. If he came with her what would be the outcome? She closed her eyes. "Fine, be here by seven," she snapped disconnecting the call.

Chapter Seven

Emily rolled over and turned off the alarm clock. "Six already?" she moaned. She lay on her back and closed her eyes. Just a few minutes more.

An hour later the doorbell woke her. She gaped at the LED numbers on the clock and moaned even louder. "Son of a bitch!"

She ran down the stairs. Before she opened the door she glanced at herself in the mirror attached to an antique coat rack. She scowled at her reflection and pulled the door open.

"Good morning," he said softly, juggling a heavy cardboard drink tray and a box of pastries.

His eyes raked over her slowly, from head to foot. She wore a gray tank top and matching panties. He shot her a brief, hot intense look, causing her to flush.

Tucking her hair behind her ears she shrugged, "I woke up late."

"So I see," he murmured. "It's a good thing I brought coffee." He passed by and walked into the kitchen.

He turned and studied her, his blue eyes trailing over her face. "I'll wait while you get dressed."

She nodded, scrambling up the stairs. How could one heated look from him turned her to mush?

It was a bad idea to let him come with.

*   *   *

Emily bounded down the stairs a half hour later. Chase sat at the kitchen table talking on his phone. She busied herself by filling a cooler with ice and bottles of water.

"No, I won't be going to the farmhouse today; I've had a change of plans." He briefly smiled at Emily, rolling his eyes. "For fuck's sake, Jason, wear your big boy pants and deal with it." He listened for a moment longer then growled, "Then hire fucking people who are men enough to do the job!"

A vase sat in the middle of the table filled with flowers. He brought his fingertips to the card nestled among the greenery. *How nice,* he thought snidely.

He slammed his phone on the table, causing Emily to jump. "Fuckley is still sending you flowers, I see."

She glanced over her shoulder and lifted her shoulder.

"Sorry," he muttered, shaking his head.

She took a sip from the coffee cup and shrugged, "It sounds like you're needed at work. I can handle this on my own."

A sexy, amused grin lit up his face. "I'm where I want to be, Emily."

A delicate flush painted her cheeks. "Well then, let's get going."

"What about the donuts?"

"We can eat them on the way," she called over her shoulder.

Chase found her bent over the coffee table picking up a roadmap and a notebook. He couldn't help but admire the view. The denim shorts she wore crept up her backside exposing more of her thighs. His eyes darted away when she stood up.

"Ready?" she asked, grabbing the cooler from the dining table.

"Yeah," he mumbled. He looked down at the bulge in his pants and

124

rolled his eyes. It seemed as if little Chase was ready and rarin' to go, too.

There was no way he'd be able to keep his lustful thoughts in check today.

No way in hell.

*   *   *

Emily gasped sharply when the heat and humidity slapped her in the face. It would be a brutal day. For more than one reason.

The moving van pulled up as she hit the bottom step, followed by a bright yellow car. A young, dark skinned man leapt from the truck with a clipboard in hand. "Are you Emily Waters?"

"Yes," she nodded.

"Sorry we're a little late. They have road construction everywhere," the man groused. "It's all fueled up and ready to go, if you'll just sign here."

Emily signed her name and took the keys from the man, thanking him.. He told her to have a safe trip before he stepped into the yellow car waiting for him.

Chase cocked his head in disbelief. "We're driving a box on wheels today?"

She grinned, "Yep. Didja think I was going to drive the Challenger?"

"Well, yeah. What do you plan on buying?" he asked, walking to the passenger door.

"Whatever turns me on," she replied walking to the drivers' side door.

He cleared his throat. "Emily? Where are you going?"

"I told you, downstate."

"No, I mean now," he clarified, looking over the hood of the truck.

Her eyebrows knitted together. "I'm going to drive so I need to be on this side of the truck." How could he be so daft?

His jaw clenched slightly. "No, I'll drive."

"No, I'll drive," she said simply with a shake of her head.

He frowned, looking mildly annoyed, causing her to wave a dismissive hand. "I know, I know. I'm exasperating."

"That you are, Miss Waters," he agreed, climbing into the passenger seat.

*   *   *

Several miles down I-57 Chase looked over the map and the notebook with several addresses. "Do you know where you're going or shall I navigate?"

She shot him a brief smile. "We're headed to Gilman first and then once we get onto I-24 I'll need some direction."

He studied her for a long moment. Her hair was pulled back with a clip and thin tendrils fell on either side of her face. He noticed that she didn't wear any makeup. Either she felt totally comfortable or didn't feel the need to put forth any effort because he was a lost cause.

The thought made him frown.

Out of the corner of her eye she noticed his scowl. "What's with the face?" she asked, teasingly.

He shrugged, looking out the window at the vast farmland. He didn't know how to respond.

"Ah. You wish you wouldn't have come with now, huh?"

He released a soft sigh. "Well, you haven't called in a week and if I hadn't called you I wouldn't be sitting here right now."

She lifted an eyebrow. "I thought you pocket dialed me."

"Well, I lied. I wanted to hear your voice then chickened out at the last minute," he confessed, with a forlorn expression on his face.

Her cheek lifted slightly at his admission.

"Did you think of me at all, Em?"

She ripped her sunglasses from her face, exposing the dark lines under her eyes. "I haven't been able to sleep because I thought about you! Last night I kept thinking about what would happen today; how I'd act, how you'd act. It's ridiculous!"

His lips twitched. "So, Fuckley isn't your style?"

She rolled her eyes and growled, "He might've been if I met him first."

He blinked his eyes. Funny how much those words hurt.

She pulled into a rest area, parking the truck in an isolated area. After unbuckling her seat belt she turned to face him. "Let's just clear the air otherwise this is going to be one long assed trip."

"Oookay," he mumbled, uncertain.

She took his hand into hers and ran her thumb lightly over his knuckles. "Chase, I like you. A lot, in fact. But you and I are two different people. I go out with men in hopes of meeting Mr. Right and you look for a girl to bang for seven days. I can't be that girl. That's not to say that I don't have salacious thoughts about you, because trust me, I do. But, I don't want to invest time in a relationship that could possibly go nowhere."

He shifted in the seat. "You want more."

She shrugged, "At least a glimmer of hope for more."

He moved towards her and took her hand. "Look, I can't promise anything, but I can tell you this. You're all I've thought about since we met. I want to try…dating, if you're willing to give it a shot."

She eyed him curiously. "By dating do you mean exclusively or will you still do the 'seven day' thing with other women?"

He lifted an eyebrow. "Well, clearly I can't go out with another woman when I'm thinking about you so…"

She grinned, satisfied with his answer, and started the truck.

*   *   *

"So tell me about trailer park," Chase said, sweeping a glance at her.

She glanced at him. "What?"

"The mechanic. Trailer park. What's the deal with him?"

Emily glanced at him briefly. A small laugh escaped from her lips. "Trailer park, huh?" Chase nodded with a lop-sided grin. She shrugged, "Well we dated for almost a year. Not much else to say."

"Who broke up with who?" he wondered aloud.

Emily shifted in her seat. "He broke up with me."

Her response surprised him. "Can I ask why?"

"He couldn't handle my crazy, complicated life."

"Oh, running the store, working late hours, shit like that?"

She nodded, "Yeah. He used to say that I cared more about the things in my shop than I did him." She smiled at her creativity. He really said she cared more for her spooks.

Chase was thoughtful for a moment. "Do you ever think about getting back with him?"

Emily snorted. "Not a chance. If it didn't work out the first time, it wouldn't work the second. How about you? Have you ever had a relationship last longer than a week?"

"Yep. Once. Then I came up with the seven day thing," he replied coolly. Even though it'd been many years since Cassie, the pain, although numb, was still there in the recesses of his mind.

"Don't want to share, huh?"

He blew out a hard breath. "Her name was Cassie," he paused. It'd

128

been a long time since he said her name aloud. "We planned on getting married. Long story short, I found her in bed with my roommate. End of story."

Emily blinked in surprise. She had a few scenarios rolling around in her head and that wasn't one of them. She shook her head. "What a bitch."

Chase smirked. "Agreed."

She returned his smirk. "Blehhh!"

Chase shot her a lop-sided grin. "Say again?"

"Let's change the subject. So...you said you were in a band when you were younger. Is that where the earring came from?"

He reached for the small gold hoop in his ear and grinned. "Yeah, I was rebellious back then. Almost got both ears pierced, but decided that it didn't look very manly." He shifted in the seat with a frown. "You don't like it?"

She blushed. "I like it fine. It fits you. In fact, I think it's sexy."

He wiggled his eyebrows, causing her to blush a deeper red. "Were you ever a rebel?"

"Nope, I was straight as an arrow. Even an 'A' student," she beamed.

"So you were a nerd..." Chase teased.

Emily stiffened. "No. I didn't have many friends growing up so I spent my time reading or studying."

It was hard to keep friends when they all thought she was either a liar or a freak when she told them she could talk to ghosts. And, since her parents didn't move from the area she never got a second chance with those kids.

If not for the intermittent spirits she'd met at her parent's antique shop, she never would've had friends at all. At twenty-five she could still count the number of friends she had on one hand.

"Em...I'm sorry," Chase said softly.

129

She shrugged, "Doesn't matter. I graduated Valedictorian of my class so my hard studying paid off."

"So, what do you do now, in your free time?"

"I still read. I like to work in my garden and I'm a groupie for Double Exposure," she laughed.

"You're more than a groupie! You've got a helluva voice on you!" She shook her head, unsure. "C'mon Emily! You've gotta know how great you sound. Not to mention how great you look on stage! Guys were practically tripping over their tongues!"

His eyes narrowed when he thought about the pricks eyeballing her that night.

His upper lip curled. She could've had any guy there that night, but she left with him.

His sneer turned into a smile.

*   *   *

After six hours of estate and garage sales, Chase hoped this was the last stop. He didn't know where she'd put more stuff since the truck was filled to the gills.

Emily gripped his hand as they walked into the farm house.

"I've always wanted one of these!" Emily beamed, running her hand along the top of a white and red Hoosier cabinet. She began figuring out how to rearrange the truck in order to fit the cabinet inside. She already knew where she'd put it in her house.

Chase scanned the old farm house for ideas as Emily bounded from one side of the kitchen to the other. His eyes rested on her as she practically drooled over the red cabinet.

From the corner of his eye he saw a woman pick an item from a dining table and drop it quickly causing other items on the table to fall onto the floor. He crossed the room to help her pick up the fallen items, but she brushed past him and scurried out the door.

As he picked the items up he gazed at Emily who stood motionless.

"Stupid damn people! Comin' into my house and touchin' my things!"

Emily shuddered at the old farmer's demeanor. As he stomped around the kitchen, items fell from shelves in his wake.

The farmer turned his head and noticed Emily staring at him. He limped towards her with one arm dangling loosely from its socket. She quickly averted her eyes, but not quickly enough for the old man.

"Hey girly! You can see me, can't ya?" he leered.

Noticing a change in Emily's demeanor Chase finished placing the items on the table and crossed the room to her.

"Em?"

She stared blankly in front of her. Chase followed her line of vision, but came up wanting.

"Em?" he repeated.

"Oh girl! They're lookin' for ya," the dead farmer cackled.

Emily's eyes widened. Who was looking for her?

She felt Chase's hand on her elbow, breaking her gaze from the farmer.

"You okay?" he asked.

She nodded. "There's nothing I want here."

"I thought you wanted that cabinet?"

She shook her head. "No, let's go."

"C'mon, I'll buy it for you," Chase offered.

"Yeah, girly! Let 'em buy it for ya! That way I can lead them to ya!" the

131

farmer chuckled.

Emily grabbed Chase's hand, tugging him towards the back door. "I changed my mind."

When they reached the truck Emily was shaking. She handed Chase the keys. "You can drive."

He eyed her cautiously as she fidgeted in the seat. The farmer stood outside the passenger door. "C'mon girl! Ya want the Hoosier! Buy it!" he screamed.

When she wouldn't acknowledge him, he banged on the passenger window, causing her to jump.

"Start the goddamn truck Chase!"

"What's wrong?" he asked, confused by her demeanor and the loud banging against her window. He looked past her, but didn't see anything.

Emily's hands flew to her ears when the farmer continued to bang on the window. "Get me the fuck out of here Chase!"

"No matter, girl! They'll find you eventually!" the farmer cackled when the truck pulled away.

*   *   *

Chase pulled into a parking lot of a greasy spoon restaurant. He noticed Emily's hands still shook. "Em, talk to me for fuck's sake."

She shrugged, brushing a lock of hair from her face. "Must be the heat."

"Well that's a bullshit answer if I ever heard one," he scoffed.

"It's the only one I've got."

*   *   *

Half-way to Emily's house the trucks air conditioner stopped working. Chase pulled into a truck stop and tried to troubleshoot the problem while

Emily used the restroom. He pulled out his phone and called Danny.

"Hey, it's Chaser. I need you to do me a favor," he murmured into the phone.

*   *   *

Emily pulled her phone from her pocket as she entered the dining area. The heavy odor of grease made her stomach roil. "Jenny? Are you alone?"

"Um, the last customer is walking out the door, why?"

"I need you to put me on speaker phone," Emily muttered, glancing around at the truckers seated at the dining bar.

"Okay, you're on speaker. What's up?" Jenny asked.

"Phyllis? Frankie? I need your help!"

"What's wrong doll?" Phyllis asked.

"Yeah, darlin'. You sound upset," Frankie murmured into the phone.

Emily glanced out the window at Chase before replying. "Look, I just met a spirit, a mean one, and he said '*they* were looking for me'. Who are *they* and why are *they* looking for me?" she squeaked.

Phyllis and Frankie eyed each other warily. They'd heard rumors of entities searching for Emily, but thought they were just that, rumors.

"Um, we're not sure, Em, but we'll look into it, okay?" Phyllis replied softly.

"Yeah, don't let it rattle your cage," Frankie urged.

When Emily disconnected the phone, she didn't feel any better.

*   *   *

Emily exited the building. Her eyes searched the horizon and she didn't like what she saw. "C'mon, Chase. Let's just get home. It looks like we're in for one hell of a storm and I'd rather be home when it hits."

133

Chase lifted his head from under the hood and surveyed the sky. "Ya gotta thing against *storms*?" he teased.

"*Thunder* storms, yeah. Chase Storm's, no," she grinned.

They settled into the cramped truck and pulled onto the expressway.

Even though it was muggy and hot as hell, Emily shivered. She couldn't shake the uneasiness she felt when she thought of the farmer.

Chase was confused by her abrupt mood change. Before they entered the old farm house she was laughing and seemed to be enjoying herself. Then his insides clenched.

"Have I done or said something wrong, Em?"

She shifted in her seat and placed her hand on his arm. "Not at all. Why?"

"Well all of the sudden your mood bottomed out and I thought I was the cause of it," he shrugged.

The pained look he wore made her want to tell him *everything*, but she couldn't risk it.

"Chase, my mood has nothing to do with you. I'm just hot and it's been a really long day."

He released his breath, unaware he held it. He thought for a moment and smiled.

"I happen to have a friend, my best friend, actually, who now plays for the Chicago Wind," he murmured.

Emily's eyes darted from the passenger window to Chase. "I'm sorry. What did you say?"

He grinned, "My friend plays for the Chicago Wind. Your favorite hockey team. He just got signed a few weeks ago. He was at Candace's birthday party. I'm surprised you didn't notice him."

She shrugged, "I guess I only had eyes for you."

He gripped her hand tightly. "You guess?"

"You were the only guy I saw," she amended. "What's your friends' name?"

"Rick O'Shea. His nickname is Ricochet."

"Holy shit! Didn't he play with the Rangers?" she squeaked.

Chase nodded. "So, you've heard of him?"

She nodded enthusiastically. "He's not only a hell of a scorer, but he's a scrapper, too! Wow! He'll bring much needed toughness to the team."

Chase nodded thoughtfully. He was glad he got her mind off of whatever upset her at the farm house.

*   *   *

Chase pulled the truck in front of Emily's house and turned off the ignition. Fuck, he didn't want to leave.

"Um, since there's a storm brewing, why don't you stay here tonight," she offered. She didn't want him to leave.

He turned his head slowly and lifted an eyebrow.

"You can borrow some of Freddie's clothes since you're about the same size and well, I have a couch you can sleep on," she amended.

A slow smile crept across his face. "Are you sure?"

"Yeah, it's the least I can do since you came with me today."

"I hope you have air conditioning," he teased, getting out of the truck.

It'd been an exhausting day, but both managed to sprint towards the front door. Chase grabbed her around the waist, spinning her around until both were dizzy.

"Chase! Put me down you Neanderthal!" she laughed heartily.

He set her gently onto the grass, but held tight to her. "God, I love to hear your laugh." His eyes brimmed with a mixture of tenderness and passion, completely turning her insides to mush.

How could any woman resist that look? she wondered. Swallowing the lump in her throat she breathily muttered, "Come on, we're giving the neighbors something to gossip about."

He laughed nervously, releasing her.

She was making him have thoughts that he ought not to be having.

But, instead of running to his car, he followed her into the house.

Maybe his schmuck of a brother-in-law, Neil, was right. Maybe it was time for him to grow up.

Maybe Emily would be the one to tame him.

The thought chilled and warmed him at the same time.

*   *   *

"Are you sure Freddie won't mind me borrowing his clothes?" Chase asked as Emily rifled through Freddie's dresser and closet.

"Well, I'm pretty sure he wouldn't like you wearing his boxers, ya know, your boys being where his boys have been, so to speak," she blushed. "So, you'll have to go commando."

He grinned salaciously, "I usually don't wear anything to bed."

She nodded, handing him a pair of denim shorts. "So you've told me before."

"No shirt?" he asked, grinning.

"Do ya need one?" she frowned. She liked seeing him without one.

"Nah, this is fine. Where can I shower?"

She moved past him. "Upstairs."

He trailed after her, doing a great job of keeping his lustful thoughts to himself. In fact, he thought he'd done pretty well for the day, as far as lustful thoughts go.

But the furniture blankets in the back of the truck did give him pause earlier.

And, if he was correct, they also gave Emily salacious thoughts as well.

"Towels and washcloths are in here," Emily waved her hand in front of a large maple cabinet. "Shampoo, etcetera is already in the shower."

The bathroom had been updated, he noted. The flooring was off-white ceramic tile, the walls painted dove gray. The clear acrylic shower was unusually large and took up nearly one wall.

"Did the owner before you update the bathroom?" he asked curiously, glancing around.

She cocked her head, the corner of her mouth lifted. "No, I updated it."

He couldn't contain his smirk.

"What's so funny, Storm," she laughed.

"Nothing. I really like the color scheme and the blue rug and towels makes it look sharp. I'm curious about the shower size." He placed his hand over his mouth to hide his grin.

She rolled her eyes and flushed. "What? Only you can have a large shower? "

She sure as hell wasn't going to tell him that having sex in the shower was high on her fantasy list and if you're gonna have sex in the shower, it damn well better be big enough to accommodate two people.

He noticed that she instantly broke eye contact with him, choosing instead to look at her hands that were knotted together in front of her.

Oh! To know what the woman is thinking!

He cleared his throat and waved his hand in front of the shower.

137

"Ladies first."

Her heart pounded heavily in her chest. Was he asking her what she thought he was asking?

The day had been very interesting indeed. She blushed when she thought about the back of the truck and the furniture blankets.

Cripes! How she wanted to pull him down onto them and rock his world.

"Em?" he half-coughed, half-laughed.

Her head snapped up, color staining her cheeks. "Yeah?"

"Would you like to shower first?"

She frowned, "No. Go ahead. I'll start making dinner."

"Okay…" he replied, waiting for her to leave the bathroom.

Realization smacked her upside the head after a few long moments. "Oh right! Okay, I'll be downstairs then," her voice trailed off as she walked from the room.

As he undressed a smile spread across his face.

She had the same thoughts he did.

Except, he wouldn't act on them.

No sir! He'd be the perfect gentleman. Even if it killed him!

*   *   *

Emily scrounged through the fridge and came up wanting. Friday was grocery shopping day and since she spent the day at estate sales…

She opened the junk drawer for menus from local restaurants.

Smirking, she ran upstairs and knocked on the bathroom door. Maybe she could sneak a little peek…

"Yeah?" Chase called, washing soap from his eyes.

"Chinese or pizza?" she said softly through the door.

"Em? Didja want something?"

Her lips thinned. Damn! She wanted to open that door! "I have to order something out. Chinese or pizza?" she growled.

Rinsing the soap from his ears he replied, "Hey, I'm having trouble hearing you. Why don't ya just open the door?"

Her throat went dry at his suggestion.

Well, it *is* what she wanted!

Gulping she turned the knob and pushed the door open slightly, just enough for him to hear her.

"Sorry, don't mean to disturb you, but we'll have to order dinner out. Would you prefer Chinese or pizza?"

"Which would you prefer?" he asked smoothly, wondering if she was gaping at him.

"Um, doesn't matter to me," she muttered, wanting so much to poke her head around the door!

He jerked his head quickly to see if she was watching him and frowned when he saw that she wasn't.

"You decide Emily. I'll be fine either way."

She poked her head inside the door.

His back was to her and he was washing his left arm. She sighed happily.

The man had a spectacular ass!

"Em?"

She pulled her head out of the doorway so fast that she banged it on the doorframe.

"Shit!" she moaned.

Chase turned, "Em? Is everything okay?"

Rubbing her head she shook her head. She got what she deserved, being a peeping Tom and all. "Yeah. We'll go with pizza."

She shut the bathroom door and checked the side of her head in the bureau mirror. Satisfied there wasn't a red mark she sprinted down the stairs and called in a pizza order for delivery.

*   *   *

After a quick shower Emily dressed in her standard tank top and boy shorts. She grabbed a light robe before going downstairs.

Chase nearly choked on his beer when she walked into the living room. She looked sexy as hell with damp hair and fresh out of the shower. He grabbed his phone and pressed a button. The song *Wicked Game* filled the room.

A small grin formed on her lips when he stood and held a hand out to her.

"May I have this dance?" he asked huskily.

The room wasn't large enough to dance in, but neither seemed to care. He held her tightly and brushed light kisses along her temple and forehead. He'd played this song many times since meeting her and envisioned dancing with her as it played.

Her hand traveled from his shoulder down to his ass. She'd seen it while he showered and now she wanted to grab it. Purely for fact gathering. Was it as muscular as it looked?

Chase's insides clenched when she brought her hand to his ass. The little vixen! Totally trying to undermine his self-control!

Emily licked her lips before she grabbed a generous amount of his butt cheek.

Chase hissed into her neck. *Fuck trying to be a good boy!* His teeth grazed her neck as he sucked and nibbled his way to her shoulder, nudging the flimsy robe away.

The doorbell chimed, causing them both to jump.

Chase pulled away and raked a hand through his hair. "I'll get that," he mumbled as he adjusted his denim shorts for comfort.

Emily forgot all about dinner. In fact, she forgot all about the creepy ghost farmer, too. Chase had that affect on her.

Chapter Eight

Emily took a pull from her beer as she watched Chase chew his pizza. "*Wicked Game* on your phone, huh?" she asked.

He grinned. "Yeah, it reminds me of you. In more ways than one, now. Ass grabber."

She glanced away from him as a pretty shade of pink dappled her cheeks. She swallowed a bite of pizza. "Only yours," she clarified.

He took a long pull of beer and shook his head. "You're playing with fire, you do realize that don't you?"

Smiling coyly she replied, "What *ever* do you mean?"

He waved his hand in front of her. "Dressed like that? Grabbing my ass? Looking so fuckin' sexy? I'm trying my very best to be a gentleman, but you're making it damn near impossible!"

"Who says I want you to be a gentleman?" she whispered.

Chase gulped a bite of pizza lodged in his throat and shook his head. Reaching across the table he gripped her hand and explained gently. "Em, I'm not ready to go there yet. Don't get me wrong, the body is willing, but I'd rather get to know you first, okay? Because as you've said before, you're not some bimbo and you deserve more."

He couldn't believe his own fuckin' ears!

Emily smiled warmly and lifted her chin. "You're right." She placed the slice of pizza in her hand on the plate and shrugged. "I don't know what's wrong with me. I mean, I'm not usually this forward. Maybe it was the heat of the day or that crazy farmer…"

His eyebrows knitted together. "What crazy farmer?"

Emily's eyes widened. Two beers and she almost blew it!

"Em?" he prodded.

She lifted a narrow shoulder and laughed nervously. "Um, you didn't notice him? At the last stop?"

He shook his head. "No, there were only a handful of people in the house and I didn't see any crazy farmer."

She rolled her eyes. "Silly! He was outside by the barn…chasing chickens." She shivered slightly and waved a hand. "No big deal. He just freaked me out a little."

Chase eyed her curiously. He wasn't a stupid man. He had a built-in bullshit meter and it was dinging loudly.

Emily was hiding something from him.

* * *

Thunder crashed in the distance as they cleaned up dinner. Emily wasn't a fan of thunderstorms and jumped as lightning struck something nearby.

Chase pulled the blue checked curtain from the living room window and whistled low. "This is going to be a doozy of a storm. Do you have flashlights or candles?"

Emily was a step ahead of him and carried a small wicker basket that held a large assortment of candles in glass jars, along with a lighter. She placed them on the pine coffee table. "I'll get the flashlights," she murmured, walking towards the kitchen.

When she returned Chase had lit six of the candles and placed them strategically around the living room. She gulped at the sight of him, shirtless,

144

bathed in candlelight.

He smiled warmly and held out a hand to her. "C'mon, let's sit on the couch and tell ghost stories."

"Huh?" she squeaked.

"Aren't you the one trying out for a play about ghosts?" he replied, pulling her towards the couch.

She rolled her eyes. "Doesn't mean I like ghost stories."

"Okay, we can talk about something else then," he laughed. "Hey, did I tell you I designed a wicked awesome movie theater?"

She shifted on the couch and faced him. "No. Is it in the city?"

"Yeah. The owner wanted it to be retro looking, like the Biograph, but grander. It has cathedral ceilings, a very elegant staircase, polished marble floors…"

"Does it have the neon lights on the outside, too?" she asked.

"Oh yeah. It's one of the best jobs I've done. In fact, I need to stop by there next week to check on things, if you'd like to go with me."

She yawned into her hand. "Yeah, I'd like that."

"Why don't you go to bed, Em? Ya look beat," he murmured, kissing her hand.

She nodded, "Let me get some pillows and a blanket for you."

While she ran upstairs Chase extinguished the candles, except for one, and laid on the couch, with his hands behind his head.

He closed his eyes and felt a cold draft pass alongside of him. He lifted one eyelid and saw a blur. Goosebumps rose on his arm as he sat up. "Em?" he swallowed thickly.

She descended the stairs. "Sorry, I put a clean covering on the pillow."

He glanced around the room and lifted his hand in the air.

"Is something wrong Chase?"

Shrugging he replied, "It was the damndest thing. I felt a cold draft, but don't feel any air coming from the vents."

Emily's eyes searched the room. She hadn't had a ghostly visitor since the original owner of the home passed over. "Ah, you know old houses. Drafty one minute, stuffy the next," she mumbled.

He cocked his head. "I suppose so. It is windy out there, too. Maybe you need an update on the insulation," he replied, taking the pillow and blanket from her.

"Maybe so," she shrugged. "Kiss me goodnight?"

Chase tossed the items on the couch and caressed her cheek as he brought his lips to hers.

She placed her hands on his hips and pulled him closer. She felt him smile as he parted her lips with his tongue.

Their tongues danced a slow rhythm and little Chase started to twitch. He quickly pulled away and smoothed Emily's hair with his hand. "Goodnight Miss Waters," he rasped.

She gently cleared her throat. "Goodnight Mr. Storm."

Chase watched her climb the stairs and groaned. Damn his new found morals!

*   *   *

Emily turned on a night light before climbing into bed. It was a habit that she never shook from childhood. The soft glow from the little light brought her a sense of security. Plus, it was her belief that it kept the ghosties away.

*   *   *

Chase rubbed the goose bumps away, annoyed. He felt like a

teenager again. Feeling cold spots near him, the gentle brush of what felt like fingers along his forehead not to mention the hair on the back of his neck lifting.

It was nerves. Plain and simple. Well, maybe a little stress thrown in for good measure, too.

Emily Waters had that affect on him.

*   *   *

The angry lake tossed the boat like a toy in a bathtub. Emily scrambled for purchase on the wet floor, gripping the metal rail.

Thunder boomed all around causing Emily to lift her hands to her ears. Before she was tossed into the churning lake she saw the old farmer. He grinned and waved his dangling arm at her. "They're lookin' for ya, girl," he cackled.

Emily screamed as she sank deeper into the murky depths. Water filled her mouth and lungs, stifling her scream. She waved her arms frantically while kicking her feet, trying to swim, but failing miserably.

She screamed again when she felt a gentle tug on her shoulder. Although she didn't want to, she turned her head and screamed when she saw the flesh eaten man.

*   *   *

Chase awoke from a restless sleep to Emily's screams. He bounded the stairs two at a time and stopped in the doorway of her room, mouth agape.

Emily thrashed on the bed. Her legs kicked the air while her right hand smacked at her left shoulder.

He scanned the room quickly, looking for an intruder. Crossing the room to her bed he grabbed her hand in mid-air. She fought against him and released a blood curdling scream that made the hair on the back of his neck stand up. "Em!" he yelled.

147

She continued to thrash on the bed, frantically trying to pull away from him. He grabbed her other hand, straddled her, pinning her hands above her head.

Ordinarily, straddling a woman turned him on, but right now he was scared shitless.

"Emily!"

Her eyes shot open and caused a shiver to form up his spine.

"Hey babe," he said meekly.

She glared and struggled to sit up. He released her arms and sat back on his knees as she pulled hers against her chest. "Who the fuck are you?" she hissed.

Chase blinked and cocked his head.

Emily glared at the white wispy image behind Chase until it formed into a human body.

A sudden draft filled the area behind Chase, causing him to turn slightly.

"I asked who the fuck you were!" Emily said icily.

The apparition knotted her hands in front of her. "I didn't cause your nightmare, child."

Emily lifted a thin eyebrow. "Your name!"

Chase gaped, "Em? It's me, Chase." *Christ! Is she still asleep?*

"I'm Andrea. Chase's mom," the ghost replied before vanishing.

*   *   *

Emily slumped against the headboard. Her chest heaved with a myriad of emotions. She felt Chase inch closer to her.

"Emily?" he said softly.

She lifted her head to meet his gaze. His heart twinged at the sight of her. She managed a weak smile and wrapped her arms around his waist.

He pulled her to him and felt warm tears fall onto his chest hairs. "I'm not sure what to do, babe," he whispered smoothing her hair with his palm.

Her voice cracked, "Just hold me."

*   *   *

Sunlight pierced through the white curtains waking Chase. Lifting his head he glanced at his body.

Wow. I spent the night in a woman's bed and didn't have sex! What a concept!

His arm was wrapped protectively around Emily. It was a damn rough night. She managed to fall asleep after an hour of shaking and sobbing softly in his arms.

Chase hated feeling helpless. It sucked even more when uncertainty was thrown in. It wasn't an emotion he allowed himself to feel. Not in a long fucking time. Especially not where a woman was concerned, but last night helpless was all he felt.

The thought of anything upsetting her unnerved him and for him to feel *that* emotion set him on edge. But fuck! What could he do? The only way he'd stop having these feelings was to walk away from her.

Fuck! Fuck! Fuck!

Shit was getting too real for him.

*   *   *

Emily shifted slightly and jumped when she couldn't fully stretch.

"Relax, it's just me," Chase murmured into her hair.

Chase lifted his arm and she pulled herself up, tucking her hair behind her ears. "Morning," she mumbled.

149

He tucked his hand under his head and smiled lazily at her. Most women didn't look amazing in the morning, but this chick, whoa. He rolled his eyes at himself.

"Gosh, do I look that horrible?" she gasped.

"Nah, ya look great. That's the problem," he sighed, sitting up.

Emily blanched at the backhanded compliment and got out of bed, her foot just missing a long strand of seaweed on the floor.

Chase watched as she walked into the bathroom and when she slammed the door shut he winced.

This is why he didn't do the dating thing. He never said the right words.

*   *   *

Emily looked at herself in the mirror and shrugged. Besides a little darkness under her eyes from a shitty nights sleep, she looked fine.

She splashed water on her face and as she brushed her teeth she thought about the nightmare and shivered.

Chase never talked about his mom so she didn't know if she was alive or dead. But, if she was dead, why would she haunt her?

Emily snorted and spit the toothpaste into the sink. Chase's mom probably didn't think she was good enough for him.

*   *   *

"I'll see you in an hour," Chase whispered into the phone when he heard Emily coming downstairs.

She walked past him and stepped into the kitchen. She needed coffee and a lot of it.

Chase sighed when she brushed past him. He walked into the kitchen and sat at the table. She wore a pair of denim shorts that showed too much of her legs and a bikini top.

"Aren't you going to unload the truck today?" he asked, ignoring the insatiable thoughts that rolled around his head.

"Yeah, but not until Freddie gets home." She glanced at him over her shoulder. "Ya hungry?"

"For you," he said under his breath.

She turned away from the coffee pot. "Chase? Are you hungry?"

He stared intently at her, causing her to flush.

After several long minutes he replied hoarsely, "Yeah."

Her eyebrows knitted together at his strange demeanor. "Okay, bacon, eggs and toast work for you?"

He pushed away from the table and stood. "Sounds great. Ya know what else sounds great?" She backed up against the counter top as he approached. "My clothes, so Freddie doesn't see me in his shorts," he grinned.

"Oh! They're downstairs in the dryer. I'll get them and start cooking," she offered.

He pulled her against him and kissed her lightly on the lips. "I'll start breakfast then."

*   *   *

As she pulled his clothes from the dryer she felt someone staring at her. She looked towards the stairs, expecting to see Chase leering at her. Instead she saw his mom.

"Go away!" she hissed quietly.

"I need your help," Andrea Storm replied haughtily.

"After scaring me shitless last night, you want me to help you?" Emily scoffed.

"I didn't mean to frighten you."

151

Emily softened slightly and sighed, "Fine, but what can I help you with?"

Andrea approached slowly. "We can help each other." Emily shot her a puzzled look and Andrea continued. "I need you to make Chase understand that I didn't leave him and Preston for another man."

Emily backed away. "Um, no disrespect, but he doesn't know I communicate with spirits and I'm not ready to divulge that to him just yet."

Chase called down to her, "Em? You okay?"

Andrea's image began to fade. "Find another way to tell him."

Emily quickly grabbed his clothes and ran to the foot of the stairs. Chase looked down at her with a lop-sided grin. "You okay?"

"Yeah, just picking up a little down here," she replied walking up the stairs.

"You look a little pale. Maybe you ought to put something warmer on," he said wrapping an arm around her.

Her nose scrunched. "I'm not cold."

He rolled his eyes. "Okay, but that outfit of yours has me hot and bothered and I'm trying to be a gentleman."

She handed him his clothes and pulled away. "Nobody said you had to," she replied over her shoulder.

*   *   *

Chase entered the kitchen as Emily was putting the plates on the table. When she turned around he pulled her into a tight embrace. She giggled into his shoulder.

"What's this for?"

"For cleaning my clothes, making breakfast and most importantly, for giving me a toothbrush so I can do this," he replied, sweeping his tongue against her lips.

She swatted at him. "You're crazy."

"Yep. I'm completely bonkers," he laughed, releasing her.

He pulled her chair out and sat across from her. He eyed the plates, "Looks great!"

"So, my parents live in Florida and I'm thinking about visiting them soon," she mentioned casually as she began to eat.

"Really? When?"

She shrugged, "I'm not sure yet. I really miss them and since I'm their only kid…"

He swallowed a bite of toast. "I didn't know you're an only child."

"Yep. My mom didn't have me until she was 42."

"She was a career woman, huh?"

"Um, no. Just had a hard time getting pregnant. Anyway, tell me about your parents," Emily replied.

Chase put his fork on his plate and wiped his mouth with a napkin. "Not much to tell. My parents got divorced when I was ten and I haven't seen the woman who gave birth to me since."

Emily flinched at his cool demeanor. His blue steely eyes bore into her, daring her to ask another question.

Instead, she reached across the table and touched his hand. "Chase, I'm sorry."

His eyes narrowed. "I don't need your sympathy, Emily."

She shook her head. "No, I'm sorry I've upset you with my question. It's just that I feel as if I hardly know anything about you, but yet you slept in my bed with me last night."

153

"Only because you had one helluva nightmare. Speaking of which, did you want to talk about it? 'Cause woman, you scared the shit out of me last night."

"It was just a stupid dream," she hedged.

When she wouldn't look at him he nudged her with his foot beneath the table. "C'mon, you shook and cried for quite a while last night. It was more than a stupid dream," he said softly.

Her hand shook as she picked up her coffee mug. He took it from her hand and placed it on the table. "Em, talk to me."

She closed her eyes and began softly. "I sometimes have nightmares of when I drowned. Being pulled deeper under the water and not being able to breathe."

Chase's insides clenched, but he knew there was something more to the story. "Is that all?"

When she opened her eyes he saw unshed tears pooling. "Christ! Isn't that enough?"

She pushed away from the table, angry at his remark and repulsed by the images of Fleshy, as she now termed the ghost who grabbed her so many years ago.

Chase caught her by the arm. "Baby, I'm sorry. I didn't mean it the way it came out."

She pulled her arm free and hissed, "I fucking *died* that day Chase! And *don't* call me *baby*!"

He lifted his hands to apologize when the doorbell rang.

Emily glared at him for a moment, wiping tears away with the backs of her hands. "Great, just great," she muttered to herself as she went to the door.

She pulled the door open and gasped, "What have you done, Chase?"

154

"Hi girly!" the dead farmer cackled.

Chapter Nine

"Um, Emily, this is Danny Martin, my friend. Danny, this is my...this is Emily," Chase mumbled, shocked by Emily's demeanor.

Emily's eyes darted from the farmer to Danny. She'd seen him at Candace's birthday party. He was a heavy-set man with a long red beard and a lot of tattoos. She nodded briefly then shifted her gaze back to the farmer.

He waved three stubby fingers at her and grinned.

Chase ran a hand over Emily's hair. "You okay? Ya look like you've seen a ghost."

The farmer released a hearty cackle, causing Emily to jump.

She steadied herself and turned to Chase. "What did you do, Chase?"

"I bought the cabinet for you. Ya know, the one you said you wanted then said you didn't?"

"I. Said. I. Didn't. Want. It!" she replied icily, crossing her arms over her chest.

Danny watched the exchange between his friend and the girl. A smirk formed on his face. He'd never seen Chase so flustered.

"Christ Emily! You know how women say no to shit but really mean yes. I thought that was one of those times!" he huffed, running a hand

157

through his hair.

"No when they really mean yes?" Her eyes narrowed when she considered his words further. She sucked in an outraged breath and hissed, "You bastard!"

His eyes widened and he stepped away from her. "No! Not like that! For fucks sake! The first night we were together, you clearly wanted it and baby, I could've had you! But *I* said no! I've *never* taken advantage of a woman!"

She continued to glare at him while the farmer cackled and Danny backed further away from the door. His eyes scanned the street, the grass, anywhere but at them.

"Fuck this!" Chase yelled. "I'm outta here!" He brushed past her and Danny and strode to his car, muttering to himself.

"Um, nice to meet you," Danny said meekly, before turning on his heel.

"Bye, girly! I'll see you again!" the farmer chuckled, following Danny to his truck.

Emily watched as Chase and Danny conversed. Chase looked at her and shook his head. After several minutes they pulled away.

She closed the door and shook.

Now that the farmer knew where she lived, he'd be back. And who knew what he'd bring with him.

*   *   *

"Andrea? If you're still here, I need your help," Emily called out.

Andrea appeared with a frown on her face. "Harold will cause you problems," she sighed.

Emily sat on the green couch, scrunching her face. "Who?"

"The farmer," Andrea replied, sitting next to her. "He doesn't mean to be bad, but he can't help himself."

Shifting to face Andrea, Emily asked, "He told me yesterday that 'they'd find me'. Do you know who he means?"

Andrea nodded sadly. "Yes, the Soul Hunters. They are misguided spirits who search for those who cheated death."

Emily's eyebrows knitted together. "Cheated death? Doesn't fate have a hand in someone's destiny?"

"Yes, but the Soul Hunters don't see it that way. Most of them are jealous entities who died unexpectedly," Andrea shrugged.

"What do they do when they find who they're hunting?" Emily gulped.

Andrea glanced away from Emily's probing eyes, unsure how to tell her.

Emily closed her eyes briefly. "Andrea, you told me earlier you'd help me if I helped you. Did you mean to help me with the Soul Hunters?"

Andrea nodded sadly. "Yes, but it won't be easy."

*   *   *

Chase turned the radio up to ear splitting levels. Although he loved Bob Marley, he was too mellow for him right now. Instead he listened to System of a Down. Women were a fucking conundrum! Now he had a fucking cabinet he didn't know what to do with.

At a stoplight he rolled up next to Danny's truck and honked the horn. "Yo! Danny! Follow me!"

*   *   *

"So…what do the Soul Hunters want?" Emily prodded.

Andrea hedged, "It's not clear to me right now."

"If I'm going to help you, you've got to be straight with me," Emily stated firmly.

"It could be one of many things. One of them may want to take over your body to finish the life that was taken from them."

Emily gulped, "Or?"

"Or they want to take the lingering spirits around you to the next plane of existence."

Emily's eyebrows furrowed. "So they are good and bad spirits?"

"Yes. I'm not sure which ones are looking for you, but I have...connections who are looking into it for me," Andrea smiled.

"You are a spirit, right? One with unfinished business?" Emily asked.

"I'm Chase's guardian angel with unfinished business," Andrea clarified. "Chase thinks I left his father and him for another man," she sighed sadly. "I was diagnosed with cancer and only given months to live. I didn't want them to see me suffer and I didn't want to be a burden to them."

Emily shook her head. "So it was better for them to believe you left for another man?"

Tears rimmed Andrea's eyes. "Looking back, no. My leaving had a terrible effect on Chase. It's my fault Chase is the way he is and I think you're the woman that can turn that around."

*   *   *

Chase pulled down the alley behind Emily's shop and parked his car. Danny got out of the truck, scratching his head. "What's up Chaser?"

Chase cocked his head to the back door of her shop. "She owns this place. I figure we'll dump the cabinet here and jet. I sure as hell don't want it, do you?"

Danny shook his head. "Uh-uh. The thing gives me the creeps like that fuckin' farmhouse of yours. Last night it felt like something was watching me the whole night."

"A big guy like you, scared of a cabinet?" Chase laughed.

"I'm not afraid of a cabinet ya jackass! I'm afraid of ghosts!" Danny sneered.

"There's no such thing as ghosts, ya pussy. C'mon, let's get this thing off your truck and get the fuck out of here."

*   *   *

"So, how was the gig?" Emily asked Freddie while she drove to the shop.

"Awesome! Gotta love our Wisconsin fans! Too bad you couldn't make it," he frowned.

She laughed, "You're really gonna wish I went with you once you see all the stuff in the back."

"Well, at least you're short one Hoosier cabinet," he reminded her. "I had a chance to talk with Ian about Chase on the drive up to Madison."

Emily glanced at him, "Do tell."

Freddie blew out a breath. "We think the guy digs you. He never contacted Ian's sister-in-law, Margo, after three days of being with her. And what's it been? A month? And he's still sniffing around you."

"Sniffing around?" she replied testily.

Freddie shrugged. "You know what I mean."

Emily pulled the truck behind her shop and groaned.

Harold, the farmer, paced by the Hoosier.

"Let me guess…your farmer is here," Freddie replied.

Emily nodded, "Damn Chase for leaving it here!"

"After we unload the truck we'll throw it in and I'll take it to the dump," Freddie offered.

Emily's eyes narrowed as Harold waved his stubby fingers at her. "Or I can bring the Hoosier in and let Frankie and Phyllis beat some answers out of him!"

*   *   *

After stopping at a liquor store, Chase cruised home, but stopped on the fifteenth floor to Rick O'Shea's condo first. He tapped at the door with a paper wrapped bottle of Jameson. "Ricochet, come out and play!" he said in a sing-song voice.

Rick opened the door with a brunette plastered to his lips. Chase stepped back and murmured, "Sorry dude, I'll come back later."

"Nah, she's just leavin', aren't ya sweetie?" Rick replied, pulling away from the girl. He swatted her ass playfully. "I hope you left your phone number." She nodded coyly and stepped past Chase.

"I hope she left her name, too," whispered Rick as he waved Chase inside.

"You're doing it all wrong, dude. Never, *ever* let the chick know where you live. Shit could get ugly fast. She could fuck up your house or worse, make up shit about you and spread it to all the papers," Chase admonished, pulling the Jameson from the bag.

Rick crossed his muscular arms over his chest and leaned against the breakfast bar. "I've done all right so far."

"Whatever, man. I can't handle my own relationship issues. I sure as hell shouldn't be handing out advice," Chase scoffed.

Rick took the proffered glass from Chase and laughed. "The only relationship issue you have is which chick you're gonna have for a week."

Chase crossed the room and sat on the black leather couch. "Those were the days…"

Rick sat across from him in his favorite leather recliner and eyed him

162

thoughtfully. "What's up, Chase?"

Chase swallowed a mouthful of Jameson and ran a hand over his face. "Well, it all started when I met this beautiful honey blond at Candace's birthday party in May…"

*   *   *

After the last items were pulled from the truck Freddie eyed Emily warily. He was damn tired and wanted to go home. "Well? What are you gonna do with the cabinet?"

She shrugged, "Frankie? Phyllis? What do you think?"

Frankie pounded his right fist into his left palm. "I say bring it in. I'll give ol' Harold a good poundin' for scarin' you."

"Why's he so creepy lookin'?" Phyllis asked, wrinkling her nose.

"I think it's because he's newly dead. He hasn't had time to change to the way he wants everyone to see him, right Frankie?"

"Yeah, I was really grody at first. Now I'm back to my original good-looking self," Frankie beamed.

Jenny hopped off the table and slapped her hands together, "Well? What's the verdict? We've got a lot of cleaning and arranging to do with all the stuff you bought."

Emily looked around the storage room. "Hey, where's Lilly?"

Phyllis shrugged, "Don't know. I haven't seen her."

"I haven't smelled her," Freddie shivered.

"Okay guys, let's bring it and him in," Emily announced.

*   *   *

Chase talked for thirty minutes non-stop about Emily and when he paused to take a sip of his drink Rick asked, "How did you feel when you saw her having a nightmare?"

163

Chase shrugged. "I felt a shitload of emotions. Helpless, scared for her, confused, protective. I wanted to kick someone's ass!"

Rick nodded. "And when you held her as she cried, how did you feel?"

"You a fuckin' psychologist now?" Chase snapped.

"Just answer the question," Rick urged.

Chase leaned his head against the back of the couch and pinched the bridge of his nose. "No! No! *No!*"

Rick grinned, "No what?"

"I know where you're going with this Ricochet! I'm *not*, repeat *not* falling for her!"

"You're right," Rick agreed. "You've already fallen."

*   *   *

"Woo-hoo! I git to come in!" whooped Harold. "Take it easy on the Hoosier. It used to be my grannies!"

Emily lifted a brow and huffed, "If you're not nice to me I'll break every damn window in it and take a sledge hammer to it."

Harold blinked in shock. "Why wouldja do that? That'd be plain ol' mean!"

Jenny, Freddie and Emily maneuvered the huge cabinet into the shop area, stopping several times to rest.

"I sure wish I could hear what these ghosts say to you," mumbled Jenny.

"Not me! It'd scare the shit out of me," Freddie blanched.

Emily ignored them and looked around the shop for a place to put the cabinet. "How about against the wall over there with the dinette?"

"Don't I get a say where it goes?" Harold whined.

"No!" Frankie, Phyllis, Emily and Lilly replied in unison.

"You! Oh! You awful man!" Lilly shrieked upon seeing Harold.

"What did I do?" Harold cried out.

Lilly moved closer with her arm and forefinger extended. "You're the awful man who had my armoire!"

"Huh?" Harold replied, scratching his head. "Wait a second! Wait one golldang second! I remember that perfume!"

Lilly crossed her arms over her chest, narrowing her eyes at him.

"You! You're the one who haunted that dresser!" he yelled.

"What is this scoundrel doing here?" Lillie asked Emily.

*   *   *

At home Chase removed his clothing at the front door. There was just something liberating about walking around naked. Although he didn't need another drop of Jameson, he poured himself a shot anyway.

He carried his cell phone and shot glass into the bathroom. Glancing at the phone he frowned when he noticed Emily hadn't called.

Why would she? He acted like a complete asshole.

He sighed as he stepped into the shower, letting the hot prickly stream singe his skin.

While he lathered up he considered his options. Chase Storm didn't do things half-assed. It was either all the way or no way.

He could cut his losses, continue with the seven day thing and forget about Emily. Or, he could give the relationship his all.

Tears formed in his eyes. "Damn soap."

But, deep down, he knew the truth.

He *had* fallen for Emily and was scared for what she could do to his heart.

And he sure the fuck didn't need another trip to the psych ward.

*　　*　　*

Frankie grabbed Harold by his good arm while Phyllis pushed his back.

"All right ya dope, you're gonna open your trap and spill it," Phyllis said hotly.

"Spill what?" Harold sniveled.

"What you know about the Soul Hunters, daddy-o, otherwise I'm gonna give you a knuckle sandwich!" Frankie warned.

Lilly watched the three of them fade into the wall. She glanced over her shoulder at Emily with a wicked grin. "He's not so tough now, is he?"

"I hope they get some answers and I hope they're ones I can live with," Emily replied, biting her lip.

Lilly shot her a tight smile, promptly disappearing.

*　　*　　*

Ten at night and Chase sat on his couch in front of his large television in his very large condo.

He scoffed at the absurdity of it all.

He should be out chasing tail or drinking with his buddies.

Glancing at his cell phone he sighed.

The only person he wanted to be with hadn't called and probably wouldn't.

He took a deep breath, releasing it slowly.

Yep, shit was *definitely* too fucking real.

"C'mon, Em, lets call it a day," Jenny yawned.

"You can go," Emily mumbled as she read a newspaper from the 1920's.

"Em, it's midnight, come on," Jenny sighed.

Emily lifted her head from the paper. "Wow, time flies, huh?"

"Yeah, so let's go. We can finish later today."

"I'm gonna stay. If I get tired, there's a cozy bed in the other room I can snuggle on."

Jenny rolled her eyes. "Do you mean the bed that we're trying to sell? The one with the antique quilt on it?"

"I promise not to dirty it," Emily replied with a lifted eyebrow.

"Fine. Stay! Hang out with fucking ghosts. See if I care!" Jenny huffed, walking out the front door of the shop.

"What's her beef?" Phyllis asked sidling up to Emily at the Duncan Phyfe table.

"Who knows? She's been acting strange lately. How'd it go with Harold?"

Phyllis removed her black boa and set it on the table. "He's been tight-lipped, but I think Frankie's got him behind the eight-ball now. I expect ol' Harold will spill his guts soon." Emily frowned and sighed sadly.

"Aw, sweetie, don't let it worry ya," Phyllis cooed, wrapping her arm around Emily.

Emily jumped slightly. "See? That's just it! Filly, I can feel you more now! Why? It's not normal!"

"Come on, doll, you're probably over tired. Let's go in the other room where you can get comfy and we'll talk. Kind of like a pajama party," Phyllis said soothingly.

*   *   *

Phyllis stretched out on the bed next to Emily, propping her head on her hand. "So… what's going on with the dream boat?"

"He's got issues and I'm not sure if I can handle them," Emily sighed, pulling a pink blanket up to her neck.

"Em, all men have issues!" Phyllis laughed.

"Aw Filly, I really like him, but I know if I tell him about you, he'd bolt. I can't even be myself with him. He was so mad at me earlier that I don't think he'll be coming around anymore."

She yawned and continued, "Probably for the best anyway. I could be dead soon."

"Emily Martha Waters! I don't want to hear that come out of your yap again!" Phyllis shrieked.

"Filly? What's it like?" Emily asked softly.

"What's what like?"

"Being dead?"

Phyllis sighed, "Well, sometimes it's fun. Like I can follow cute guys around and grab their butts."

"C'mon. I'm being serious! When I died the first time, I don't remember seeing a light beckoning to me. Just darkness, well that and Fleshy. Did you see a light?"

Phyllis nodded, "Yeah, but I was afraid to go to it."

Emily sat up and rested on her elbow. "Filly, how did you die?"

A sad smile formed on Phyllis' lips. She rolled on to her back and looked up at the ceiling. "I wasn't married and got pregnant. I was excited,

168

ya know? When I told Tommy he said to get rid of it or he'd get rid of me. Anyway, during the abortion I died on the table."

"Oh Filly!"

Phyllis jutted her chin out. "Don't feel sad for me, Em. I got what I deserved. I tried to take a life and my life was taken."

"But…" Emily stammered.

"But nothing, doll. I chose him over my baby." Phyllis turned to face Emily; tears shimmered in both their eyes. "I won't let anything happen to you, sweetie. You're the baby I never had."

$*$ $*$ $*$

Chase awoke at six in the morning in his bed. He didn't remember leaving the couch.

Pulling his legs over the side of the bed he checked his phone and frowned.

A trip to the gym downstairs would help to de-stress and clear his fucking head.

$*$ $*$ $*$

Phyllis watched the rise and fall of Emily's chest as she slept. She smiled wistfully and pushed a strand of hair from Em's face. She'd watched her grow from a child into a beautiful, funny and smart woman. No way in hell was anyone, dead or alive, gonna hurt her girl.

$*$ $*$ $*$

Sweat formed on Chase's forehead as he curled the twenty five-pound barbells intermittently.

After kick-boxing, using the treadmill and lifting weights, he came to a decision.

He placed the barbells in the holders and rolled his head back onto his shoulders.

169

He had to see her.

*   *   *

His pulse raced as he knocked at the front door. After a few minutes the door opened.

A very disheveled Freddie answered, looking highly pissed.

Chase blanched at his demeanor. "Hey, is Emily awake?"

"I wouldn't know since *I* was sleeping," Freddie growled.

Chase looked past Freddie then met his steely gaze and shrugged. "Sorry. I really need to see her."

Freddie pulled the door open wider, lifting his eyebrows.

"Thanks," Chase muttered, moving past Freddie.

A few minutes later he bounded down the stairs and went into the kitchen.

Freddie stood over the sink brushing his teeth. "Wha?" he muttered.

"She's not there, but her car's the driveway," he remarked, looking out the back door window.

"Maybe she spent the night with Jenny," Freddie replied after spitting the toothpaste from his mouth.

Chase pulled his phone from his pocket and dialed Emily's number. His call went to voicemail.

"Can you call her?"

Freddie snorted, "Why don't you call her?"

Chase rolled his eyes. "No, I mean can you call Jenny? Emily's not picking up."

An amused grin lit Freddie's face. "Maybe she doesn't want to talk to you."

170

"Please Freddie?" *Christ! I sound pathetic!*

Freddie leaned against the kitchen counter, crossed his arms over his chest and eyed Chase thoughtfully. "You've got it bad for her."

"Yeah, I've got it bad for her," Chase admitted.

*   *   *

Freddie yelled at his sister, "What do you mean she slept at the shop?"

"Look, she wanted to stay, I wanted to leave! No big deal," Jenny huffed and hung up.

"The key to the back door," Freddie said, dangling a key from his finger.

Chase took the key, passing Freddie a tight smile.

*   *   *

Emily awoke to Phyllis' finger jabbing her in the arm.

"Doll, you've got company!" she giggled.

"Huh?" she replied sleepily.

"Your dream boat with sexy blue eyes is here."

Emily brushed the hair from her face, sure she was dreaming, when she saw Chase sitting on the red fainting couch across from her.

"Chase?"

He nodded, walking to the bed.

She sat up, unsure what to say.

Sweat soaked his palms and he discretely wiped them on his khaki shorts before sitting next to her.

"Hi," he said softly. "I missed you."

171

A corner of her mouth lifted.

"Em...I'm sorry. I'm doing and saying all the wrong shit." He ran a hand through his hair and sighed deeply, "I need for you to be patient with me. Can you do that?"

"Em! Say something for Pete's sake!" Phyllis urged.

"But..." Emily hesitated.

"Em!" Phyllis moaned.

Chase's eyebrows furrowed. "But what?"

"Emily! Tell him yes!"

Emily placed her hands over her ears and closed her eyes.

Then she realized she must look like a loon and quickly opened her eyes, smiled and removed her hands from her ears.

She cleared her throat. "But...I...yes. Yes, I can do that."

*   *   *

"Thanks for coming with me," Chase murmured, a week later, as he sped down I-57.

Emily grinned, "No problem. I'm interested in seeing this old farmhouse that's been giving everyone the creeps."

Beth had told her stories about lights turning on and off by themselves as well as cabinet doors slamming shut.

He turned off at an exit and carefully drove down a pot holed street. "I hope the hell they resurface the road soon. Who the hell is gonna want to drive down this goat path?" he muttered.

After a short while the farmhouse came into view. A large sign had been erected on the land stating the property was owned by Storm Design Group and coming soon seventy five new luxury houses!

The house sat on a hill which overlooked the valley. Land had been scraped and huge sewer pipes littered the area.

"Wow! The house looks magnificent!" she beamed. "So will it be the focal point of the subdivision?"

He grinned at her. "No, it's going to be razed and the hill will be leveled to accommodate two or more houses."

She gaped at him in horror. "Why? It's a beautiful old house!"

He pulled to a stop in the gravel driveway and laughed. "It's a dump!"

She sat in the car until he came around and opened her door.

"Have I told you how lovely you look today?" he said gripping her hand tightly.

"Twice," she grinned. It was the outfit he bought for her on their first date to Navy Pier.

"Be careful on the porch," he warned. "Some of the boards are rotted."

She released his hand and carefully walked the length of the porch, smiling. It wrapped around to the back of the house and even with rotted boards and chipping white paint, it was beautiful.

"Oh what a waste to trash this house," she murmured to herself.

"Yeah? You won't think so when you see the inside. It needs a ton of work," he mumbled.

Neil opened the front door with a haggard expression on his face.

"Chase. Em, it's so good to see you," he shot her a lopsided grin and kissed her cheek.

"Oh my!" she squeaked when she stepped into the house. A curved stairway met her gaze. The stairway was tapered at the second floor and as it wound to the first floor it widened. Emily guessed that four or five

173

people could stand side by side on the bottom step easily.

"I love this house!" she exclaimed.

Neil and Chase shot each other quizzical looks.

"Em, this house is a dump!" Chase laughed.

Doors began slamming and several workers ran from various parts of the house and skidded to a stop when they saw Chase.

A loud scream shortly followed.

Danny, Chase's friend, whimpered. "What the fuck was that?"

The hair on Chase's nape lifted and he shifted his feet, "Probably just the wind blowing through broken windows.

Emily shot him a small grin.

Neil laughed nervously. "I'm glad that happened while you're here. Now maybe you'll believe us when we tell you this place is haunted."

"Now Neil, you know there's no such thing as ghosts," Chase replied condescendingly.

Noticing Neil's eyes narrow Emily spoke up. "Hey, Chase, why don't you talk to Neil while I take a look around? I see some antiques here that you could put in the shop and make some serious money on."

Chase eyed her warily. "Be careful, okay? The house is falling apart." She nodded and set off for the kitchen area.

The kitchen was huge, as she assumed it would be. Back in the day that's where the families would congregate. She spotted a dead mouse in the corner and shirked away, bumping into a frail old lady.

The old lady glared at her with her lips pursed. She brought her hands up and pushed Emily's shoulders.

She's pretty strong, for an older lady, Emily thought as she was jostled backwards.

174

"Hello," she whispered to the woman.

The woman blinked in surprise. "You can see me?"

Emily nodded and grinned, "You have a lovely home."

"That's what I keep trying to tell them!" the old lady sniffed. "They want to tear down my home!"

Emily nodded sadly. "My name is Emily. What's yours?"

"Alma. Alma Raines."

"Alma, it's nice to meet you."

Alma lifted a hand to her graying bun, smoothing stray hairs. "I'd say I was happy to meet you, but I think you're up to no good like the rest of them."

"I'd like to help you save your home," Emily said wistfully.

Alma eyed her suspiciously. "You're not just saying that are you?"

"I'll do what I can, but if it doesn't work out, you can come with me."

Alma backed away slowly. "You ain't one of them Soul Hunters are ya?"

Emily blinked in surprise. "You've heard of them?"

Alma nodded, "Yeah. Most of them ain't no good. One of them came here and tried to take me into the light. I wouldn't have nothin' to do with it. She said I could see my husband, Lenny. Got no reason to see him. He was an asshole when he was alive, doubt he changed much in death."

*   *   *

"Em?"

Alma faded away with a scowl at his voice.

175

"There you are!" he remarked, pulling her into a hug.

"It's a great kitchen. I'm envisioning a white table in the corner over there and perhaps a kitchen island in the center of the room," she sighed into his shoulder.

He laughed, "I'm afraid to show you the rest of the house if you're enamored by the kitchen." He gazed down at her and planted a kiss on her forehead. "C'mon. There's a bunch of stuff here you can put in your shop, if you want it."

*   *   *

After a quick tour of the house, Chase was pulled aside by Danny and Emily grabbed Neil's arm and pulled him onto the porch.

"Her name is Alma and she's pretty pissed that you want to raze her house."

"What the fuck am I supposed to do about that?" Neil muttered, irritated.

Emily shrugged, "Don't raze it."

*   *   *

At dinner Chase shivered when he thought about the scream at the farmhouse. Not to mention the banging doors.

Emily noticed. "Ya cold?"

Chase took a bite of his steak and shook his head, "Just thinking about the house. It was kinda weird how the doors slammed shut, huh?"

"The place is haunted," she shrugged.

Chase groaned, "Not you, too!"

She put her fork down on the plate and cocked her head. "Why are you so against believing in ghosts?"

"Because it's just not possible. You live, you die. No gray area."

176

She smirked, "What about Resurrection Mary? Bachelor's Grove Cemetery? Hell, even Oprah Winfrey's studio, Harpo Inc. is said to be haunted by victims of the Great Chicago Fire!"

"Rumors," he shrugged, taking a sip of Chablis.

"Bullshit! You're just afraid to admit that ghosts exist," she huffed, chugging her Chablis.

He lifted a dark eyebrow. "Babe, there are a lot of things that I'm afraid of, but ghosts aren't one of them."

But love? That was a different story.

*   *   *

Freddie ripped the front door open when he heard the closing of car doors.

"Dudes! You aren't going to believe this! I got a call today from some hot shot CEO who wants Double Exposure to play at Petrillo Music Shell on July fourth!"

"Freddie! That's great!" Emily squealed, hugging him.

Chase shook Freddie's hand. "Congrats, man. That's huge!"

"Right? I'm so excited I could piss myself!"

Emily's nose scrunched. "Have you told the guys yet?"

He nodded, "They're on their way. The guy is e-mailing the contract for us to sign. Plus, we have to come up with a song set. It's only two weeks away!"

Chase frowned. "Why did he wait so long to hire you?"

Freddie shrugged, "Don't know, don't care. This could launch us!"

Chase pulled Emily's hand and sat on the couch. He didn't like her to be too far away from him. "Are you looking for a record deal?"

"That'd be epic!" Freddie laughed, picking up his beer bottle.

"Yeah, Freddie writes a lot of his own songs, but doesn't play them nearly enough in public!" Emily frowned.

Chase and Emily watched as Freddie loped towards the basement where his instruments were set up.

"Hm…Freddie is giving us alone time," Chase murmured.

Usually Freddie hovered over them like a mother hen.

"Let's not waste time," she whispered against his lips.

He gathered her in his arms and held her snugly on his lap. His kiss was slow and thoughtful, but she wanted more.

She gently grabbed the back of his head and parted his lips with her tongue.

A low, deep moan escaped from his lips while his right hand pressed firmly against her lower back and his left hand cradled her head.

She opened her eyes and met his searing gaze, causing her stomach to tingle.

With her lips pressed against his she said, "Do you want to go upstairs?"

He didn't get a chance to reply because the doorbell rang.

Chapter Ten

With a sigh Emily unfolded herself from Chase's lap and walked to the door.

Freddie's band mates walked in smiling. "Hey Em! How's it going?" Ian asked, kissing her briefly on the cheek.

"Hey, I want you guys to meet someone," she said, walking towards Chase.

"Ian, Ted and Steve, this is Chase Storm…," she hesitated.

Chase extended his hand to them. "Her boyfriend," he added.

Ian shook Chase's hand, laughing. "For a week. This is the guy I was telling you about," he chortled to his buddies.

Ted shook Chase's hand and bowed, "I'm at your service."

Steve smacked Ted on the head. "Shut up, asshole." He shot Emily a wink and ignored Chase's proffered hand. "Freddie downstairs?"

The mood in the room was palpable, causing Emily to fidget. "Yeah," she nodded. As they began their descent she called to them. "Congrats on the gig!"

Chase blew out a hard breath. "Well, I can see Steve's not a fan."

Emily laughed lightly. "He's a deep guy. Very sensitive. Kind of the conscience of the group."

He brushed his nose against hers. "Where were we?"

"I asked if you wanted to go upstairs," she replied breathily.

His eyebrow arched. "You're playing a wicked game."

She tugged his hand. "I don't play games, Chase. C'mon."

When she got on the first step he spun her around to face him. A smile slowly spread across his face. "Just the right height," he murmured, crushing his lips against hers.

She grabbed two fistfuls of his hair, pulling him closer.

Their tongues danced together slowly building to a deeper, quicker pace. She tried to walk up the stairs, backwards, but he held her firmly in place.

His hands cupped her backside, pulling her tightly against him. God, how he wanted her.

And she totally wanted him.

"Em? Can you come down here?" Freddie called from the basement.

She pulled away from Chase, breathless. "Later Freddie! I'm busy!"

Chase shot her a lop-sided grin before pressing his lips against her neck.

"I really think you need to come down here," Freddie urged.

She pulled away from Chase, her eyes lifting heavenward. Freddie had a shitty sense of timing! "Fine!" she hissed.

She tugged Chase's hand, but he didn't budge, causing a frown to form on her face. "Aren't ya coming?"

He waved a hand in front of his crotch. "Gimme a minute, while little Chase deflates."

She smirked, "Little?"

He lifted an eyebrow. "It's an expression, Em."

"Um-hum," she snickered, walking down the basement stairs.

*   *   *

The room was too quiet. She wondered if Andrea or something worse made an appearance when four sets of eyes stared at her warily.

Freddie waved several sheets of paper in his hand. "Small problem," he mumbled to Emily.

She laughed, "What's with the grim expressions?"

"The guy has, um, conditions," Freddie replied bleakly.

Emily cocked her head, "Such as?"

"He wants you to sing a few songs," Freddie blurted, then held his breath awaiting her reply.

She glanced around the room, measuring his band mates' expressions, and then looked back at him.

She felt Chase's warm palm on the small of her back. "What's up?" he asked, gauging the vibe of the room.

"Apparently the guy who hired Double Ex wants me to sing a few songs, but I think there's something Freddie's not telling me, judging by everyone's frowns."

Chase tore his eyes from Emily and lifted his brows to Freddie, "Is there something else?"

"Gah!" Freddie roared, stomping away.

"Freddie!" Emily laughed. "What is it?"

"He wants you to sing at least eight songs and after the first set's finished he's extended an offer for dinner," Freddie replied, sulkily.

"Eight songs? But that's almost your whole set!"

181

Freddie's eyes lit up. "Yeah, but we're doing two sets. So you're not mad? You'll do it?"

She shrugged, "I guess so. Who the hell is this guy, anyway?"

Ian blinked. "You're not mad about the dinner invite?"

"Should I be?" she half-grinned.

Freddie pushed the contract into her hands, along with a blue ink pen. "Ya gotta sign here." His finger ran along a black line with her name printed beneath it.

She signed it hastily when Steve snipped. "Dick move, Freddie."

Chase eyed the curly brown haired, green-eyed man for a moment then snatched the contract from Emily as Freddie tried to grab it.

He quickly scanned the paper and after a few minutes a hiss escaped from his lips. He shoved the contract into Freddie's hand. "I agree with Steve. That *was* a dick move, Fred."

Emily's brows knitted together as she looked back and forth between Chase and Freddie. "Okay…what am I missing?"

"The dinner invitation is only extended to you, Emily," Freddie muttered, unable to meet her gaze.

*   *   *

"Who the hell is this guy and how does he have the ability to pull this off? Is he a politician?" she griped, stomping around the basement. Steve wrapped an arm around her, pulling her closer. She leaned into his shoulder.

Chase ran a hand through his hair. "Well, he's someone who must have clout and the resources to pull this off. Freddie, what's his name?"

Freddie shrugged, "Don't know. When he called he said that his name was J. Arthur something. But on the contract it just says 'Art Attack Corp."

Chase stroked his chin thoughtfully. "I'll reach out to my business associates; see if they've heard of the company."

"I hope he's only expecting dinner," she frowned.

*   *   *

At home, Chase called his friend, Greg Travers, a Chicago cop.

"Well, I'll be a son-of-a-bitch!" Greg laughed when he picked up the phone. "How ya been Chase?"

"I've been…well. You?"

"Got no complaints! Got a great lady to spend my time with and I'm flying to Ireland next month to see my best friends."

"Ireland?" Chase snorted.

"Yeah. Remember Camryn O'Mara?"

Chase did remember her. Poor Greg was like a lost puppy with that chick. Then, some crazy fucker started stalking her. Nearly drove Greg nuts!

"How is she?" Chase murmured into the phone.

"Real good. She married an Irishman and they just had a baby girl. My girl, Tamara, and I are going to be little Failend's godparents. That's why we're flying to Ireland."

"Tamara, huh? Wasn't she Camryn's best friend?" Chase replied, smiling.

Greg laughed, "Good memory."

Chase poured a copious amount of Jameson into a glass. "So are you and Tamara serious?"

"As serious as a heart attack, my friend."

Chase lifted his eyebrow, skeptical. "No more Camryn? I mean,

183

dude, you were fucked up over her."

Greg was quiet for a moment. "Yeah, I was, but I'm very happy with Tamara. Ah, besides, Declan, her husband, is good for her."

Chase didn't know if he'd be as gracious if he lost Emily to another guy. The startling admission to himself made his hand shake.

"Dude? Ya still there?" Greg laughed.

Chase swallowed hard. "Yeah. Um, look, the reason I'm calling, other than to see how you are, is because I met a girl…"

"Cripes! Another stalker?" Greg moaned.

Chase frowned. Many years back when he first started seven days of heaven he wasn't careful and gave a chick his address. When the seven days were up, she wasn't ready for it to be over. She stalked him ruthlessly-it boarded on the movie *Fatal Attraction*.

With the help of Greg and the Chicago police department she was quickly taken care of.

Afterwards, Chase moved, changed his phone number and bought a new car. It was an expensive mistake he never made again.

"Nah, not a stalker," Chase smiled. "I've met a woman who I've been with for over a month."

Greg choked on his beer. "Hold the fuckin' phone! Are you serious?"

Chase sat on the couch. "It's true and I gotta say, it's been pretty great."

"So what's the problem then?"

Chase quickly explained the concert and the mysterious strangers request for Em to have a private dinner with him. "I don't like the thought of her having dinner alone with someone who won't divulge his name on a contract."

"Good point. He could be a perv or worse. What can I do to help?" Greg asked.

"Be her bodyguard for the night?" Chase asked, hopefully.

*   *   *

As Emily climbed into bed she had the strange feeling someone was watching her. "Andrea?" she said aloud.

Grey warned her the mortal was gifted so Marianna stood silently in the shadows.

"My nerves are frayed," Emily laughed nervously, pulling the sheet over herself.

Marianna shifted on her feet. Grey told her to wait until Emily was asleep before jumping into her. She watched the time tick by and grew frustrated. The mortal tossed and turned for an hour. Marianna's patience wore thin.

She would wait no longer.

*   *   *

The next afternoon Emily found herself driving to the farmhouse. She reasoned that it was on the way to the herb farm where she wanted to purchase plants for her flower beds.

Several vehicles were parked on the gravel driveway.

She sat in her car for a moment staring at the house. She had to convince Chase not to tear it down…somehow. Why couldn't he see the beauty of it?

She got out of the car and walked in the tall grass to the back of the house.

The ruins of what was likely a barn lay off in the distance. A sudden melancholy filled her.

"Hey, can I help you?" A voice called from the back door.

She looked at the man and smiled weakly. He looked familiar, but she couldn't place his name.

With his head cocked and his arms folded over his chest he stepped away from the door, onto the porch. "You're Beth's friend, right?"

"Yeah," she murmured, walking onto the porch. She shook his hand. "Emily Waters."

He gripped her hand tighter. Hell, he wanted to hug her! So, he did. "You're Stormy's girlfriend!" She giggled into his shoulder. "I've heard some great things about you," he replied, pulling away to get a better look at her.

Her lips curved into a smile. "Do tell," she said conspiratorially.

He stuffed his hands in his blue jean pockets. "Well, you've completely transformed my brother into a human. I should really bow to you."

"Aw, Chase is a good guy."

"Pfft. You didn't know him before. Stormy was always getting into fights. Hell, the man still has a temper, but I gotta be honest with you. I haven't seen that temper in a while," he replied.

She folded her arms across her chest and lifted an eyebrow. "Stormy?"

"Yeah, after my mom married his dad, Preston, she was always going to school to see the principal because Chase was always gettin' into scraps. He was a moody em-effer! So I began calling him 'Stormy'. The nickname stuck over the years."

She shrugged, "Well, I've never seen that side of him."

"I hope you don't, either. He can get pretty ugly and ruthless," Jason replied. He smacked himself in the head. "Where are my manners? I'm Jason Storm."

"Jason! You're Sarah's husband! I knew you looked familiar!"

"Guilty!" he laughed. "Is Stormy supposed to meet you here?"

She glanced away shyly. "Um, no. I was on my way to an herb farm and wanted to stop by. Chase said there were some things here that I could take to my shop for him.

"I hope that includes the creepy ghost," he shivered.

She eyed the tall, dark haired man who was built like a brick shithouse and laughed. "A big guy like you scared of a little old lady?"

He nodded. "Dead ones, yes." He thought for a moment and shrugged, "Does Stormy know you can see her?"

A panicked expression filled her eyes. "No, and please don't tell him!"

He cocked his head, "Why? From what I understand you two are kind of tight. Hell, he hasn't been with a woman this long since college."

"You know him better than I do. What do you think he'd do if he found out I talk to ghosts?" she muttered.

"He'd jet." Jason patted her arm gently. "Your secret is safe with me, Emily."

Alma stood in the kitchen, glaring at Emily. "You said you'd help me keep my house! I don't see you doing anything! They're still here!"

Emily rolled her eyes and glanced at Jason. "Alma is here and not very happy about her house being taken over." She turned her back on Alma. "Jason, isn't there anything you can do to stop the demolition?"

"I've got no say in the matter."

"Can you call Preston and tell him that I want to buy it?" she blurted out.

"This house needs a lot of work. The electrical alone would cost a fortune to update."

She gripped his forearm firmly. "Please? Can you call him?"

"But…" he hesitated.

She didn't know what came over her when she said, "This is my home."

*   *   *

As she pulled away from the farmhouse she looked out the rear-view mirror and slammed on the brakes.

She got of the car and held her phone up, snapping a photo of the house with the sun settling behind it.

*   *   *

"You failed!" The Grey One hissed.

"Sh-h-e's too strong willed," Marianna trembled.

"You will suffer the consequences!" he roared, pacing. He didn't suffer fools gladly.

Mitch Rhodes appeared next to Marianna. "I have an idea on how to deliver Emily to you Grey."

*   *   *

Emily's phone vibrated in her pocket. She knew it was Chase, calling to bitch at her about the house. It wasn't something she wanted to deal with. She was happily planting perennials and herbs in her flower garden.

Besides, she had some thinking to do.

If Preston Storm came back with an agreement to sell her the house she needed to get some cash and quick. She didn't want to call her parents and ask for money, but if push came to shove…

She turned the volume up on her MP3 player and reinserted the ear buds in her ears as she planted her way through the flower bed.

A shadow formed behind her as she was digging, causing dirt to fly everywhere.

She quickly stood, wielding the trowel as a weapon.

"Jared! You scared the hell out of me!" she shrieked, pulling the ear buds from her ears.

He picked a small dirt clump from her pony tail. "Sorry," he grinned. "I thought I'd deliver these flowers in person." He held out a thick bouquet to her.

She sighed, "Jared, you shouldn't waste your money on me."

"I told you, I don't give up easily," he shrugged sheepishly.

Tugging off her gloves she said quietly, "I don't deserve them."

He lifted her chin with his thumb and forefinger. "I beg to differ."

She felt like a total shit head. Jared was a nice guy and *could've* been the one.

His chocolate colored eyes stared into her toffee colored eyes, making her stomach flip-flop a little. She started to back away when he held her chin firmly. He lowered his head and kissed her chastely on the lips.

His body jerked suddenly. "Do you smell that?" he mumbled.

She shook her head. "Smell what?"

"It smells like the lake. Water, seaweed, sand…" he mumbled, looking around, flummoxed.

She shrugged, "Nope. All I smell are these flowers."

He turned and palmed her cheek. "I've gotta go. Enjoy the flowers, baby."

*   *   *

After showering, Emily checked her phone and grimaced. No calls from Jason, but a shit ton from Chase. She chose to ignore his calls and called her parents instead.

189

"Hi honey!" her mom, Martha, sang into the phone.

"Hi mom, did you get the pictures I sent you?" Emily asked as she poured a glass of water.

"I did! My, Chase is very handsome! Oh! Hold on! Your dad wants me to put you on speaker phone."

Emily grinned. "How's my handsome dad doing?"

"I'm doing well. I have to say that I'd rather see pictures of you instead of the man you're dating or a house," he laughed.

"Hush now, Sam. I think Chase is quite a looker!" Martha admonished.

"Chase aside, what did you think of the house?" Emily asked, biting her thumb nail.

"What are your plans, young lady?" Sam asked, grinning at his wife.

"Well, I really like it dad. And Chase's company is going to tear it down and build houses. There's a little old lady who is haunting the place and well, I want it," she blurted out.

"Well, why don't you just tell this Chase that you want it?"

Emily sighed, "It's not like that dad. We've only been dating a little while."

"I see. What about the house you own with Freddie? Will he buy you out if you were to get the farm house?"

"I don't know. This happened so suddenly and I'm not even sure if they'll sell it to me," she replied wistfully.

Sam Waters laughed, "Okay, sweetheart. Find out all the details and call us back. We may be able to help if they're willing to sell. Now, what's this I hear you're going to be singing with Freddie?"

Emily relayed the entire story to her parents even though she e-mailed them about it a week ago.

"Make sure Freddie takes a video! I sure wish we could be there, but your mom has us going on some damn tour of the Florida Keys."

"By the way, honey, we're sending you an e-mail," Martha broke in.

"Okay…" Emily grinned.

Martha laughed. "We bought you a plane ticket to come see us!"

Emily's eyes teared and she tucked her legs under her bottom. "Really? When?"

"The end of July, the prices were cheaper then."

"Emmy, are you okay?" her dad asked.

She nodded. "Yeah, I miss you guys so much and to hear that you've gotten me a ticket, well, dad, I'm having a female moment here!"

Sam laughed, "You girls! Your mom is tearing up too!"

Emily's doorbell rang, "Mom, dad, I gotta go. I'll call you later in the week. I love you!"

*   *   *

She hastily wiped the tears from her eyes with the back of her hands before she opened the door.

Chase's angry expression faded when he noticed the tears in her eyes. "What's wrong?" he asked, cupping her cheek.

She shook her head and closed the door. "Nothing. I was just talking to my parent's."

"Are they okay?"

"Yeah. I just miss them, ya know? They bought me a plane ticket for the end of the month to go see them."

"Next week?" Chase asked, leading her to the couch.

She sat next to him. "No, next month. It'll be good to see them."

He nodded, lifting an eyebrow. "Why haven't you answered my calls?"

"I knew you were only calling to berate me about the house," she shrugged.

He stood and tucked his hand into the pocket of his khaki shorts. As he paced the small room she checked him out.

He wore an untucked dark blue polo shirt which accentuated his light blue eyes and well formed upper arms. Her eyes raked along his body down to his hairy legs. He wore slip-ons with no socks. Something about that turned her on.

She rolled her eyes at herself.

"Why are you rolling your eyes at me when you're the one who wants to buy a dilapidated farm house? Are you out of your mind?" he hissed.

She lifted her chin. "The house needs a little TLC, Chase!"

A smile curved on his lips. "No, it needs a little TNT! Emily, be reasonable! You can't afford to rehab that dump!"

She glared at him and stood. "It's not a dump! It's a great house! Here, I'll show you!"

She grabbed her phone and pulled up the photo she'd taken earlier in the day. "Do you see the sun is setting behind it? It's beautiful, Chase. Why can't you see that?" she asked softly.

He glanced at the photo and she pressed her phone into his hand to look at it further.

Silhouetted against the sun, it did look pretty fuckin' cool. He started to tell her so when he noticed a flower filled vase on the coffee table.

Chase growled, "What the fuck?"

Emily followed Chase's gaze.

"What's going on, Em?" he hissed.

"With?" she frowned.

His eyes narrowed. "Why is he still sending you flowers?"

"Because he's a masochist," she snorted.

His fists clenched at his sides. "Are you leading him on?"

"How dare you imply that!"

"He's been sending you flowers weekly for the past month! I've gotta think there's something more to this," he shouted.

"I've told you that I have no interest in him and I've asked him not to send flowers, but clearly you two are a lot alike because neither of you listen to me."

"What's that supposed to mean?" he snorted.

She walked to the front door and pulled it open.

He rubbed the back of his neck, shuffling towards her. "Em, I'm sorry." When he reached for her, she pulled away.

"Goodbye Chase," she choked out.

Chapter Eleven

"You alone?" Chase said into the phone.

"Whaddya got in mind, cutie?"

"I'm downstairs in the bar," Chase smiled.

"I'll be right down."

*   *   *

Chase downed two Corona's before his guest joined him. He held up a hand to the waitress. "Two more of these and two shots of Cuervo," he mumbled to the buxom raven haired girl.

"About fuckin' time!" he snapped.

Rick mumbled. "Why are you in such a shitty mood?"

Chase ran a hand through his hair. "Cause I fucked up with Emily."

Rick rolled his eyes. "What didja do?"

The waitress placed the drinks on the table and quickly walked away. Chase picked up a shot glass, tilted his head back and drank the amber liquid quickly, slamming the glass on the table. "I told ya, I fucked up. Accused her of leading some other guy on. Fuck! I know she isn't and I knew it when I accused her. What the fuck's wrong with me? Why can't I allow myself to have a healthy, normal relationship?"

Rick took a long pull from the long neck and shrugged. "Only you can answer that question."

Chase lifted his eyebrows, incredulous. "That's all you got for me?"

"Beg for forgiveness," Rick replied, shifting in the wooden booth. "You're crazy about her, fuckin' tell her that! Quit being a pussy."

"That's more like it," Chase smiled and shrugged. "I don't know how, ya know, to beg."

"Jewelry works. So do flowers," Rick offered.

Chase flinched. "Don't talk to me about flowers!" A smile spread across his face. "I know something even better." He sat straighter in the booth. "Dude, I need you to do me a huge fuckin' favor."

*   *   *

Soft music filled the shop when Emily began to dust. She smiled when she realized it was Filly's favorite song, *Love Ain't Nothin' but the Blues.*

"Hey doll," Filly grinned, snuggling on the wrought iron bed.

"Hi," she smiled wistfully. "Appropriate song choice."

Phyllis frowned. She saw the argument Emily and Chase had the night before, but couldn't let on that she knew. "Aw, Em, why ya so sad?"

Emily knotted the dust cloth in her hands and explained the previous days events.

"Ya know, his being jealous of Jared isn't a bad thing, kiddo."

"Yeah, but to accuse me of leading Jared on *is*, Phyllis," she replied, throwing her hands up in the air. "Gah!"

Phyllis huffed, "So that's it then?" Emily turned, shrugging. "Wow, you give up easy. Em, don't ya like this guy?"

"Well, yeah, but I'm not going to chase after him."

Frankie chortled, "She's not going to *chase* after *Chase*. That's funny, Em!"

"Don't ya have some knuckle sandwiches to make?" Phyllis sneered.

"Daddy-O is a hard cookie to crumble. Lilly is working him over now," Frankie shrugged.

"He didn't tell you anything?" Emily frowned.

"Nah. Just said he heard about the Soul Hunters because they came lookin' for him when he died. He said he wouldn't go into the light and they left him alone." Frankie sat on the bed next to Phyllis and tugged her boa.

Phyllis snatched it back and stuck her tongue out. "Beat it, we've got girl jawing to do." When Frankie made no move to leave she poked him with her index finger. "Tick tock…"

"Cool it ya party pooper. I'm cuttin' out," Frankie snipped before he disappeared.

Emily chewed on her bottom lip. "Frankie's not any closer to finding out what the Soul Hunters want with me."

Phyllis giggled, "Maybe the bluenose will use her feminine wiles on him."

"Bluenose?" Emily half-grinned.

"Prude," Phyllis smiled.

When Emily turned her back to dust Lilly's armoire Phyllis glided next to her.

"Doll?" Emily cocked her head at her transparent friend and Phyllis continued, "Do you think you're pushing Chase away because you're afraid of getting hurt?"

"He's pushing me away, Filly," Emily sighed when the chime over the door rang.

"Welcome to Play it Again Sam," she called as she entered the main room. She stopped in her tracks when she saw Rick O'Shea, all six foot two inches of him, in her shop.

"Hi Emily," he said smoothly.

"Hubba hubba, Em! He's god like!" Phyllis sighed as she gazed at his face. Dreamy hazel eyes, full kissable lips, sandy blond hair and a tight, hard body. She felt herself swoon.

Her eyes widened. "Is Chase okay?"

He came closer and took her by the elbow. "Actually, he isn't. He's suffering from a rare disease."

Emily gasped and brought her hand to her mouth. "What?"

Rick grinned, "Asshole-ism."

Her eyes narrowed and she folded her arms across her chest. "Not funny."

"Sorry. It was meant to be," he shrugged sheepishly. "Look, he's really sorry about last night."

"So he sent you to apologize?" She walked away, turned and lifted her hands. "Gah!"

Rick's lips curved, "Gah?"

"He's impossible! He accuses me of something really shitty and he asks his best friend to apologize for him? He's ridiculous!"

"Emily, I've never seen Chase so happy and sad at the same time. Whether you believe this or not, he's crazy about you," Rick said softly.

"But..." she stammered.

"In the years I've known him, you're the only woman he's been with for this long. Shouldn't that tell you something?"

She lifted a narrow shoulder and glanced away.

Rick sighed heavily. "Look, I probably shouldn't be saying this, but the guy's in love with you."

She lifted her chin, ignoring the stinging in her eyes. "Did he tell you that?"

Shaking his head Rick softly said, "He didn't have to."

*   *   *

Chase knocked at the front door. Freddie opened the door and lifted an eyebrow.

"She's not home," he muttered.

"I know. Look, I was wondering if you'd do a huge favor for me?"

Freddie crossed his arms over his chest. "And that would be?"

Chase held up his guitar case. "Can I practice with you tonight? I have a song I'd like to sing to Emily."

Freddie grinned, "You love struck pup! C'mon."

*   *   *

When Emily drove down the street, her breath caught in her throat. Chase's Porsche was parked in front of her house. Well, along with Ted and Steve's cars.

She thought about turning around, but damn it! She had a shitty day and wanted to go home and relax.

*   *   *

"Show time!" Freddie yelled into the basement when Emily got out of the car.

199

When she walked to the front door Freddie promptly pulled it open, taking her purse and canvas tote bag from her. "C'mon. There's something you need to hear," he said tugging her towards the basement.

"Freddie, I'm not ready to see him," she moaned.

"Trust me, Em," he replied seriously.

The piano slowly began as she walked down the stairs. The beginning riff of *Jealous Guy* filled the room. Chase sat at the piano, singing to her with a tenderness she'd never seen before.

The other guys gradually began playing their instruments, too, smiling like idiots.

Tears stung the backs of her eyes and she tried to hold them back, but the little bastards came out anyway.

When the song was over Chase approached her warily. "My singing skills are a little rusty," he replied huskily.

She shook her head and wrapped her arms around him. "That was beautiful," she cried into his chest.

"Em, I'm so sorry," he said softly, holding her tightly against him.

In the corner of the basement Phyllis and Frankie gave each other a high five, promptly fading off into the sunset.

*   *   *

At the shop the next day, Emily noticed a strange demeanor in her cousin.

"Jenny? Have I said or done something to make you angry with me?" Emily asked as her cousin brushed past her quickly.

"Jeez, Em, why would I be angry with you?" she snippily replied. "I mean just because you'd rather talk to dead people instead of me and date an asshole instead of Jared." Jenny stopped and rested her hands on her hips. "Now why would I be mad?"

"Chase isn't an asshole," Emily replied, her hackles raised. "You don't even know him, so how dare you say such a thing!"

"He's a spoiled little rich kid, Emily. Once he has sex with you, you can kiss him goodbye." Jenny lifted her arm over her head. "He's up here and you're down here," she cackled, lowering her hand to the floor.

"Wow, PMS is kicking your ass pretty hard this week," Emily spat.

"And your obsession with your ghosts? Ya need help Emily. I think you say you see ghosts so people pay attention to you. It's pathetic! You're parents should have committed you a long time ago," Jenny concluded with a sneer.

She stormed out of the shop, slamming the door in her wake.

*　　　*　　　*

"Aw, doll, don't let her get to you," Phyllis said softly, wrapping an arm around her.

Tears pooled in Emily's eyes at Jenny's harsh remarks. "Why would she say those things?"

"Who knows? She's been in here talking to herself for the past few days and then, that Jared guy's been in here too. I'm beginning to wonder if there isn't something going on between them," Phyllis replied.

"Jared's been here?"

"Yeah. She talks to him on the phone, too," Frankie interjected, plopping himself down on the mortician table.

"I wish I knew what's gotten in to her," Emily frowned sadly.

201

Jenny stood outside the shop door, a slow, cunning grin slid across her face.

*   *   *

After a week of intense practicing, Emily was ready for the next day. Well, not mentally. A large crowd was expected for the concert. She tucked that fact into the back of her mind.

She packed a small bag as well as a garment bag and placed it by the front door. Chase would be picking her up to take her to the city for the evening.

"So, ya ready for the big day?" Freddie asked when he walked in the back door.

"As ready as I'm ever gonna be," she sighed. "I just hope I don't stumble over the words. Hey, have you talked to Jenny lately?"

"Nah. Why?"

"Last week she verbally attacked me. Basically said I was certifiable because I talk to ghosts and that Chase is out of my league. She only talks to me when I initiate conversation and then she responds with one word answers. Something's not right with her."

Freddie scoffed, "You're tellin' me? I grew up with her!"

Emily rolled her eyes. "Would ya talk to her? See what's wrong?"

"Sure. Now, how are you feeling about tomorrow?"

She bit her lip. "I hope I don't eff up the words."

Freddie hugged her. "You'll be great."

She pulled away. "Freddie? Do you like Chase just a little?"

He rolled his eyes. "I'll admit I didn't like him at first, but he's grown on me, like a fungus."

They heard the alarm on his car and Freddie laughed, "Speak of the devil."

Emily grinned over her shoulder as she walked to the front door. "Hi."

Chases eyes raked over her thoroughly appraising her outfit. "You look mighty sexy, Miss Waters," he crooned, crushing his lips against hers.

It was the same brown dress she wore the first time she met him.

"Ahem…" Freddie bellowed. "You! Take good care of her tonight and be sure to get her there on time tomorrow."

Chase smiled against Emily's lips. "Yes sir. Four, right?"

"Not funny, Storm. She needs to be there at three," Freddie growled.

Emily admonished them. "You two! C'mon, let's go."

Chase shot Freddie a wink as he closed the door.

*   *   *

Chase and Emily met his friends at a restaurant.

"Emily, this is Greg Travers and his girlfriend Tamara Youngblood," Chase said loudly over the crowd in the bar.

Greg pulled her into a hug. "Nice to meet you Emily!"

Emily gazed up at him and smiled. He looked like a cop with his short spiky blond hair. His hazel eyes had a hint of mischief to them, too.

Tamara smiled warmly and shook her hand.

They were seated in a secluded area. Chase didn't like sitting in the open. Ya never knew where the cameramen were hiding. He tried to keep his private life, well, private, but things had a way of making the papers.

Emily wondered what Tamara did for a living. She looked familiar, but she couldn't place her face. She looked to be American Indian with her long black silky hair and high cheekbones. She was stunning! Maybe a model?

After they placed their orders Chase initiated conversation. "Greg, were you able to find out anything?"

"Nah. Whoever this guy is, he's good," Greg muttered, taking a swig of his beer.

Emily cocked her head. "Who're you talking about?"

Chase gripped her hand. "The guy who hired Double Ex. Greg's a cop, Em. I asked him to check the guy out."

"I even used my resources, but came up wanting." Tamara explained, "I work for the Daily paper. I'm beginning to wonder if the guy is using a pseudonym."

"A reporter?" Emily giggled. "I thought you were a model or something."

Tamara laughed, tossing her hair over her shoulder. "My friend, Camryn says I should be on the cover of magazines and not reporting."

Emily smiled. "Well, she's right!" Her eyebrows furrowed then. "I don't understand why this guy would go to such lengths."

Chase's jaw clenched. "Because he doesn't want anyone to know who he is."

Emily rubbed the goose bumps on her arms. Chase wrapped his arm around her and pulled her closer. "Em, Greg will be with you when you have dinner with Mr. X." He arched an eyebrow when she began to talk.

She put a finger over his lips and smiled. "I'm not going to argue with you. This time." She reached across the table and touched Greg's hand.

204

"Thank you for agreeing to be my body guard."

Greg blushed, "It's nothing. I'm glad to do it. Besides, it's been a while since I kicked anyone's ass."

* * *

While Chase drove to his condo Emily gazed out the window. The conversation flowed so easily with Greg and Tamara. She enjoyed the banter between Chase and Greg and talking with Tamara was like talking to Phyllis.

"You're awfully quiet," Chase murmured, reaching for her hand.

"I like your friends. It's been a very long time since I've had such an entertaining dinner. They were comfortable to be with."

Chase thought for a long moment and smiled. "I've never done that before."

She turned away from the window. "Done what?"

"Shared a dinner with my girlfriend and my friends."

* * *

Chase kicked off his loafers at the door and placed her bags on the kitchen nook. He winked and walked into the den briefly.

She noticed that he moved two armchairs which were sitting in front of the tall window further into the room, along with the small table. Her eyebrows furrowed. Why would he do that?

An instrumental played softly, causing her to smile. He came towards her with his hand outstretched. "Dance with me?" he asked softly.

She took his hand and he lead her to the large window. She grinned, "Now it makes sense."

He placed his palm on her lower back, pulling her closer. "What makes sense?" he asked, nuzzling her ear.

"Why the furniture is moved."

"Oh. All the better for us to dance," he crooned, bringing his lips to her neck.

Small tremors of excitement rippled her insides.

He tore his lips from her neck and gazed into her eyes. His gaze shifted to her hair which was pulled up with a clip. He removed the clip, tossing it into the black chair, allowing her hair to fall onto her shoulders.

Her breathing quickened when he ran his fingers through her hair and stared at her lustily. The corner of his mouth lifted before he crushed his lips against hers.

Her heart pounded as he deepened the kiss, pulling her tighter against him. She could feel his heart thudding against her own.

Chase had many thoughts rolling through his head as he kissed her. Like how he wanted nothing more than to strip her right there and make love with her.

He pulled away, assessing the situation and the thought he had.

He wanted to make love with her.

Not sex.

Love.

Fuck! No, no, *no*!

*   *   *

"What?" Emily whimpered. "What's wrong?"

206

Chase backed away. "It's late and you need to rest for tomorrow."

She reached for him, but he smoothly walked towards the window, tucking his hands inside of his pants pockets.

"The bedroom's yours tonight. I'll sleep on the couch," he mumbled.

Emily chewed her bottom lip as she crossed the room to retrieve her bag. She hesitated at the doorway of the bedroom, turning to look at him.

Not turning his gaze from the window, he cleared his throat gently. "Night, Emily. Sleep well."

*   *   *

Three in the morning and he was wide awake. Even a few shots of Jameson didn't help.

He hated the way he felt. Insecure, scared, vulnerable.

But he knew, deep inside, that if he told her how he really felt, his whole life would change with three simple words.

And he didn't know if he was ready for such a change.

*   *   *

Emily rolled over and checked the time on the digital clock on the nightstand.

She'd never slept past eight in the morning and the clock read eleven. Another shitty night of sleep again. Courtesy of Chase Storm.

Not bothering to check on him, she took a quick shower and fixed her hair and make-up. She threw on shorts and a t-shirt. She'd bring her dress with her to the park and dress there.

Chase sat at the kitchen nook nursing a cup of coffee. Lack of sleep and feeling conflicted took a toll on him.

When she came out of the bedroom, she walked past him and filled the coffee mug he had set out for her.

She didn't need to get into another argument with him, especially before going on stage, but damn it, she needed to know what his problem was.

"Having second thoughts about me?" When he didn't respond she turned to see an empty chair.

Walking towards the bedroom she stopped when someone knocked at his door.

When she opened the door Rick O'Shea sauntered in with a grin on face.

"Good morning, Emily. What a surprise to see you here."

She snorted, "I'm sure."

He rubbed her arm. "You okay?"

"No! Last night he coulda damn near did anything he wanted with me because I was ready and willing, but instead I slept alone," she huffed.

"This relationship is a big leap for him, Emily. Just give him time," Rick urged.

"The man has commitment issues. I'm nothing like Cassie!" She paced the room, waving her hands. "I don't care about his stupid money, his stupid condo…I just…

Rick's lips curved. "You just what?"

She turned and smile sadly. "I just want him."

*   *   *

The ride to the band shell was glacial, at best. She was jittery enough without having to deal with his icy demeanor. She turned her head and shot him a glare. If he noticed, he didn't say anything.

When they arrived at the bandstand Freddie and the guys were setting up their instruments. A few of Freddie's students worked the sound machines and the lights.

Chase glanced at the men under a canopy. "Who are they?" he asked.

"Freddie's students."

Chase's eyebrows lifted. "His what?"

"Freddie teaches music theory at the community college."

"Wow, I didn't know that," Chase mumbled.

"Ya ready?" Freddie yelled to his students. They gave him the thumbs up sign. "Check one, check one," Freddie murmured into the microphone.

Chase spotted a large blue tent. "I'll be right back," he mumbled.

Women and men dressed in red and white uniforms entered and exited the tent.

He casually walked up to the tent and poked his head inside. Instantly he heard a gruff voice. "Sir, unless you're a VIP you can't be in here."

A small mountain of a man walked towards him with big beefy arms outstretched. "Just having a look," Chase smiled, although the smile didn't meet his eyes. "Is this for the Mayor?"

The mountain laughed, "No. It's for the promoter of the concert."

Chase nodded, "That's right. John Marks or something, right?" He hoped the guy would take the bait.

"Jared Buckley's running this show," the mountain proclaimed.

Chapter Twelve

Chase ground his teeth back to the bandstand.

Jared Fuckley was running the show. Jared Fuckley planned on having dinner with *his* girl!

He hoped Jared was having steak for dinner because it'd be the last time he'd be able to eat solid food for a while once he got through with him.

"Hey, you okay?" Emily asked, noticing the scowl on Chase's face.

His fists clenched at his sides, but he faked a smile and shrugged. "I tried to see what was going on in the tent, but was given the brush off."

"So we still don't know who the mystery man is. Ugh! I'm a freakin' bundle of nerves now," she moaned.

He rubbed his hands up and down her arms. "Hey, c'mon, you're gonna be great today."

She leaned into him. "Can I have a hug?" He obliged and held her tightly in his arms. "Rick said he'd be here today," she murmured into his chest.

"Yeah. I told him what a great band Freddie has." He didn't tell her that some members of the Chicago Wind would also be there. She was nervous enough.

Families and groups of young adults picked out spots to place blankets and chairs. She pulled away from Chase and yelled to Freddie. "Hey, I see some of your regulars!"

He grinned down at her from the stage and nodded. "Hey, Chase, can you come up here for a minute?" Freddie said into the microphone.

Chase hesitated, but Emily urged him to go. "I'll be okay."

Freddie pointed to a guitar and Chase slung the strap over his shoulder. "I want to check the sound. Play something easy guys," Freddie said as he bounded from the stage.

Steve tapped on the piano keys and Chase shook his head, smiling. *Jealous Guy* filled the air.

"Use the mike, dude," Ian called from the drums.

Chase approached the mike and softly began singing.

"Louder man!" Ted yelled at him.

They began again, this time music and Chase's voice filled the air.

It made Emily's stomach flip-flop. Two woman bustled past her to get closer to the stage her stomach flipped for another reason. Chase ignored them, even though they barely had anything on and kept his eyes on her.

The heart rending tenderness of his gaze made her forget why she was angry with him.

*   *   *

"Showtime!" Freddie yelled into the dressing room.

Emily took a deep breath before opening the door. "Whoa! Damn woman! It won't matter if you screw up the words, what you're wearing will more than make up for it!" Ian hooted.

Freddie elbowed him in the ribs. "She'll be fine, won't ya, Em?"

She rolled her eyes. "I hope so. C'mon, let's do this."

Ted, Steve and Ian surrounded her as she scanned the area for Chase. Ted led the way and stepped aside.

Chase stood near the steps to the stage with a bouquet of pink and white roses. He swallowed hard when he saw her.

She ran to him, crushing her lips against his. "You're here," she murmured against his lips.

He pulled away slightly. "Of course I am." His eyes traveled the length of her and he blew out a low whistle. "Good god woman, you've barely anything on! Now, go up there and kick ass, okay?" he managed to eke out.

*   *   *

Greg Travers and Chase waited with Emily until Freddie announced her. The crowd cheered when he said her name, causing her stomach to flip. She felt like she would vomit.

Chase nudged her. "They're calling your name."

She shook her head. "They're chanting it for fuck's sake!"

The band started the intro to *I've Got the Music in Me* as she took her place in front of the microphone. She gripped it tightly with her eyes closed.

Slowly she began to sing, moving her hips to the rhythm of the music. Eventually she opened her eyes and wished she hadn't. The lawn in front of the band shell was packed with people. It was the biggest crowd Double Exposure ever played for.

Cameramen were set up on either side of the stage filming. It unnerved her until she spotted a section directly in front of the stage where she saw Chase, Greg, Tamara, Rick and holy shit! Members of the Chicago Wind!

She closed her eyes again and concentrated on the words and getting through the first song.

*   *   *

After the first song was over the guys began the opening riff to her all time favorite Rolling Stones song. She took her place at the side of the stage since she'd only be singing the chorus.

Chase's eyes traveled from her head down to her short red dress. *Fuck!* She probably had to shave more than her legs to wear the damn thing! His nostrils flared when he looked back up to her chest. She was showing too much cleavage and too much leg. Her red *fuck me* pumps completed the outfit.

When she belted out the chorus to *Gimme Shelter* his jaw dropped. Holy hell! The lady could sing!

The crowd whooped and hollered, cheering her on. As much as he hated to admit it, Fuckley called it right. She should be on stage more. Freddie and his band were good, but she made them better.

He watched as she took a long pull from a glass after the song was over.

Although he only had a side view of her, he saw her lift her arms, like she was embracing someone, but no one was there.

*   *   *

"You're here!" she screeched when she saw Frankie and Phyllis.

"'Course we're here!" Frankie bellowed. "We had to make the scene!!"

"Aw, doll, you sound great!" Phyllis squealed. "Now go back out there and sing that song for Chase.

She elegantly walked back to the microphone at the front of the stage. When she began to talk the crowd quieted.

214

"This song is for Chase," she said breathily, gazing at him.

Chase held his breath in anticipation. He had no idea she planned to sing a song for him.

Steve began playing the piano. She followed shortly afterwards. Ian and the rest of the group fell in later.

Rick nudged him, smiling. Chase couldn't tear his eyes from her. She was singing about wanting to be his one and only and how it's not easy giving up your heart.

"She loves you, bro," Rick yelled in his ear.

A lump formed in his throat as her eyes searched his.

It overwhelmed him. To the point where he wanted to run. To the point where he felt tears stinging the backs of his eyes. He groaned and pulled the Ray Bans from the vee in his shirt, covering his eyes.

*   *   *

Concert goers made a path when she came down the stairs and walked towards him.

He rolled his head back onto his shoulders. *Fuck!* No! No! No!

He looked for options. If he ran to the right, Rick would stop him.

If he ran to the left, Greg would stop him.

His heart accelerated when she stood in front of him, palming his cheek.

The people who surrounded them cheered and slapped him on the back. Seth Brice, captain of the Wind muttered what a lucky fucker he was.

He would've grinned, but he was scared shitless. Then an amusing

215

thought lifted his spirits.

Fuckley was getting a full blown show of her declaration of love.

After the song she leaned into him and whispered, "I love you."

He thought his heart would burst from his chest at her admission. Rick nudged him in the back, urging him on.

Chase took her in his arms and kissed her deeply in front of the crowd, Freddie and more importantly, Jared Fuckley.

*   *   *

Freddie and the guys started the next song. She winked at him over her shoulder and ran back to the stage and belted out a Janis Joplin song.

Wow! She couldn't believe she told him! It felt liberating, exhilarating but most of all, it felt *right*.

*   *   *

Chase tried to watch the rest of the show, but it was difficult when people, mostly men, came up to him clapping him on the back. One guy actually told him that he'd be glad to take her off his hands.

Greg and Rick had to hold Chase back from the guy. "C'mon Chase. The guy's drunk. Let it go," Greg yelled into his ear.

Later, as Emily sang *Rescue Me*, Beth sauntered over to him and linked her arm into his. "Wow, she sure knows how to work a crowd, huh?"

He glanced down at his little sister, grinning. "That she does." He pulled her into a hug. "Thanks for coming."

"I wouldn't miss it. She's really great up there," she beamed.

"Did I hear her say that she loves you?" Beth pushed. Chase nodded

216

once. "Well?" she huffed.

Chase looked down at her. "What?"

"Do you *kinda* feel something like that for her?"

"*If* I feel the same for her, I sure as hell wouldn't tell you before I told her," he replied with a grin.

*   *   *

After Emily's last song Freddie asked the crowd for a round of applause. When the roar died down he plucked a guitar string and grinned. "Our final song of this set is one that I usually sing, but instead I'd like to bring up a friend of mine to sing it for me. Chase, c'mon up."

He shook his head at Freddie, but Rick nudged him hard in the ribs.

"Go on!" Rick urged. "Do it for her!"

Chase rolled his eyes and walked up the steps to the stage. Emily stood off to the side, a puzzled expression on her face.

Freddie handed him a guitar with a shit eating grin on his face. "You can do this, dude."

"I hope so," Chase muttered, walking to the microphone.

He took a deep breath. "Since Emily sang a song for me, it's only fair that I reciprocate with her favorite song. Babe, this is for you."

The beginning riff of *Wicked Game* filled the air.

Emily walked down the stairs to where Greg and Rick stood.

His eyes sought her at the side of the stage, but he followed the index fingers of the people back stage and saw her in front of the stage next to his friends.

He lifted an eyebrow when Rick wrapped his arm around her waist. He nuzzled her neck, causing her to slap him away, making Chase grin.

She stared so intently at him, that he felt it deep in his soul. He knew just by the way she gazed at him that she meant what she said earlier.

She loved him.

*   *   *

When the song ended Emily ran backstage, meeting Chase on the steps. Tears filled her eyes.

"Was I that bad?" he laughed, rubbing his hands up and down her arms.

"You have a wonderful voice," she choked out.

"Miss Waters? Your dinner date awaits you," Mr. Mountain stated smugly.

She gaped at him and warily looked at Chase. "Go on. Greg will be with you," he mumbled past the lump in his throat.

She turned back, "You'll wait for me right?"

"You can count on it," he assured her.

Greg placed his hand on her lower back and followed the Hulk through the throng of people into the blue tent.

Emily's jaw dropped when she saw Jared with a bouquet of roses.

*   *   *

Her jaw dropped further when she spotted Jenny and Keith sitting at a table.

"How nice, you brought friends," Jared sneered, staring at Greg, Frankie and Phyllis. "Well, at least it isn't Storm."

Greg looked around and shrugged. Who the hell was that guy talking about? As far as he knew, he was the only one in the room who knew Emily. He narrowed his gaze when the rich dude began talking.

"Really, Emily, why are they here?" Jared asked, taking her by the elbow.

"Because I didn't know who the hell set this up, that's why," she snipped. "Why the secrecy, Jared?"

He laughed, "Why not?" He measured her mood and continued, "Emily would you have agreed to this if you knew if was me?"

She lifted her eyebrow. "To dinner or the concert?"

"Either," he shrugged.

"Well, yeah. I've got nothing against you, Jared. I just wish you would've been up front and honest," she shrugged.

"So can we cut this guy loose then?" Jared whispered, jerking his head towards Greg.

Greg stepped closer and grinned, "Don't think so pal."

"Fine!" Jared hissed, grabbing Emily's hand.

"Aye! Show some manners!" Greg growled following them.

*   *   *

"Dude, chillax. She's fine. Probably in the tent eating lobster and drinking expensive wine; yucking it up with a big shot," Freddie told Chase.

"She's not fine, Freddie. The mystery man is Jared," Chase hissed.

219

"No shit? I didn't know he had this kind of cash," Freddie mumbled.

Chase pulled out his cell phone and Googled the asshole. He frowned when there were several pages dedicated to him. He was a hot shot in advertising and owned the company *Art Attack*. His net worth was way more than Chase's.

He grinned. For once making less was a good thing. Especially since Emily wasn't comfortable with it.

He dialed Greg's number.

Greg rolled his eyes when he answered the call. "Seriously? It's only been a few minutes."

"I know that!" Chase spat. "How is she?"

"She knows him and he tried to get rid of me, " he chuckled.

"Keep me posted, okay?" Chase asked, nibbling on his thumb.

*   *   *

"Baby, you looked great out there. Although I can't say I was too impressed with the song you sang to Storm," Jared scolded.

"Frankly, Jared, I don't give a rat's ass what you thought about my song. Are we going to have dinner or what?" she snipped.

His warm breath fanned her face. "Don't worry, I'll take care of you baby."

A scream caught in her throat.

*   *   *

"Emily, are you okay?" Jared asked, grabbing her hand.

She stiffened at his touch, "I don't like to be called…that."

"Baby?" She nodded and he continued, "It's a term of endearment." She shot him an icy glare. " I won't say it again," he mumbled.

Jared led her to a table in a secluded corner and pulled a chair out for her. She hesitantly sat when she wanted to leave.

A server immediately brought glasses of white wine.

She lifted her hand in a huff. "Really Jared? All this to have dinner with me? Kinda weird, don't ya think?"

He lifted the wine glass and took a sip, encouraging her to do the same. When she finally relented he answered her question. "I wanted to finish the date we started." He ran a hand through his hair. "I didn't know what else to do, plus, I really love to hear you sing."

A server brought warm bread and butter to the table then another server followed up with salad along with several types of dressing.

Emily made no move to eat, causing Jared to frown. "Emily, please eat something."

She shrugged. "I'm really not hungry."

He sighed and put his fork down. "Emily, I've paid a lot of money to make this happen. The least you can do is join me in a meal."

She leaned in. "It's not my fault your wallet is bigger than your brains!"

Greg laughed as she pinned Jared with a glare. He flinched at her demeanor.

"He's really gotten to you, hasn't he?" Jared muttered.

She waved to the television sets placed strategically around the tent. "Didn't you hear the words I sang to him? I think it's pretty evident how I feel about him."

"Ouch," Jared whispered. "Then you should go to him. I don't want to cause you any discomfort."

Emily's bottom lip trembled. "But…"

"Don't worry. Your friends have already been paid. You're free to go."

"I haven't had my dinner yet," she replied, lifting her chin.

Jared lifted his head. "It's okay, Emily, you don't have to stay."

She cocked her head. "I want to stay."

A small grin appeared on his face. "Then let's eat."

Conversation flowed easily between them and it reminded her of their first date. He was charming, witty and well, handsome. She found herself relaxing despite the situation.

Seeing Emily had things under control, Phyllis and Frankie left in search of answers from their friend Harold.

Greg answered two calls from Chase during the time she and Jared had dinner. The third time he called, Greg wanted to ignore it, but thought if he did, Storm would bust through the tent and make an ass of himself.

"They're wrapping it up now. Relax!" Greg hissed into the phone.

"I guess I can't keep you any longer from Storm," Jared sighed sadly.

"I had a good time, Jared. Thank you," she said softly, taking his hand.

He bent and kissed her chastely on the cheek.

She blushed, "Thanks again."

Greg brushed past Jared, giving him the once-over.

Jenny sidled up next to Jared and together they watched Emily and Greg walk towards Storm who paced a few feet from the tent.

"Well?" Jenny asked.

Jared watched as Emily ran into Chase's outstretched arms. "I think I jumped into the wrong body," he sighed sadly.

*   *   *

With his guts knotted up, Chase didn't notice the guy snapping pictures of him and Emily.

*   *   *

Chip Sanders chuckled heartily to himself on the way to his apartment. Ol' Chase Storm was gonna help him make it out of the obituary section straight to the *Talk of Chicago* section.

*   *   *

Emily went into the dressing room and gave all the guys high fives while Chase stayed outside and talked with Greg.

"Well?" Chase asked.

Greg shrugged. "They had dinner and talked."

Chase's eyebrows narrowed. "Is that all?"

"Well, at one point he told her she could leave and she didn't," Greg replied.

"That proves she still likes him," Chase hissed.

Greg shook his head. "No, it means she's not a bitch and has a heart.

223

He jabbed his index finger into Chase's chest. "She wants *you*, so don't fuck it up."

Chapter Thirteen

The ride to his condo was eerily quiet. In fact, it was an uncomfortable silence for him. But what could he say? *Do you really love me or were you just caught up in the moment?*

She gazed out the window, tears stinging the backs of her eyes. Was he so dead inside that the song she sang meant nothing to him?

They sighed simultaneously and glanced at each other with lifted eyebrows.

Then they broke out in laughter. He rubbed his chin and grinned at her bubbly giggles.

His grin quickly turned into a frown.

He was swimming through a haze of feelings and desires.

Hell, he wasn't swimming…he was drowning.

*   *   *

It was hard for Emily to not notice Chase's sudden change in demeanor.

As they entered the condo she removed her high heels and padded to his bedroom with her over night bag, slamming the door in the process.

Chase leaned over the kitchen nook, resting his head on his forearms. *What the fuck am I gonna do?*

He didn't have time to consider his options because Emily came out of his bedroom dressed in the shorts and t-shirt she wore on the way to the band shell.

His eyebrows furrowed. "Are we going out again?"

She shook her head. "No, *we* aren't. *I* am. I'm going to catch a cab to Petrillo and wait for Freddie's set to end. Maybe I'll watch the fireworks while they pack up," she shrugged.

He cautiously moved towards her. "I thought we were going to watch from here?"

"Yeah, me too, but it feels weird between us now," she stammered. "I don't know if it's the song I sang to you or the words I said afterwards, but…It. Just. Feels. Weird."

"Yeah, it does," he said softly, removing her purse strap from her shoulder. "But it has a lot to do with me and less to do with you."

"I don't understand," she frowned.

He released a throaty laugh. "You're fucking me up in the head! I want you, I don't want you. I miss you, I don't miss you!"

He turned away, raking his hands through his hair. "Remember the first night I brought you here?" She nodded, frowning. "When I said that you scared the hell out of me? Well, that's not changed."

He took her hand and lead her to the couch. "For so many years I've literally fucked around because I never, *ever* wanted to feel anything for a woman. I didn't want to get hurt." He rolled his head onto his neck and continued, "God! I knew you were trouble the minute I met you, but yet I couldn't fucking stay away!"

226

"Back at ya, Storm," she countered.

He snorted. "I lie awake at night trying to find something wrong with you so I can just walk away. Hell, I even tried to use Fuckley sending flowers as an excuse! Christ! I knew you weren't leading him on, but I accused you of it anyway! I'm such an asshole that when you sang that song to me, I wanted to run!"

Her eyes widened at his admission and she started to rise when he gently, but firmly, pulled her onto his lap. "Emily, I know you think I have commitment issues, but the truth is, I have *trust* issues."

She rolled her eyes and tried to get off his lap, but he held her firmly in place. "Damn it Chase! I'm nothing like Cassie! You won't find me in bed with Rick or anyone else!" She gripped his head in her hands. "I. Love. You. I know it sounds crazy since we've only been together a short time, but damn it! I've never felt this strongly about any man, not that there's been a lot…"

He cut her off. "How many?" he asked with a lifted brow.

"I've only been with one guy, Chase," she sighed. "And the truth is, I didn't love him even a little."

His lips curved. "You hussy!"

She slapped his arm, "You're one to talk!"

"One guy? Really?"

"Why's that so shocking?"

He shrugged, "Because of all the things I've told you. You're beautiful, warm…how can it be that only one guy saw that?"

She sighed, "Because they all thought I was a freak."

*   *   *

"Okay, daddy-o, you're going to give me some answers or I swear, I'll give you a beatin' like you ain't never got before," Frankie said darkly, leaning over Harold.

"Leave him be!" Lilly admonished. "He's told you all he knows."

"She's been workin' him over alright! Just not with her fists," Phyllis sneered.

Lilly blushed, "Harold and I have come to a…stalemate of sorts."

Phyllis walked around the two of them with her eyebrow lifted. "Is that what they're callin' it these days? A stalemate?"

Frankie's face scrunched. "Am I missin' something?"

"Don't be such a dope! Look at them! Hell! Look at *him*! Can't ya see how he looks younger, thinner and not so scary? She's gotten to him!"

Frankie gaped. "You're right! Hey, what's goin' on here anyways?"

Harold took Lilly's hand into his and proudly stated, "I'm smitten."

"Oh applesauce!" yelled Phyllis. "Why'd ya have to be such a weak-sister?" She turned and glared at Lilly.

"Applesauce?" asked Harold, scratching his now full head of chestnut brown hair.

Phyllis hissed, "In your time it means shit, ya boob! Emily's in a jam and you two are making googly eyes at each other! *Unbelievable!*"

Frankie crossed his beefy arms over his chest and cackled. "Don't go all ape, Filly."

She crossed the room and stood in front of him. "Our girl's in trouble, Frankie. That Jared guy isn't who he seems. Didn't ya get that feeling from him tonight?" She turned, gripping the ends of her boa and slid it back and forth across the back of her neck. "I'm scared for her, Frankie."

"Ah, doll, don't worry your pretty head. We'll keep her safe," Frankie vowed, cupping Phyllis' cheek.

*   *   *

"What do you mean they thought you were a freak?" Chase frowned.

Emily shook her head, stood and walked towards the window. She wanted to tell him about her ability, but they were already on tenuous ground. Divulging something like that would only send him running and he'd have good reason to not look back.

He crossed the room slowly. When he reached her he took her chin between his thumb and forefinger so she was forced to meet his eyes. "Hey, we have that in common, too," he said huskily. Her eyebrows furrowed and he continued with a shrug. "People thought I was a freak, too."

He sure as hell wasn't going to reveal his stint in the psych ward for a short time when he was a kid. That confession might make *her* want to run and he sure as hell didn't want *that* to happen.

She smiled weakly at him and kissed him on the corner of the mouth. "Thank you."

"For?" he grinned.

"For trying to make me feel better," she shrugged.

He wiggled his eyebrows lecherously and grabbed her around the waist, pulling her tightly against him. "I know something that may make you feel better," he said silkily planting hot, wet kisses on her neck.

She groaned into his ear. "You tease."

He withdrew his lips from her neck and gazed at her. "No teasing tonight. Unless you'd rather not…"

Christ! He hoped she wanted to! She clearly wanted to the night before!

Her nose wrinkled. "I worked up a sweat onstage and probably smell like a barn yard."

He ran his nose over her neck, to her bosom, where he lingered for several moments then got on his knees and ran his nose lower, causing a bright red stain to color her cheeks.

"Mmm...you smell fine to me, Miss Waters," he purred. "But, if you'd rather shower first..." his voice trailed off as he pulled her along to the bedroom. He casually waved a hand. "I think you know the way."

*   *   *

When he heard the shower run he fought with himself. Be a gentleman and wait patiently for her to finish or...*fuck it!*

*   *   *

He stood naked inside the bathroom and gaped. He'd imagined her many times naked, but actually seeing her? A low primeval growl built in his chest.

"Chase?" she squeaked, rinsing soap from her eyes. She turned and her eyes widened. She subconsciously started to cover herself then stopped.

His eyes looked everywhere but her. "I um...sorry, bad idea. I'll go."

When she found her voice she said sexily, "Won't you join me?"

He stopped in mid-grasp of the door knob and turned. Her hands were knotted in front of her, making her tits jut out. His eyes smoldered at her pose.

She watched in anticipation as he crossed the room in two strides, opening the shower door. Her insides became a fluttery mess!

His heated eyes raked over her slowly. He lifted his hand to her hip and turned her slowly, to view all of her assets.

Her breath hitched when his hands softly caressed her backside. He pulled her against him and ran his hands up to her heavy breasts. Cupping them, he gently pulled at her taut nipples as his teeth grazed the back of her neck and shoulder.

"Christ, Emily. I feel like this is the first time for me," he rasped into her ear.

She giggled softly. "Well, it is, silly."

His warm kisses sent shivers of desire through her. "No, I mean…"

She turned to look at him. His eyes burned with intensity. "Tell me," she said low.

"Later," he rasped, flicking his tongue across her lips. She wrapped her arms around his neck, pressing her breasts against his stomach. He gripped her ass cheeks, lifting her. "Wrap your legs around me."

Excitement trilled through her as he pressed her against the wall of the shower. The tile felt cool against her hot skin, but she didn't mind. After all, her shower sex fantasy was coming true!

He held her with one arm as his fingers slid into her folds. Christ she was wet and ready! His fingers skillfully played her like a fine tuned guitar. She groaned in his ear, her breathing became shallow. "Give it to me, Emily," he said silkily against her cheek.

She wasn't normally verbal during sex, but something about Chase and what he was doing sent her over the edge with a loud moan.

While she was still quaking from her eruption, he entered her, gripping her ass tightly. After he slid in and out several times he stopped and gazed at her. "Em? Please open those pretty eyes of yours," he rasped.

231

Slowly, her eyes opened. A smile curved her lips as she gently gripped a handful of his hair.

The tenderness of her gaze, the feel of her inside and out, undid him. He slid deeper into her and didn't think about anything other than this moment. This feeling.

This perfect feeling. The love she held in her eyes, for him only. His pulse accelerated and a feeling of total warmth blanketed him. He knew what he felt was pure and true. But, still, he couldn't say those three words.

*   *   *

Looking at Emily wrapped in the thick blue towel with her damp hair tousled made Chase groan.

"What?" she giggled.

He wrapped a towel around his waist and shook his head. "You! You look pretty sexy in that towel."

She shot him a sexy wink, "Back at ya."

He followed her into the bedroom and pulled open a dresser drawer. "I, um, have a drawer here for you."

Emily peered into the drawer, a grin on her face. "One small step for man, one giant leap for mankind?"

Chase grinned, "Smart ass."

"And look! There's already something in there," she teased.

He pulled the item out and held it up. "Rick brought this over for you. He couldn't stand the fact Brice is your favorite player."

She grabbed the blue tank top with the number 8 and the name O'Shea on the back and the Chicago Wind logo on the front, from his hands.

"Hey, Seth Brice is not only a great player, but he's easy on the eyes," she smiled, pulling the shirt over her head. "But, number 8 ain't so bad, either."

"Yeah, and Seth Brice is in love with my woman," growled Chase. "So, rest assured I won't be buying you any more of his shit."

She smiled sweetly at him and wrapped her arms around his neck. "You're overreacting. Besides, I only have eyes for you."

"I'm not overreacting," he pouted.

She pushed him away, laughing. "C'mon, let's go watch the fireworks."

His right eyebrow arched and he smirked. "No panties?"

Emily glanced down at the tank top which just skimmed the tops of her thighs and shot him a sexy grin over her shoulder. "Nope."

*   *   *

Emily stared at the fusion of colors in the sky and sighed happily. A rich palette of lavender, fuchsia, pale yellow along with a tinge of red painted the sky over the lake. Oh, she loved the suburbs, but could get used to seeing the sunset in Chicago on a regular basis.

She felt Chase behind her and nuzzled the back of her head into his chest. He wrapped his arms around her and rested his chin on top of her head. "I agree," he said softly.

"Huh?"

"The sunset *is* beautiful. That reminds me. I found a song that fits this very occasion," he replied, pulling away from her.

He walked into the rec room and within moments music filled the living room. He sauntered into the room, singing, with his hand outstretched to her.

She giggled and took his hand. Slowly they danced, while Chase sang into her ear. Abruptly he stopped dancing, ran his fingers over her cheek and sang. "I've been a dead man runnin' all my life and I never felt a thing woman, 'til I met you."

He crushed his lips against hers. Their tongues danced in a light caress as their bodies moved slowly to the music. He tore his lips from hers and gripping her hair with both hands, he rested his forehead against hers.

Tears of happiness and fear burned the backs of his eyes. He kissed her forehead and roughly pulled her tightly against him. "God, Emily, what I feel for you scares me."

She pulled away to search his eyes. The color was darker blue than normal and definitely had a glaze over them. "What can I do to ease your mind?"

He shrugged. "Be patient with me and my irrational fears."

*   *   *

A soft breeze brushed against Emily's skin, awakening her. Groggily, she lifted her head. Moonlight filtered through the gauzy curtains, casting an eerie glow in the room. She jumped when she saw someone sitting in the chair near the window.

"Relax," Chase murmured. "It's just me."

She propped herself up on an elbow. "Is everything okay?"

In the merest light, she noticed the lift in his cheek. "Yeah, I had an urge to draw so here I am," Chase replied, waving a hand over his sketch pad.

Emily pulled herself out of bed, crossing the room to him. Standing next to the chair she peered down at the drawing and gasped. "Chase! I'm naked!"

He brought his left hand to her backside and caressed it. "In real life

234

and now on paper," he grinned.

"But…" she stammered.

"Emily, all you can see in this drawing is the gentle curve of your luscious ass. Your arm is covering your breasts."

"Nuh uh! I can see my cleavage!" she admonished.

He sneered, "Hell, you didn't worry about that last night with the dress you wore onstage! Christ! Everyone saw your cleavage! Especially Fuckley and Brice!"

She rolled her eyes, sat on the arm of the chair and ran a hand through his hair. "Do I really sleep with my lips pouty?"

"Yep. It's very sexy, don't ya think?" he grinned.

She pulled his head back so she could see his eyes. "Ya know what's sexy?" He gulped and shook his head. "You, naked, drawing me, naked. Now that's pretty hot."

He swallowed hard, threw the pad on the floor and pulled her onto his lap.

When he slid his hands up and down her back she shivered against his touch. She lowered her head and claimed him with her mouth. Her tongue gently circled his lips, causing him to moan softly.

Chase moved her bottom gently away from his sensitive parts. She stopped the ministrations on his lips, pulled away and cocked her head. He half smiled. "Little Chase wants to come out and play," he waved a hand to his lower region.

Emily shot him a hot, intense gaze and cradled his head in her hands. "Then let's play."

Holy fuck! She's going to be my undoing!

235

He removed her hands from his head and planted a warm, moist kiss in each palm. His kisses spread from her wrist to her elbow then to her shoulder. He ran his tongue across her neck to her other arm where he slowly planted kisses down to her chest.

She wiggled her hips in impatience, causing a smirk to form on his lips. "Why Emily, I get the feeling you want to skip the foreplay and get down to business."

When she didn't respond he looked up and gazed at her. Her eyes were hooded and she almost looked ashamed. He lifted her chin to meet his gaze. "Emily? I realize that guy you did it with was just a sex thing for you, but didn't he…didn't he make love to you?"

She shrugged and tried to pull away, but he held her firmly. "It was nothing like this. I mean, no foreplay or anything," she stammered.

Chase considered her words for a moment. The first two times they had sex it was all very fast. Mostly it was his fault because he'd been holding back for so long that when they finally did it, all he wanted to do was bury himself in her.

Selfish fucking asshole!

His eyes smoldered with intense heat as he palmed her cheek. "Can I be the first to make love to you?" he asked, huskily.

"Um, didn't we already do that twice?" she replied with a grin.

He gently shook his head. "No, Emily. That was just great fucking sex." Carefully, he stood, cradling her in his arms and carried her to bed. His eyes raked seductively over her before his body covered hers.

His lips gently closed over hers, coercing her lips apart with his tongue. Their tongues swirled to a slow easy rhythm, sending shivers of desire racing through her.

He eased his tongue away and gently circled her lips. The look he wore was so seductive it drove Emily wild with need.

Chase ran his tongue down her neck, licking and sucking, causing Emily to squeal. Then she felt the gentle pressure of his mouth and tongue swirling over her nipple, while his hand reached down between her thighs. He cupped his hand over her, then gently inserted two fingers into her. "Christ Emily! You're so wet!" he moaned against her breast.

She blushed at his words, but damn! What he did to her and how sexy he made her feel made her body do weird shit!

She drew a ragged breath as he suckled the other nipple, gently pulling it deeper into his mouth. She grasped his head between her hands and pulled his hair softly as a groan escaped her lips.

He got harder with each moan and whimper she released. He grinned when he thought about how loud she'd moan as he worked his way further south.

Chase continued to sear a path down her stomach, pausing at her belly-button, where he dipped his tongue deeply inside, eliciting a shudder from Emily.

As he lowered his head between her thighs, he shot her a look so hot and intense she thought she'd melt into the sheets.

He'd done this with the seven day girls, but it wasn't something he normally enjoyed. But Emily was different. He *wanted* to do this to her. He wanted to taste her. To feel inside her with his tongue. Desire, want and need coursed through his body as his tongue plucked and teased the most sensitive areas of her sex.

She gripped his head between her hands, feeling the climax build. His tongue swirled slowly then fast, pushing her over the edge. Her hips bucked, while her insides trembled.

Chase felt her shudder under his tongue but continued to swirl his tongue until she begged him to stop. He lifted a wicked eyebrow and with his tongue still firmly planted on her hot spot he mumbled, "Are you sure you want me to stop?"

"For now, yes," she flushed, caressing his head.

Pulling himself up he trailed kisses up her stomach to her breasts back to her mouth. He kissed her hungrily for several minutes before pulling away. Her lips were swollen from his firm, deep kisses.

She flushed when the heat of his gaze bore into hers as he eased his hips forward gently pushing inside her.

"Fuck!" he moaned, breathily. His hands gripped her shoulders as he slid deeper inside her.

Finally, he wrapped his arms around her, gasping raggedly, covering her lips with his. Each hip thrust was followed up with a deep kiss. Chase slowed the pace. He wanted to feel the warmth of her around him. As he gazed at her, his heart jolted at the tenderness and love he saw reflected in her eyes. "Em, don't ever leave me. I couldn't bear it," he said huskily.

She swallowed the thickness in her throat and tears stung the back of her eyes. "Not gonna happen," she choked out.

He lowered his head, kissing her and moved his hips slowly with hers. She groaned into his ear, "Faster!"

Not one to ignore a request such as that, Chase thrust harder and faster until Emily's nails dug into his upper arms and she let out a deep groan, followed by a satisfying shudder.

Chase followed her release with his own, gasping her name. He hovered over her until both their spasms subsided and sweetly kissed her on the nose.

He laid on his back, pulling her against him. She nestled her head onto his chest and wrapped her leg around his. "I'm spent," she giggled into his chest.

He lifted his head and looked down at her, gripping her tightly. "Emily Waters, I love…being with you."

She didn't return his gaze. Instead she kept her head on his chest and sighed sadly. "I love…being with you, too."

As Emily drifted off to sleep in his arms he wondered why the fuck it was so damn hard to say those three words he knew she wanted to hear. Words he wanted to tell her, but just couldn't bring himself to say.

*   *   *

Cassandra Seton sat at the white tiled kitchen nook of her new condo, eating a grapefruit and drinking decaf coffee with the Daily newspaper in front of her.

She didn't normally read the paper but the previous owner forgot to cancel so she'd been getting freebies for nearly a week.

Images of the night before covered the front page. The grand firework display over Lake Michigan along with spectators eating ice cream, running with dogs or little kids building sand castles.

She sighed disgustedly at the photos and turned through the pages. It was always the same old shit in the paper. Kids killing kids because they were on the wrong side of town. Asshole drunk drivers killing innocent people and the damn politicians who couldn't keep their dicks in their pants.

Mid-way through she spotted the *Talk of Chicago* section. Her breath hitched when she saw Chase's picture. Bastard hadn't aged a bit. Her eyes narrowed when she glanced at another picture of him with a blonde wrapped around him.

She read the bold wording at the top of the page and scoffed. *Can this woman tame the wild Storm?*

As she read further she found that Chase had been living the life of a player for the last ten or so years. *Seven days of heaven?* She frowned and read the

239

article twice. Afterwards she lit up a smoke and exhaled, laughing. He only dated women for a week then dumped them?

He used to be such a nice, gullible guy, too. Fuck! He *worshipped* her! It was actually kind of nauseating. He talked about her having her own law office while he erected skyscrapers after they were married.

But, damn, the sex was good with him! No, it was great! He knew how to fuck with his ample asset!

She tried to remember why she cheated on him, then suddenly remembered. He once said they'd travel the world together and have babies. Lots of babies, if she remembered correctly.

She trembled slightly. She hated kids and dogs. He wanted both. She wondered if he still wanted those things.

*   *   *

Emily awoke to the scent of bacon frying. She got out of bed and searched the floor for her tank top. Afterwards she put her hair in a pony tail and sauntered out of the bedroom.

Chase was in the kitchen flipping pancakes. He turned when he saw movement from the corner of his eye. He eyed her seductively and grinned. "Morning, babe."

"Wow, good looks and he knows how to cook?" she teased.

"I hope you like pancakes," he shrugged.

Her nose wrinkled. "Sorry. I prefer French toast or eggs."

"Scrambled or over easy?" he asked before kissing her.

"Chase, it's not big deal. You don't need to go to the trouble…"

He pulled her tightly against his chest and cut her off. "It's no trouble.

Besides, after last night I'm sure your appetite is as voracious as mine," he leered.

She blushed slightly as he pulled away and opened the fridge door.

"What are the plans for the day?" he asked, scrambling eggs in a red ceramic bowl.

"I don't have anything planned really. Just to go home, shower, do some housework."

He stopped mixing the eggs and lifted his eyes to her. "Oh. You don't want to…um, never mind."

She clasped her arms around him and nuzzled her face into his shoulder blades. He smelled of soap, so she pressed her face further into his t-shirt. "Don't want to what?" she murmured.

He released a hard breath. "Spend time with me?"

She playfully gripped his butt cheek. "Of course I do. I just thought you had stuff to do."

He spun around and captured her face in his hands. "My mind is currently preoccupied by a luscious blonde right now. I can't seem to think about anything else." His lips crushed against hers and he felt her smile beneath his lips. "I'll drop you off at home and give you a few alone hours then I'm picking you up, along with your overnight bag, and taking you to the theater that I designed."

"My overnight bag, huh?" she grinned.

"Yeah. I can't imagine sleeping in my bed without you now," he replied softly.

*   *   *

After Chase dropped Emily off he drove to his dad's. Joanne

answered the door and her smile widened when she saw him.

"Chase! How wonderful to see you!" she squealed, pulling him into a hug. Normally, he kept a fair distance and patted her on the back, but today he pulled her into a fierce hug and even kissed her cheek.

"Ya look great, mom," he grinned. "Is the old man around?"

Joanne reeled from his hug, but when he called her 'mom' her heart swelled. In the eighteen years she'd been with Preston, Chase begrudgingly called her 'ma'.

She regained her composure when Preston entered the foyer. "Chase!" His father embraced him tightly. "What brings you to the 'burbs?"

"Let's go in the study to talk," Chase said softly. He turned and looked at Joanne. "All of us."

Chase paced in front of the couch, nibbling his thumb nail. It was a nervous habit he picked up as a kid and it recently reared its ugly head again.

"Chase? Is everything okay?" Joanne asked with worry.

He stopped pacing, raked his fingers through his hair and released a long breath. "Yes. No. Fuck! I don't know."

Joanne didn't blanche at his language. She'd heard it enough from Preston. She waved her hand towards the dark blue leather chair. "Sit down."

His khaki slacks made a rustling sound when he crossed his leg over his knee. His fingers tapped lightly against the arm of the chair while his right foot kept in rhythm.

Preston eyed him curiously. Something troubled his son and now it troubled him. "Chase?"

Chase sat forward, pushing the sleeves of his white silk shirt up past his elbows. "Dad, mom, I want to buy the farmhouse."

Soft lines crinkled around Preston's eyes when he smiled. "Now it seems as if I have two interested parties in that particular house."

Chase shook his head. "Just me. I want to rehab it and…"

When he couldn't finish his sentence Joanne gently prodded him. "And what, Chase?"

He swallowed the lump in his throat. "And build a life with Emily."

Chapter Fourteen

"Well! It's about time you came home!" roared Andrea.

Emily gripped the green towel around her tightly, jumping at the sound of Andrea's voice. "Jeesh! You scared the hell outta me!"

Andrea sighed, "Sorry, sweetie. But I've been wanting to talk to you and I can't if Chase is always around."

"It's bad, isn't it? The Soul Hunters?" Emily gasped.

"They've found you. I'm not sure how to put this…" Andrea hedged.

Emily closed her eyes. "Just tell me."

"One of them has taken over your cousin, Jenny."

Emily's eyes opened. "No wonder she's been acting like a bitch! Are there more?"

"I'm afraid so," Andrea replied knotting her hands in front of her. "Jared is the other one."

*   *   *

Preston clapped his hands together. "I believe a celebration is in order!"

Chase held up a hand. "Hold on, Dad. Don't get all crazy about this.

245

I'm still trying to digest this."

"We saw the two of you last night at the concert," Preston grinned. "Emily's a fine singer. She sure grabbed the crowd's attention, huh?"

Chase rubbed his chin and grinned. "Yeah, she did."

"Will we get to meet her?" Joanne asked.

"Really? Ya want to meet her?"

"Of course we want to meet the woman our son's in love with," Preston smiled.

Chase groaned and rolled his eyes. "It's not like that, Dad."

Preston and clapped his son on the back. "The hell it ain't!"

*   *   *

Emily quickly dressed in a pair of cut-off denim shorts and a Double Exposure t-shirt. "C'mon Andrea."

"Where are we going?" Andrea asked as Emily shoved her feet into a pair of flip-flops.

"To the shop. I have to see if Phyllis and Frankie beat any info out of Harold."

*   *   *

After giving his dad a dollar for the farmhouse and four acres surrounding it, a price Chase literally couldn't argue with, he drove to the house.

Neil and Jason's vehicles were parked on the gravel driveway. Chase made a mental note to have the driveway redone. Cobblestone would be cool, he thought. Or maybe brick.

He avoided the rotting boards on the porch and pushed the door open. He heard sounds of a hammer and drill when he entered. "Hello?" he yelled loudly.

"Fuck!" Jason yipped.

Chase followed the voice into the parlor. Jason gripped his thumb as a hammer fell to his feet. "You scared the fuck out of me!" he yelled.

"Pussy!" Chase glanced around the room and frowned. "What are you doing?"

"I'm smashing the walls, looking for anything of interest. People used to hide their valuables in walls. I'm just lookin' for something valuable," Jason shrugged.

"Well stop!" Chase yelled.

Neil came down the stairs in a hurry. "What's going on?" When he spotted Chase he stopped in his tracks. "Oh, it's you."

Chase lifted his eyebrows. "Thanks for the warm fuzzies, bro."

"I heard yelling and thought the crazy ghost was back," Neil shrugged.

"Enough of the ghost business! Christ! You two act like little girls." Chase rolled his shoulders and closed his eyes. "Stop demolishing the house. I bought it, but you two have to keep your big mouths shut because it's a secret."

A collective gasp filled the air followed by a loud whooping female sound from the kitchen.

"What. The. Fuck. Was. That?" Chase gulped.

*   *   *

Alma Raines danced a jig of glee in the kitchen. The girl came through for her! Her house wouldn't be demolished!

*   *   *

247

"Em? Is everything okay?" Phyllis asked, gliding next to her.

"Yes. No. Hell, I don't know. Andrea said…Andrea?" Emily turned and Andrea materialized.

"This is Chase's mom, Andrea," Emily replied.

Phyllis gave her the once over and turned her attention to Emily. "What gives, honey?"

"Andrea told me that Soul Hunters are inside of Jenny and Jared."

Phyllis' eyes narrowed. "What can I do to help?"

"Don't forget about us!" Frankie crooned as he slid across the tile floor, followed by Harold and Lilly.

"Whoa!" Emily replied when she got a good look at the new, improved Harold. "What happened to him?" she asked, aiming a thumb at him.

Phyllis nodded her head at Lilly. "She did."

Lilly ignored her comment and gasped when she spotted Andrea. She stepped closer to her, with her arm outstretched. "You're not like us, are you?"

Phyllis, Frankie, Harold and Emily stared at the two of them. Andrea replied with a slight grin, "No, I'm not. I'm an angel."

Phyllis and Frankie slowly backed away from Andrea and stood behind Emily. She turned and shot them a frown. "What's up?"

Crossing her arms over her chest Phyllis growled, "We're not going with her. Into the light or anywhere for that matter. So she can kick off!"

Andrea cocked her blonde head. "Kick off?"

"Yeah! Die! Ya ditz!" Phyllis spat.

"I'm already dead. Besides, I'm not here to bring you to heaven. I'm

248

here to help my son and Emily."

Phyllis eyed her. Her hair was long on the sides, but short and spiky on top. She wore blue jeans that narrowed at the ankle and bright red pumps. When Phyllis glanced up, she noticed Andrea wore a white shirt with gaudy looking red beads around her neck that matched her earrings. She wore a denim jacket and to complete her outfit she wore lots and lots of bracelets. Her lips puckered at the ensemble.

"What the hell era are you from?" Phyllis scoffed. "Or is that what Angels wear instead of white robes?"

"Apparently you've never heard of Madonna," she waved a dismissive hand.

"Okay, enough. What do I have to do to bring Jenny back?" Emily spat.

"You have to convince the Soul Hunter inside of Jared to take her away," Andrea replied matter-of-factly.

*   *   *

Not one to run from bodiless sounds, Chase strode towards the kitchen. The hair on the back of his neck stood at attention when he spotted a figure in the room from the corner of his eye.

When he turned to get a full view, the figure vanished.

He shook his head several times and slowly backed out of the kitchen. A check-up with the optometrist was in order.

Ghosts? No fuckin' way.

*   *   *

When Emily drove home, Andrea appeared in the passenger seat. "The flapper doesn't like me," she frowned.

Emily shrugged, "She worries about me. She's my best friend."

249

"She loves you," Andrea commented. "What will you do when she's taken from you?"

Emily slammed on her brakes. "What do you mean?"

"Eventually someone will buy the item that she belongs to or she'll find her way to heaven," Andrea shrugged.

"I don't know what I'll do," Emily replied sadly. The thought of never talking with Phyllis made her heart ache.

*   *   *

Chase arrived at Emily's shortly after she got home. When she opened the door he held a wrapped bouquet to her.

She took the bouquet and he took her in his arms and dipped her backwards, kissing her deeply and making her a little dizzy in the process.

He stood her up and appraised her outfit. "Did I come back too early?"

She waved a hand. "Nah. I had to run to the shop to do a few things. I'll change in a minute."

"I thought the shop was closed this weekend?" he asked, following her to the kitchen.

"Yeah, it is, but I needed to talk to Phyllis," she murmured as she unwrapped the flowers.

He pulled out a chair from the kitchen table and sat. "Who's Phyllis?"

Emily's forehead wrinkled. Did she say Phyllis? Holy hell! She ignored his question and sighed happily when she saw red, pink and white Calla Lilies, her favorite flower. "They're beautiful! How did you know?"

He smirked, "Cause I'm *just* that good!" She rolled her eyes and he laughed, "I called Beth and she told me. Ya know at first I thought it might be a problem that the two of you are friends, but now I see it as a blessing."

250

She put the flowers in a vase and kissed him on the top of his head. "I love them. Thank you."

He pulled her onto his lap and kissed her. "You're very welcome. Now, back to my earlier question. Who's Phyllis?"

She lifted her chin. "My best friend. I met her at the store. Um, there was something she wanted there."

He laughed, "Don't get so defensive, jeez. I mean, you've met my friends. Maybe I'd like to meet yours."

She smiled wistfully. "Maybe some day."

He cleared his throat. "Speaking of meeting people, would you like to meet my parents?"

She stifled a giggle. She'd already met his mom!

"What's so funny?"

"Nothing. You um, look so serious, that's all," she hedged.

"I probably did. Kind of a big step for me," he murmured. "Anyway, they'd like to see the theater, too and I thought we could all have dinner together, if that's agreeable to you?"

"Tonight?" she squeaked.

He cocked his head, "Too soon?"

"No, I'll just run upstairs and change." She got off his lap and walked towards the doorway and stopped. "Should I get dressed up or is this a casual affair?"

"In the middle," he smiled.

*   *   *

"What the hell does that mean?" she muttered to herself as she searched through her closet.

Then a startling thought occurred to her. She grabbed the pink phone on the nightstand and dialed Beth's number. When she answered Emily whispered into the phone. "Beth! Does your mom and dad know I talk to ghosts?"

Beth laughed, "Maybe, why?"

Emily closed her eyes and pinched the bridge of her nose. "Cause I'm meeting them tonight and I don't want them to say anything to Chase about it." She gulped, "I hope they haven't already!"

"I'll call them and tell them to keep quiet but Emily, you're going to have to tell him sooner or later."

"I know," Emily replied sadly.

*   *   *

Chase squeezed Emily's hand when he rounded the corner to the Grand View. "We're here," he announced, then checked his watch. "And, we're early. That's okay, we'll wait for them outside."

He ran around the car and opened the door for her. He was absolutely a freak about doing that.

"Wow, I can't wait to see the inside," she murmured.

The outside of the building was grey brick and on either side of the doors were windows that held movie posters. The marquee extended from the top at an angle with neon lights surrounding it.

The roof had tall pointed tips which jutted up from the top of the building. She removed her sunglasses and shifted her gaze to Chase. He had a hopeful expression on his face. "Well?" he asked, biting his thumb nail.

She removed his thumb from his mouth and grinned. "It's amazing, Chase. I'm in awe."

His eyes perked up. "Really? Ya like it?"
She beamed, "I think it's fabulous."

She liks it!

Emily palmed his stubbled cheek and kissed him.

"Storm?" a man called from inside the theater.

Chase turned away and grinned, "Hey Percy! How's it going?"

He tugged Emily's hand forward. "Percy, this is my lovely girlfriend, Emily Waters. Emily, this is Percy Lang, the owner of the Grand View."

Emily smiled warmly at the older rotund gentleman, taking his hand into hers. "Mr. Lang. You're theater is absolutely beautiful."

Percy laughed and gripped her hand firmly. "Call me Percy. Yeah, ol' Chase here did a great job, didn't he? Come inside!"

As they walked inside Chase heard Preston's voice behind them. "Dad! Mom!" Chase grinned.

Percy lead the way and a smile of satisfaction lit his face when Emily oohed and ahhed over the foyer.

The floor was polished marble and as she walked further into the building the flooring turned into red plush carpet. Her eyes scanned the large room and her breath caught when she saw a large, grand white staircase with black handrails leading up the stairs.

To the right was a coat room along with a wine bar. On the left of the staircase were several retro concession stands.

Her eyes drifted up. A large, ornate crystal chandelier hung just above the staircase. Along the ceiling were old movie posters. She looked back at Percy. "Is it okay if I go upstairs?"

He nodded and waved the backs of his hands to her. "By all means!"

She ran her fingers along the polished banister as she ascended the long flight of stairs. On her way up she counted twenty-five steps to the top. She walked to the curved ceiling and gasped.

Chase wrapped an arm around her waist. "Unreal, huh?"

She pointed to the pictures. "These are hand painted, aren't they?"

"Yep," he grinned.

Her eyes ran along the ceiling. *Casablanca, Gone with the Wind, Bus Stop, Psycho* and a host of other old movies decorated the area.

"Wow," she replied breathlessly. "Whoever did that has some serious talent!"

Percy climbed the stairs to them, his breathing laborious. "That'd be my granddaughter, Courtney," he beamed. "She's an artist."

"I'll say," grinned Emily. She wandered farther and squealed. "Is this a fountain?"

"Well, it would be if it worked," groused Percy. "Damn thing isn't circulating the water, Chase."

Chase frowned and moved along the backside of the fountain. This was Jason's doing, but he'd try to figure it out. After he toyed with the motor and a few switches the fountain came to life. Red and gold neon lights seemed to dance in the bubbling water.

Emily clapped her hands at the display while Percy grinned. Then when the water stopped flowing and the lights faded and fizzled, Chase groaned. "I think there's a short," he muttered.

Preston whipped out his cell phone. "Jason, the fountain's not working." He paused for a moment then replied, "I want it fixed by tomorrow!"

He tucked the phone into his pocket. "I'm sorry about this Percy. Rest assured it'll be fixed tomorrow."

Percy's phone rang loudly in his pocket. "Excuse me, folks."

"Em, I want you to meet my parents," Chase murmured.

Preston took Emily's small hand into his. "I'm very pleased to meet you Emily."

Emily blushed when Mr. Storm kissed the back of her hand while Chase rolled his eyes. "It's very nice to meet you, too, Mr. and Mrs. Storm."

Preston winced. "Mr. Storm makes me sound old. Call me Preston."

"Yes and call me Joanne," Joanne replied hugging Emily. "It's so nice to meet you!"

Emily shot Chase an arched eyebrow when he began biting his thumbnail. He quickly removed his thumb from his mouth with a lopsided grin.

Percy returned from his phone call. "You'll all be here for the opening right?"

"Of course! Wouldn't miss it for the world, Percy!" Chase replied patting him on the back. "Thanks for letting me show my girl the inside."

"Not a problem! Glad you came! Hey, for the grand opening we're planning on doing something retro, as my granddaughter calls it. You'll get an official invite, but I'll fill you in now. Everyone should be dressed in costume."

Joanne interrupted with a frown, "Like a clown?"

"Heavens no!" Percy laughed. "I'm going to be dressed in something from the 1970's, when disco was big. I was quite the dancer back then."

"What a cool idea!" Emily squealed. "Chase could dress as a gangster from the 1920's!"

He slid her a grin. "And you can come as a flapper!" Emily stifled a giggle. She knew who to ask for ideas.

255

Joanne clapped her hands together. "It sounds like it'll be a lot of fun! What movie will you be showing?"

Percy crossed his beefy arms over his belly and grinned. "We haven't decided yet, but we plan on serving a lavish dinner along with dancing afterwards."

"Speaking of dinner," Preston mumbled, patting his stomach.

The five of them stepped into the gold toned interior of the elevator and rode it down to the first floor.

Emily laughed when they walked to Chase's car. "What's so funny?" he asked quizzically.

"An elevator in a movie theater?" she giggled.

"For people in wheelchairs," he replied, affronted.

He opened the car door for her and spoke to his mom and dad for a few minutes before sliding into the drivers seat.

"I'm sorry, Chase. I didn't think about that," she said softly.

He shrugged, "It's okay. I guess it could seem a little over the top." He pulled away from the curb and grabbed her hand. "Speaking of over the top...my dad and mom sure warmed up to you quickly."

She snorted and giggled, "What's not to like?"

He brought her hand to his mouth and kissed it. "Indeed."

*　　*　　*

"Where are we going?" Emily asked.

"Tuscan Tramonto," Chase murmured with a smile.

"Am I dressed enough for it? I mean it sounds fancy," Emily frowned.

He glanced at her outfit. She wore white slacks, Capri's, and a black sleeveless blouse. She looked sexy as hell to him. "You're dressed fine, Em."

She shrugged, "Can't help feeling a bit inadequate."

He shook his head. "Stop. You look great, okay?"

She waved her hand at him. "No, you look great." She touched his shirt with her thumb and forefinger. "Is this silk?"

He lifted his chin, "Yeah. You have something against silk?"

She rolled her eyes. "Only the fact that I can't afford it."

He ground his teeth at her remark. At a stoplight he shifted in his seat. "Tomorrow we'll go clothes shopping so you won't feel…inadequate, as you say."

She lifted her chin. "I can make do with what I own."

"Emily, if I want to buy you clothes, I'll buy you goddamn clothes!" he snapped.

"No. You. Won't!"

He pulled into the parking lot and quickly stepped out of the car. She opened her door and stuck a foot out when he grabbed her hand.

"You know I like to open the door for you," he ground out. She rolled her eyes at him. "Why do you have to be so…so…" he stammered.

"So what?" she sneered.

"Goddamn impossible!"

"Chase, Emily? Are you ready to go in?" Preston asked with a smirk.

Emily pushed past Chase with her chin lifted. Chase rolled his head onto his shoulders. When he opened his eyes he saw Emily and Joanne walking into the restaurant. Preston stood with his hands in his pockets, a slight smile on his face.

He patted Chase on the back. "All women are goddamn impossible, Chase. She's not the exception."

Chase cocked his head. "Yeah, dad, she is. She's an exception to *my* rules."

*   *   *

"Ha, ha, you two. This is all fine and dandy bringing up my shortcomings as a teenager!" Chase laughed.

"We were simply explaining to Emily how you got the nickname of Stormy," Preston grinned.

"It should've been bruiser or buster," Joanne giggled. "I actually took a part-time job at his high school because I knew I'd eventually get a phone call from the principal!"

Emily giggled and stared at Chase. "He's grown into a fine man."

"Indeed he has," murmured Preston.

Chase rolled his eyes, "Nah, I'm still an asshole, but I'm getting better." He glanced at Emily. "Must be the company I keep."

"*Psst.*"

Emily picked up her wine glass and tapped it against Chases. "I'll drink to that."

"*Psst!*"

Emily's glanced around the table.

"For the love of god! *Psst!*"

Turning, Emily spotted Andrea beside her with hands on her hips. "It's about time you!" she admonished.

She lifted her eyebrows and Andrea continued. "Tell Preston about me. Maybe he can hire a detective or something to verify the information."

"Um, if you'll excuse me, I need to use the washroom," Emily said to the Storm family.

She walked towards the washroom and pulled out her cell phone. Andrea was close at her side.

"I need to talk to you! Who are you calling?" Andrea whined.

"I'm going to talk to you like this so I don't look like a loon talking to air!" Emily hissed quietly.

"Good idea! Tell Preston about me. It's one step closer to telling Chase," Andrea said.

"And when the hell am I supposed to tell him? Over dessert?" Emily growled.

*   *   *

Emily glanced around the dining room. It was packed for a Sunday night and waiters bustled from table to table serving their customers.

The walls were decorated with prints of sunsets and painted grape vines.

She nudged Chase with her elbow. "Look at all the sunset photos!"

"I know. I thought you may like this place. The name of it is Tuscan Tramonto, which means Tuscan Sunset," he grinned.

"Oh! How lovely!" she exclaimed.

"You're a fan of sunsets, Emily?" Preston asked.

"Oh yeah. In fact I took an awesome picture the other day of one. Here, let me show you." She pulled out her phone and pulled up the picture of the sunset behind the farmhouse. "This is my absolute favorite," she replied, handing Preston her phone.

"Ah! Yes, that is quite magnificent," he nodded.

She nodded. "Yes. It's such a wonderful home and I know it needs work, but…"

Chase cocked his head, "But what, Em?"

"It's silly, but I feel like it's my home," she shrugged.

Preston lifted a grey eyebrow to his son and Chase shook his head. Preston sighed, "I'm sorry Emily, but someone else has made a…a generous offer and it's not one Storm Design Group can pass up."

"Someone else put an offer in on it?"

He nodded. "Yes, before you made your offer, I'm afraid."

Her bottom lip quivered. "Are they going to tear it down?"

"It's my understanding that the buyer plans on rehabbing it and build a life there," he smirked.

*   *   *

As they left the restaurant Andrea was hot on Emily's heals. "Tell him!" she beseeched.

Emily pulled away from Chase. "Can you walk Joanne to the car? I'd like to talk to your dad for a few minutes."

"He's not going to renege on the offer he received," Chase said sadly.

She shrugged, "I have to try."

"Okay…" he muttered.

Preston laced his arm through Emily's. "Emily, dear, I'm sorry I can't sell you the house," he said softly.

"I, uh, actually have something else to talk to you about," she replied, keeping an eye on Chase and Joanne.

"Is it Chase?" he asked, concern etched his face.

Emily frowned. "No, it's Andrea." Preston lifted an eyebrow, encouraging her to continue. "She's here and wants me to tell you she didn't leave you for another man."

He sagged a little, "Go on."

"She had inoperable cancer and didn't want to be a burden to you and didn't want Chase to see her sickly so she came up with a ruse." She glanced at Andrea and frowned. "A very bad ruse that she now regrets."

"Tell him that I've always loved him and Chase!" Andrea whimpered.

Emily glanced at her and shook her head.

"What did she say?" Preston asked with wet eyes.

"She's always loved you and Chase," Emily sighed. "Okay! Okay!" Emily snipped at Andrea.

She pulled a note pad and pen from her purse and jotted down the information Andrea spewed in her ear. "Is that all?" Emily asked her.

Emily handed the paper to Preston. "This is the name of the hospital she was at, along with the name of her lawyer. He was supposed to contact you after her death, but he died a short time later. She's not sure who took over his practice, but she thinks you can at least start with this."

Preston took her in his arms and hugged her. "Thank you."

She pulled away, with tears in her eyes. "One more thing." She glanced to her right and sighed, "Okay two more things. She thinks Joanne is a wonderful woman. She also wants you to help me tell Chase the truth. She wants him to know how much she loves him."

He grinned though his eyes held unshed tears. "She's still a demanding woman."

Back at his condo Chase took Emily into the den and handed her the remote to the television. "I'll be right back," he said with a gleam in his eye.

She put the stereo on instead. Soon, smooth jazz filtered from the speakers. She kicked her shoes off and laid on the couch, wondering what Chase was up to.

Chase entered the den and frowned slightly when he saw Emily asleep.

He knelt on the floor next to her and brushed a soft, feathery kiss on her cheek. When she didn't rustle he kissed her gently on the lips.

Her eyes slowly opened and a grin slid across her lips. "Ah! Prince Charming," she sighed.

"I'm not sure about that," he chuckled. "I kinda have something planned, but if you're too tired…"

"Whaddya got in mind, cutie?" she smiled, brushing a hand through his hair.

He swept her up in his arms with a wicked grin and carried her into the bathroom.

The room was aglow with candles. So many that she couldn't count them all! They lined the marble counter tops as well as around the pool he called a tub.

"Why, Mr. Storm, I think you're trying to seduce me."

He wiggled his eyebrows. "Is it working?"

Her hand curved around the side of his neck, bringing his face closer to hers. "I'd say so."

Slowly he set her feet on the floor and began unbuttoning her blouse. She blushed at his heated gaze when he threw it to the floor. His hands moved lower to her slacks while she unbuttoned his shirt.

As he lowered her slacks, his hands explored the soft lines of her waist and hips.

Emily ran her hands over his chest then his arms. His muscles bunched beneath her fingers.

They stared into each others eyes as they touched one another. Everything they had to say was expressed in their eyes.

Chase's mouth went dry as he looked at her, touched her. His heart clenched at the enormity of feelings he felt for her.

She shot him a wicked grin as she lowered his pants. She trailed warm, wet kisses down his chest, circling his nipples with her tongue. He groaned softly as she licked and kissed her way down to his navel.

Chase's legs stiffened when she pushed his briefs down to his ankles. Then, when he felt her mouth on him, his body flexed in response.

He gently gripped the sides of her head as she slid her tongue over him, circling the tip. A low groan bubbled in his belly when she took all of him in her mouth.

Slowly and seductively Emily licked and teased him. His moans only encouraged her further. Her tongue caressed his soft sac, causing Chase to groan and keen.

"Babe, I think you'd better stop," he rasped.

"Nu-uh," she replied with a grin.

She continued licking and sucking at a leisurely pace until he couldn't hold back any longer. "Em…" he warned, trying to pull away.

Emily grabbed his ass cheeks and pushed him closer, sending Chase into an eruption. His body convulsed as each drop was drained from him.

Satisfied that she just rocked his world she kissed and licked her way up to his chest.

His expression was that of wonder and glee. "Holy hell, woman," he choked out.

She took his hand and led him to the tub. "Is that wine chilling for us?"

"Yeah," he managed to eke out in a voice that didn't seem to be his own.

While she slid into the tub he shakily poured Merlot into a glass and held it out to her.

She drank it and handed the empty glass back. He grinned sexily and refilled the glass. Afterwards, he slid into the tub with her.

"Well, that was a surprise," he finally said.

"A good surprise?" she asked, rubbing her foot against his inner thigh.

"A great fucking surprise!"

She confessed, "I've never done that before."

His eyebrows shot up. "Never?"

"Nope."

Chase's lips curved. "I like that. I mean, that I'm your first."

She cocked her head. "You're the only one, ever."

Chase slid closer to her, pulling her onto his lap. "I like the sound of that."

She wrapped her arms around his neck and kissed him. "I like the pool," she murmured into his ear.

He grabbed the wine glass and took a sip, then handed it to her. "So…I have to fly to France at the end of the month and I was wondering if you'd like to go with me?"

"I'm flying to my parents, remember?" she asked, placing the glass down.

"Yeah, but you're only going for a week, right?"

She lazily ran her fingers through his thick hair. "Yeah."

"Well, afterwards you can fly to Paris. I'll have a ticket waiting for you," replied, nibbling her shoulder.

She pulled away and cocked her head. "How long are you going to be there?"

"A month or so, depending how things go."

"How many days do you want me to stay?" she asked, biting her lip.

He kissed her cheek, "A month or so."

"Chase, I can't be away from the store for that long. I'm on shaky ground now with Jenny. This would just send her over the edge."

He shrugged, "Have Beth help her out. I'm sure she'd love to work there. Christ, she always talks about what a great place it is."

"We'll see," Emily hedged. The real Jenny wouldn't mind a bit, but the new and not so improved Jenny will have a royal shit fit if Emily was gone a month.

He shifted her slightly, causing a grin to form on her face. "Already Mr. Storm?"

"Well, I can't help it if little Chase wants to come out and play again."

"I can sit at the other end…it's a safe distance away, I think," she teased.

"Uh-uh. You're not going anywhere woman. I've got things to do," he replied in a velvet voice.

He filled his hands with soap. Slowly and meticulously he began to wash her from the neck down.

Her skin tingled beneath his soft caresses.

Chase turned her to wash her back. Afterwards, his hands slid to the front and cupped her breasts. His warm breath fanned her neck, eliciting a shiver from her.

Her hips ground over his lap with each gentle tug on her nipples. A small hiss escaped from his lips with each movement.

He brought his hand down to her slick folds. She gripped the sides of the tub and her head fell against his shoulder at his touch.

Deftly he rolled her clit between his thumb and forefinger, feeling it engorge with each stroke. "Give it to me, Em," he whispered into her ear.

He placed his palm on her silken belly, to hold her in place, and inserted two fingers inside her, keeping his thumb firmly on her clit. He teased and caressed until she exploded around him.

She lay limp in his arms, still shuddering from her orgasm. "Wow," she managed to eke out.

"Wow, indeed," he grinned against her neck. "You're very receptive."

"I think it's you who makes me that way," she replied breathlessly.

She sat up and grabbed the soap. "Your turn," she replied with a lop-sided grin.

He watched her as she washed him. Her hands were so soft against his skin, her touch was feather light, almost tickling.

His heart clenched each time she giggled or shot him a smile. He thought about the time he wasted when he tried to push her way. When he knew all along that she was good for him. She made him want to be a better man.

She made him feel alive and *deserving* of love.

He spun around in the tub, splashing water over the sides and pulled her onto his lap.

"Hey! I didn't finish washing your back!" she giggled.

He cupped her face into is hands, his eyes burned with intensity. "I love you, Emily."

Chapter Fifteen

Her eyes glistened with moisture and her heart clenched at his words.

"Em?" His eyes probed hers.

"I'm sorry. I'm having a female moment here," she replied shakily.

He sighed a breath of relief. "Don't cry, Em. I've felt it for a while, but was afraid to say it." He shrugged and continued. "For a long time I felt like I didn't deserve to be loved." He took a deep breath. " I lied when I said my parents divorced."

She lifted her eyes, tears spilled slowly down her cheeks. He brushed them away with his finger tips. "My mom left us for another guy. It was…difficult…for me because she was my life when I was a kid. Dad was always out of town on business, trying to make a name for himself. Anyway, it was just me and my mom for weeks on end."

He absently looked at his wrinkled fingers. "Let's get out of the tub before we turn to prunes and I'll finish telling my story."

Stepping out of the tub he gripped her hand and wrapped a warmed hunter green towel around her. He grabbed another towel and put it around his waist.

He took her hand and led her into the bedroom and sat on the bed. "My mom used to take me to see the Bulls play because I was such a basketball fanatic and then there were times we'd hang out at home and watch movies together and eat pizza and popcorn. My life revolved around her and I thought hers revolved around mine. Don't get me wrong, I had plenty of friends when I was a kid, but she, well, she was my *best* friend."

Emily leaned against the headboard and Chase placed his head on her chest. She ran her fingers through his hair, encouraging him to continue.

"She went to all of my basketball games and was the loudest parent there when I made a basket. At Christmas time she'd coerce me to make cookies with her and she always made an extra batch of peanut butter, because they were my favorite.

"One day I was dribbling the ball, coming back from the park and I saw a limo in the driveway. Dad had only been home for a few days, so I was surprised he was leaving again. But it wasn't my dad getting in the limo, it was my mom."

His voice began to waver and Emily said softly, "Chase, you don't need to say anymore."

"Yeah, I do. I've been holding this inside for too long, Em. I want you to know why I've been so fucked up."

He cleared his throat. "Mom never left in a limo. I picked up the ball and ran as quick as I could, but the limo pulled away too fast. When I got to the house I saw tears in my dads eyes. Preston Storm never cried," he scoffed.

His voice cracked. "Dad told me she wasn't coming back. I ran to my room, looking for a note, something, anything, from her. She couldn't leave me without a note! I ran into their bedroom, looking for one. Hell, I ran through the whole fucking house looking for a goddamn note explaining why she left!

"For days I waited for a phone call or a letter in the mail. Then I started to blame my dad. It was his fault she left! Because he was never home! But then the mind of a ten year old is a precarious thing. I started to believe that *I* was the reason she left. I dunno, maybe because I didn't get good enough grades or I'd made a mess in the kitchen and didn't clean up?"

He sat up and ran a hand through his hair. "Then it hit me. She didn't love me because I was unlovable."

Emily's heart clenched at his words. She reached to him and cupped his cheek in her hand.

He turned to her, tears shimmering in his eyes. He shrugged, "I wasn't lovable."

"No, Chase, that's not true," she replied, tears fell freely from her eyes. "You *are* lovable."

He shook his head. "Not to my mom. What kind of woman leaves her kid with a man that he hardly knows? My dad was *never* around when I was growing up, Em! The only thing I knew about him was that he designed homes! To say life sucked for me at that age would be an understatement."

He drew a ragged breath. "I used to pray that my mom would come back. I cried myself to sleep for months. I wouldn't eat, I quit playing basketball and hanging out with my friends. Quite simply, I closed up. I even tried to kill myself."

Emily gasped when he held out his left wrist to her. A white jagged line etched his skin.

"I was thrown in the psych ward for a time," he snorted. He straightened and cracked his neck. "Eventually I got better. My dad stopped traveling and spent more time with me and a few years later he married Joanne." He lifted his fist to his eye. "I wanted to get close to her, but was afraid. Afraid that she'd leave too, so I kept my distance. Jason and I got along okay and then later, Beth was born. Man, I loved that little girl and she worshipped me. I wasn't afraid of her leaving me, ya know?"

He shifted on the bed and crossed his legs. "When I met Cassie, I was in a better place mentally. I didn't fall for her quickly, but I did fall." He snorted, "Man, I wanted the whole package with her. Marriage, babies, a few dogs and a huge house. She lead me to believe that she wanted those things too. I fucking worshipped the ground she walked on! It's nauseating, now that I think of it," he shuddered.

271

"Anyway, I've already told you how that ended. I didn't have to go to the psych ward that time, but it was dark times for me. That's why I came up with the seven day thing. I could have the illusion of affection and love and then discard it, before I got hurt. So when I met you, yeah, I had it planned out that you'd be a seven day girl and nothing else," he shrugged, ashamedly. "But you managed to strike something in me. You made me giddy when I saw you! And when you tried to avoid me? Hell, that was the icing on the cake. I actually found myself chasing after you! I've never, *ever* done that before."

She grinned and poked her index finger into her cheek.

He returned her smile and cupped her cheek into his hand. "Seeing you with Buckley that night sent me over the edge. So much, in fact, that I broke my own fucking rules and brought you to my home. It was game over for me, man, when I met you." He shook his head. "This is going to sound completely irrational, but I knew the minute I saw you that you would change my life."

He moved closer to her and kissed her lightly on the lips. "The first time I saw you on stage with Freddie and you belted out *Chain of Fools*, you had me. Hook, line and sinker. I was in love with you from that day on, but was afraid to admit it to myself. Who the fuck falls in love that fast?"

She shrugged and smiled, "We do."

He licked his lips. "Emily, I'm trusting you with my heart. Please be gentle with it."

*   *   *

One week later Emily was busy at *Play it Again Sam*, scrounging the jewelry cases.

"What are ya doin' doll?" Phyllis asked.

Emily jumped at the sound of her voice and blew a wayward strand of hair from her face. "I'm looking for your pendant."

Phyllis frowned. "Why?"

"Because I want to wear it to the theater premier since I'm going to dress up like you!" She shot Phyllis an embarrassed glance. "Plus, I want to have it at home. Frankie's leather jacket, too."

Phyllis began to protest and Emily held up a hand. "Look, I know what you're going to say, but you're my very best friend in the world, whether you like it or not and Frankie, well, I can't be without him, either. So deal with it! You two are coming home with me!"

Phyllis' eyes turned misty and a lump formed in her throat. She clapped her hands together. "Well, I guess we'd better find those things for you."

Jenny stood in the doorway of the shop, her eyes narrowed. "How sweet. Having a ghost as a best friend! Couldn't you have picked someone more appealing, Emily? Someone who doesn't murder babies?"

A small whimper escaped from Phyllis shortly before she disappeared.

Emily strode towards Jenny, venom in her eyes. She jabbed her in the chest with her forefinger. "You need to go back to wherever you came from and get the hell out of Jenny's body!"

Jenny shot her a grin that didn't meet her eyes. "I don't think you're calling the shots here, freak. So, why don't you take your pathetic little self home so I can run this piece of shit shop."

When Jenny pushed past Emily she felt an arctic breeze. It made the hair on her arms stand up. Although scared as hell, she went after her. "Get out of her!" she yelled. "Jump into me!"

Jenny turned and lifted an eyebrow. "Ya think I didn't try that? You're too strong willed. I had to settle for this weakling, but that's okay. Because with each day that passes Jenny's spirit fades and mine gets stronger. Now beat it. I got a shop to run."

Emily chewed her bottom lip and made a wide arc around Jenny to get her things from the storage room.

Sitting next to her purse was a spider brooch and a black leather jacket.

*   *   *

"Jared! Please call me back! I need your help!" Emily whimpered into the phone as she drove away from the shop. She'd left messages for him for the past week, but he didn't return one.

Her stomach churned when she thought about what was happening to Jenny's soul. "Andrea! Where the hell are you?" she screeched.

"I'm here. You'd better keep your mind focused on driving!" Andrea warned as Emily nearly blew through a red light.

"I have to save Jenny and you're going to help me!" she snapped.

"Only Jared can help you with that," Andrea muttered.

Emily accelerated when the light turned green. "He's not answering my calls! I don't even know where he lives!"

Emily's phone rang and she fumbled through her purse to find it, nearly running her car off the road. "Hello?"

"Hi babe. I'm kinda caught up here at work. Patrice, in Paris, wants to add something to the building plans. I'm not sure if I'll be able to see you tonight," Chase said.

She frowned. Lately he's been the only one who kept her sane. "Oh. Well, that's okay."

"Are you sure?"

"Yeah. It's been a day. Jenny's still bitchy, like something's gotten into her," she rolled her eyes at her own cheekiness.

"Maybe Freddie can talk to her. After all, she's his sister," he offered.

Emily pulled into her driveway and saw Jared standing outside of his car. "Yeah. Good idea. I gotta go. Call me later?"

"You can count on it!" Chase grinned into the phone. "I love you."

Her lips curved. "I love you, too."

She had the car door open before she put it in park. "Jared! I'm so glad to see you!" she shrieked, running into his arms.

He grinned when she wrapped her arms around his waist. "Well, this is a nice surprise!"

She pulled away and tugged his hand towards the house. "C'mon, we've got to talk."

When they got into the house she waved her hand at the couch. "Have a seat. Can I get you anything to drink?"

"No, I'm fine. What's wrong, baby?" he said smoothly.

Her scalp prickled from the endearment. Slowly she sat next to him. "Please don't call me that."

His eyebrows furrowed. "Baby?"

She nodded. "It gives me the creeps."

He nodded, "So you've told me. You've been calling all week, what's wrong?"

"I know you're not really Jared," she stammered. "I also know that Jenny isn't really Jenny."

He motioned his head towards Andrea. "Did she tell you?" Emily nodded and he blew out a breath.

Emily swallowed the lump in her throat and slowly moved away from him. "Who are you?" she whispered.

Jared grinned, "I'm the one you call Fleshy."

*　　*　　*

275

Cassandra Seton pulled her white BMW next to the curb of *Play it Again Sam*. Her pulse raced. She wasn't sure why she was nervous, but there it was. She finally tracked down the gold-digger who was dating Chase and wanted to meet her. Besides, it was easier to approach Emily Waters than Chase Storm.

It had nothing to do with the fact he wasn't returning her calls.

She stepped into the shop and peered around. Suddenly a voice called from another room. "Welcome to…ah hell! Welcome!" Jenny grumbled at the blonde. She hated the façade of being nice.

Cassandra's eyebrow lifted. The woman before her certainly wasn't Emily Waters. "I'm here to see a Miss Waters," she announced.

Jenny snorted. "You just missed her. Can I help you with something?"

Cassandra considered her options. She sure as hell didn't want to go home empty handed. "I, um, am a reporter for the Daily News and since she made such a sensation at the fourth of July fest, I thought I'd do a little article on her."

The Soul Hunter grinned her first smile since taking over Jenny's body. "Well, you've come to the right place for a story on Emily! Let's go in the back and I can fill you in!" she purred gleefully.

*   *   *

It was after eight before Chase left the office. His neck was sore from bending over a drafting table for several hours straight.

He wanted to see Emily, but was tired as hell and in a bitchy mood. So, instead, he drove to his condo and went to the fifteenth floor. He rapped twice and called, "Ricochet, come out and play!"

Rick opened the door and shook his head at his friend. "You have immaculate timing." A buxom blonde gripped Rick's ass as she kissed him. Her eyes raked over Chase thoroughly and she shot him a wink.

She turned to Rick and purred, "I can stay, if you'd like." She licked her lips in Chase's direction.

Chase's upper lip curled in disgust. "Not interested, sweetheart."

Rick pressed his hand against the small of her back. "Goodbye Dora."

She stood in the doorway and hissed, "It's Nora!"

Rick shrugged, "Whatever."

The two men watched as she stormed to the elevator, both biting back laughter.

"You're a pig!" Chase admonished.

"You're one to talk," Rick chided. "What brings you to my happy abode? It's obviously not problems with Emily otherwise you might've jumped at Dora's offer."

"Nora," Chase corrected. Rick shrugged. "No, Emily's great. I just got out of work and thought I'd drop by and see if you wanted to have a drink or two. I haven't seen you in a while."

Rick snorted, "That's because your free time is being consumed by Emily." Chase began to protest and Rick lifted a hand. "Relax, bro! I'm happy for you. You're a transformed man since you met her. Ya lucky fucker."

Chase grinned, "That's for damn sure."

*   *   *

Cassandra pulled away from the shop, shocked down to her Jimmy Choo's. This Emily chick talked to ghosts? Un-fucking-believable! And the beauty part of it? Chase had no idea!

From what she remembered about him, he was a black and white kind of guy. No gray area with him. She wondered how he'd feel if he found out that the woman he was dating talked to ghosts! And even better than that? Her best friend is a fucking ghost!

Cassandra chuckled on the drive to her condo.

She pulled out the invitation for the opening of the Grand View theater.

In a week Chase's life would shatter and she'd be there to pick up the pieces.

*   *   *

The bar bustled with harried business men and women after a long day. Chase and Rick opted for a booth and were quickly serviced with Corona's. Chase rubbed the back of his neck.

Rick smirked. "Something buggin' ya?"

"I had to rework the plans for the building in Paris and I've been getting phone calls since Monday from Cassie," he shrugged.

Rick's eyes grew wide. "No shit? The chick you were engaged to?"

"Yeah," Chase snorted.

"What did she have to say?" Rick pressed.

Chase scrunched his face. "How the fuck would I know? I haven't called her back and don't plan to."

Rick chugged the Corona and placed the bottle on the table. "Did she leave a message?"

"Yeah. Said she moved here from New York and thought it'd be nice to catch up. Christ! She's left a message every day for the past three days. I'm surprised she didn't leave one today," Chase muttered, lifting the bottle to his lips.

"Didja tell Emily?"

"No reason to. I have no intentions on calling Cassie back. She's old news." Rick shook his head at his friend and Chase sighed. "I think we're past that stage. I mean, why get her in a tizzy for nothing? Ah! Enough about that. Did I tell you I bought a dilapidated farm house?"

Rick choked on his beer. "For what?"

Chase shrugged, "For Emily. I made the mistake of taking her there one day. We bought some property and this house…this money pit, has a shit load of antiques and I thought she could put them in her shop. I didn't count on her falling in love with the place." He took a sip of beer. "Anyway, she wanted to buy it. Said that it felt like it should be her house."

Rick lifted his eyebrow and wiggled his empty bottle to the waitress. "So, just like that you bought it?"

"Pretty much. I haven't told her yet. I want to finish rehabbing it first. The funny thing is, the contractor's think the fucking place is haunted."

"Really?" Rick smirked.

Chase scoffed, "I don't know how many contractors I've hired in the past two weeks! No one will work there for more than a day!"

*　　　*　　　*

"Don't be afraid of me," Jared sighed sadly. "I saved you from drowning when you were a child."

Emily frowned, "That was you who pulled me up?"

Jared nodded. "To the surface so your father could find you."

Emily's bottom lip trembled. "Thank you."

"I couldn't save my daughter, so I saved someone else's," he shrugged.

"What's your name?" Emily asked.

He extended his hand, "Mitch Rhodes."

Emily shyly shook his hand, frowning. "What was your daughter's name?"

His eyes glistened. "Emma." He hung his head momentarily and brushed away escaped tears. "God, I miss her."

Unsure what to say, Emily gently rubbed his shoulder.

He lifted his head and sighed sadly. "I created a problem for both of us when I saved you."

A crease formed between Emily's eyebrows. "A problem?"

He released a long breath. "Yes. The Grey One was mighty angry that you lived."

Andrea glided closer to Emily and rested a hand on her shoulder. "Who is he?"

"He's a soul collector." He shifted his gaze to Emily. "You were the soul that was taken from him. He doesn't accept loss so easily, nor does he forget."

*   *   *

A week later Emily stood in front of the antique maple mirror admiring her dress. It was a repro she found on the internet, but Phyllis said it looked authentic. It was red and sleeveless with red fringe on the bottom. She wore black stockings along with a pair of high-heeled Mary Janes. To finish the outfit she had a long strand of white beads around her neck as well as Filly's spider brooch.

"Aw, Em, you look beautiful!" Phyllis cooed watching Emily put the finishing touches on her flapper outfit.

Emily frowned. "I shouldn't be having fun while Jenny's body has been overtaken by an evil nasty bitch."

Phyllis grabbed Emily firmly by the shoulders. "Listen to me. Jenny will be fine. You're the one I'm worried about."

"But…" Emily whimpered.

"But nothin'! You've got a great guy who's finally admitted he's dizzy for ya and you're dizzy for him, right?" A smile spread across Emily's face and Phyllis nodded. "So, it's about time you shake off the gloomies, have a good time with your man and live, Em!"

When the doorbell rang Phyllis pulled her into a tight hug. "Now, blow and have a blast as Frankie would say!"

*   *   *

When Emily opened the front door she heard Phyllis gasp. "Gosh, he sure looks like Tommy in that outfit."

"Wow! I mean, damn!" Chase stammered when he saw Emily. "You look incredible!" His eyes traveled slowly down her body. She blushed under his heated gaze. He palmed the back of his neck and shook his head. "Sorry. I don't mean to be gaping."

"Back at ya, Storm," she giggled. He wore a gray suit with a black shirt and white tie. She stifled a grin when she noticed the two tone wing tip shoes. It was so out of character for him. Even the black fedora hat atop his head was a different look. She'd only seen him in a baseball cap once.

A wicked grin lit his face. "Like what you see, Miss Waters?"

She licked her lips. "You look mighty sexy, Mr. Storm."

"Those were my intentions," he murmured, taking her hand.

"What the?" she squeaked as he lead her to the driveway.

A chauffer stood outside of a large red car with runners and white tires with red hubcaps. Her eyes cut to Chase who grinned like an idiot.

"Awesome, huh?" he chuckled.

The chauffer lifted his black cap to her and held the passenger door open. "Miss," he nodded.

"Chase! Are you crazy?" she gasped.

281

He laughed as he sat next to her. "Crazy would've been me renting the Batmobile, but it was only a two seater." He shrugged, "Besides, I wanted to be able to do this." He pulled her onto his lap and brought his lips to hers.

She pulled away. "Um…so what kind of car is this?"

"It's a 1929 Packard. Pretty awesome, huh?"

She shook her head, a grin played at her lips as she shifted off his lap. "The man ain't got no money sense."

*   *   *

Search lights lit up the sidewalk in front of the Grand View. A stream of cars and pedestrians clogged the area so Randy, the chauffer, parked the Packard in front of the Grand View and let Emily and Chase out.

"I'll find a place to park Mr. Storm. Just call me when you're ready to leave," Randy said loudly over the noise.

Chase nodded and wrapped an arm around Emily's waist, ushering her to the sidewalk.

"I didn't expect all this hoopla, did you?" Emily muttered into his ear.

He laughed, "Yeah. Percy doesn't do anything on a small scale, either."

Lights flashed in Emily's face from cameras, as they walked on the red carpet into the theater. Men and women called out to Chase.

"Mr. Storm, care to tell us your dates name?"

"Hey, Chase! Got a second for an interview?"

"Storm! How's the project in Paris going?"

Chase smiled thinly at them all and avoided their questions.

Once they were safely inside he tugged her towards the bar and ordered them each a glass of merlot. Afterwards, he found a small alcove for them to sit.

Emily sat wide-eyed. She'd never been to anything so extravagant as this. She saw Chase nod to the mayor of Chicago.

"You know the mayor?" she squeaked.

He shrugged, "Yeah. I know that guy, too." He cocked his head to the right.

"Holy crap! The quarterback for the Bears?"

Chase leaned in. "He's a douche bag," he whispered conspiratorially. When the quarterback spotted him, Chase nodded. "How's it going?" he asked over the din.

Emily giggled. "You're terrible."

"It's all a game with these people. They only want to talk if you can do them a favor. Otherwise, it's a nod or a limp handshake." A smile lit his face. "But there are times when you form a rare and wonderful bond." He stood and grabbed Greg Travers hand. "I didn't know you'd be here!"

"Storm!" Greg bellowed. A low whistle escaped his lips when he spotted Emily. He took her hand and kissed the back of it. "Emily, you look beautiful tonight."

She blushed. "Hi Greg. Is Tamara here, too?"

He rolled his eyes. "Yeah. She's workin' this gig for the paper. Hey, maybe she can interview you?"

Chase nodded his head. "Sure. I can do that for her. Hell, I'll even give her an exclusive."

Greg lifted his eyebrows, "No shit?"

"No shit," Chase laughed. "Get her ass over here."

Greg sped away in search of Tamara and Emily laughed. "You say 'exclusive' like it's some big deal."

He took a sip of wine and carefully placed the stemmed glass onto the highly polished round table. "It is, Emily. I don't normally grant interviews or answer reporters questions. I like to keep my life private."

"But how was that possible when you did the seven day thing?" she asked, running her index finger over the top of her glass.

"For the most part I was careful. Of course, I had a few who went to the papers to tell their story. Some made the papers, some didn't," he shrugged.

"An exclusive?" Tamara shrieked as she approached the table.

Chase rolled his eyes and laughed. "Within reason!"

Tamara hugged Emily before grabbing a notepad from her purse.

"Take my chair and I'll take a walk around with Greg," Emily offered.

Chase pulled Emily onto his lap. His mouth brushed the side of her neck, causing her to giggle softly. "If asked, don't answer any questions, okay?" he murmured into her ear.

She lifted an eyebrow to him. "I hardly think I'm the one they want to talk to."

"You'd be surprised," he smirked, releasing her.

"I'll take care of her," Greg assured him.

*   *   *

Nearly an hour later Chase found her chatting with Seth Brice, who stood way too close to her. "Fuck!" he cursed under his breath.

Chase came up behind her, wrapped his arms around her waist and planted a noisy wet kiss on her neck. He lifted his head momentarily and muttered, "Brice."

Seth's nose wrinkled. "Storm. Emily, it was great to see you again." He nodded at Chase, who still had his lips attached to Emily's neck. "Don't forget what I said," Seth grinned before he walked away.

"What does that mean?" Chase growled.

She rolled her eyes. "Why didn't you just piss on my leg? It would've had the same effect."

His lip quirked up. "Not gonna lie. The thought passed my mind. What aren't you supposed to forget?" he pushed.

"That if you and I break up, he's available," she sighed.

Chase twisted around. "That son-of-a-bitch!"

Emily grabbed his hand. "Calm down, willya? Jeesh! I told him I was only interested in his actions on the ice, not off, okay?"

Chases eyebrows drew together. "Really?"

She shook her head and lifted her eyes. "C'mon, the movie's going to start soon and I want to get a good seat. I hear they're playing *Dr. Jekyll and Mr. Hyde.*

*   *   *

While the movie played Chase gazed at Emily's profile. She turned her head, smiling and pointed to the screen.

He shook his head and pointed at her.

He'd much rather look at her than an old black and white movie about some guy with two personalities.

He turned his attention away from Emily and scanned the seats for Brice. He'd like to go *Hyde* on his ass for flirting with his girlfriend. *Asshole!* His blood pressure lowered when Emily playfully gripped the inside of his upper thigh. He released a low hiss, causing her to giggle.

He rolled his eyes. Only *he* could get a hard-on watching *Dr. Jekyll and*

Mr. Hyde.

*　　　*　　　*

After the movie was over the guests began milling out of the theater. Emily stood and looked at Chase with a frown. "What's up?" she asked.

He pointed to his crotch. "This is. Don't roll your eyes at me! It's your fault!"

She sat and shook her head. "A small grab, a half hour ago and you're still…that way? What am I gonna do with you?"

He wiggled his eyebrows at her. "Trust me, I've got ideas and that's why I'm still like this!"

She giggled, "You're impossible!"

Chase glanced around the theater, lifted an eyebrow and smirked. "Have ya ever done it in a theater before?"

She glowered. "No and it's not on my bucket list, either, so forget about it." She glanced at the tent in his pants, then grinned. "Seth Brice."

His eyes narrowed and his head twisted around. He didn't see Brice anywhere. He turned his head back when she began giggling. "What's so funny?" he sneered.

She pointed to his crotch. "His name alleviated your delicate condition."

*　　　*　　　*

Chase and Emily were ushered to a large round table where the Storm family sat. Preston and Joanne both hugged Emily upon seeing her. After everyone was settled Preston took Emily's hand. "Well, what do you think?"

Emily took a sip of water from a crystal goblet. "It's amazing! Everyone I've talked with tonight is very impressed with Chase's design. I think Percy will be very successful."

286

She glanced around the table. Preston and Joanne were dressed as hippies. Both wore peace sign pendants around their necks. Joanne wore a brown peasant blouse with bell bottom blue jeans and Preston wore a tie dye t-shirt with a fringed leather vest over it. He also wore flared bell bottom jeans.

Beth wore a red polka dot dress with a matching scarf around her hair. Neil's hair was greased back and he wore an outfit similar to what Frankie wore.

Jason and his wife Sarah also dressed in 50's fashion, but Sarah opted for a gray poodle skirt and short sleeved white blouse. Her long brown hair was pulled into a ponytail and she wore a pink scarf around her neck. Jason wore blue jeans with a two-tone shirt. It reminded Emily of a bowling league shirt.

Her attention was diverted from the table to the top landing of the grand staircase. A small band began playing *The Way You Look Tonight*.

Chase took her hand. "May I have the pleasure of a dance, Miss Waters?"

He lead her to an open area and shot her a grin before pulling her against him.

They were the only two dancing so Chase took full advantage and whisked her around the marble flooring.

When the song ended Chase felt a firm, testy tap on his shoulder. He expected to see Brice so turned with a scowl. Preston shot him a grin. "My turn," he jeered.

Chase backed away and bowed. "Until later, Miss Waters."

One of Phyllis' favorites, *It Had to be You*, played next. Preston grinned down at her. "You're a lovely dancer, Emily."

Her lips quirked up. "Back at ya, Preston."

His facial expression turned serious. "Emily, I checked into the information about Andrea."

"And?" Emily prodded.

Skin around his eyes crinkled. "You were right. Everything you told me was true."

She lifted her chin. "Preston I don't…"

He quickly shook his head. "I didn't mean to imply that I thought you made it up. Please don't misunderstand me. I'm glad I finally know the truth." He hesitated and glanced around. "Is she here now?"

Emily shook her head sadly. "I'm sorry. But if it helps at all, she did love you and Chase very much. She regrets not telling you the truth."

His eyes misted over. "She's in a better place now, right?"

She shrugged, "I think so. I need to tell Chase about her, but it's hard because he has so much anger towards her."

"Your best course may be to just tell him how you're able to interact with spirits first, then work your way up to telling him about Andrea," he offered.

Her shoulders sagged. "I'm afraid when I tell him, he'll think I'm crazy."

Preston hugged her. "He won't do that. He loves you, Emily."

She frowned into his shoulder. "Yeah, but everyone has a breaking point. This may be his."

*   *   *

Grey watched her dance and scowled. The nerve of her! She acted as if she didn't have a care in the world! As if *he* wasn't coming for her.

The corner of his mouth quirked up when he spotted the brash blonde walk towards the angel's son.

"You understand your purpose, Marianna?" he asked the spirit beside him.

"Yes, father," Marianna grinned.

"And Gerald? You understand your purpose?" he asked the other spirit beside him.

Gerald nodded, "Yes father."

For the first time in decades Grey smiled.

Chapter Sixteen

Cassie crept up behind Chase. "Hello handsome," she purred.

Her voice sounded like fingernails on a blackboard. His drink sloshed onto the floor when he turned. His eyes hooded in disgust. "Fuck off, Cassie," he growled.

"Can't we let bygones be bygones?" she pouted.

He lifted an eyebrow and smirked. "Sure. *Now* will you fuck off?"

Unruffled, she continued. "I'm surprised you're with that woman." He pinned her with a glare. The coldness in his eyes shook her, but she pressed on. "I mean I never thought you'd be with someone whose best friend is a flapper from the 20's and a ghost no less," she shrugged.

He rolled his eyes and snorted. "What the fuck are you talking about?"

She feigned innocence and placed her hand over her ruby red lips. "Sorry, I thought you knew. It was nice seeing you, Chase."

She turned her back and grinned when she felt a tug on her upper arm.

"What the fuck are you talking about Cassie?" he snipped.

She shrugged, "I met her cousin last week and she told me how your girl, Emily, talks to ghosts and her best friend is a ghost named Phyllis."

"You're pathetic, Cassie," he snapped, brusquely walking away from her.

He went in search of Emily and spotted her at the table with his family.

He shook off Cassie's accusations and walked up behind Emily's chair, placing his palm on the back of her head. She turned, giving him a smile that almost knocked the breath from him.

Cassie approached. "Well, didja ask her?"

Emily turned, unsure who the woman was.

"No I haven't. If you can't behave yourself I'll have you removed from the party," he said menacingly.

She rolled her eyes and stared at Emily. "Why haven't you told him that you talk to ghosts? Are you afraid he'd dump your ass?"

Emily's eyes widened and she looked across the table at Beth.

"See Chase? She's not denying it," Cassie pointed out.

Suddenly Chase felt woozy, lightheaded. Not himself. He needed to sit, but couldn't make his legs move. As quickly as the feeling came on, it left..

"C'mon Em. I've got reporters all over this place tonight," Chase said low. "Imagine the headlines! 'Chase Storm is dating a crazy woman'!"

Emily's throat was hot and dry. After chugging her glass of champagne she stood slowly to face him. "Yes, you're right Chase. My talking to ghosts is way more scandalous than you whoring around with your seven days in heaven bimbo's," she replied scathingly, shooting a glare at the bitch who stood closely to Chase.

Beth stood so fast that her chair fell backwards. "Chase! Back off! You don't understand!"

He pinned Emily with a blue-eyed glare. "Beth, this is none of your fucking business," he hissed.

"So do you have a tent at carnivals and wear exotic clothing and read palms, too?" his tone was acidic, causing Emily to flinch.

"Chase, that's enough," Preston warned.

"No dad, it isn't. She's a *freak*!" he replied icily.

She didn't dare cry. She wouldn't give him the satisfaction.

He bent, lowering his face to hers. "Get. Lost. *Freak*."

He might as well have slapped her. His words had the same effect.

She lifted her sequined purse from the table and when she was sure her legs wouldn't betray her, she walked away.

She heard Chase faintly behind her. "Come on Cassie. Lets dance."

*   *   *

Marianna jumped into Emily's body when she stepped onto the sidewalk. Rain fell heavily, making it difficult to see. Well, that and she had tears pooling in her eyes.

Absently, she stepped between two parked cars. Simultaneously tires squealed and she felt a firm tug on her left arm, pulling her to the safety of the sidewalk.

Marianna scowled at the man holding her in his arms and promptly floated from Emily's body.

*   *   *

Grey approached a glaze-eyed Chase. "You've done well tonight, Gerald." He eyed the brash blonde momentarily. "You may enjoy the rest of your evening."

Marianna, on the other hand, failed again. He didn't tolerate failure.

As he glided towards the entrance he stopped at the sound of *her* voice.

"Tsk, tsk, Grey. You don't play fair at all, do you?" she admonished.

His black cloak swished as he turned to face her. "Shekinah, what a displeasure to see you."

Shekinah lifted her chin. "I have to take care of what's mine."

"She's *not* yours! She belonged to me the minute she died in the lake!" he growled.

"Still beating that dead horse are you? Get over it! Why don't you take ruby red lips instead? Her soul is as black as yours," she sneered.

"Are you offering to barter?"

Shekinah rolled her eyes and looked at her manicured nails. "Maybe."

*   *   *

"Emily! Are you okay?" Jared yelled, wiping rain from her face.

Disoriented, Emily pushed him and walked away.

"Come on, I'll take you home," he offered.

"We'll take her home," Beth snipped, wrapping an arm around Emily.

Emily glanced at Beth and Neil. She saw the pity in their eyes. "Thanks, but Mitch, I mean, Jared can take me home," she muttered.

"Oh, Em! I'm so sorry for what he said to you. Tomorrow I'm sure he'll call and beg for forgiveness," Beth said encouragingly.

Emily shook her head. "Who is that woman and how did she know?"

Beth grimaced. "His old girlfriend Cassie. I don't know how she found out though."

Jared wrapped an arm around Emily's shoulders. "Lets get you out of this rain."

Emily peered up at the sky. "It's raining?"

Neil, Beth and Jared gaped at each other perplexed by Emily's strange demeanor.

She turned away and walked on wobbly legs. Abruptly, she stopped and glanced back at Beth and Neil. "I won't forgive him," she shakily said.

*　　*　　*

Chase barked at the bartender for Jameson. When the bartender filled a glass, Chase took the bottle, keeping his arm firmly wrapped around Cassie's shoulders.

After chugging a good portion of the bottle, he slammed it on the bar and pulled a fifty from his front pocket and slammed it down next to the bottle. He turned away from the bar, reaching back for the half-filled bottle.

"Let's go back to your place," he murmured into her ear.

*　　*　　*

Being chauffeured was the only way to go, Gerald thought. He could get as fucked-up as he wanted in Storm's body.

And he was half-way to fucked-up.

He lifted a lazy eyelid to the woman sitting next to him, rubbing his crotch with her left hand. He'd never been with a woman so...so aggressive! He grinned at his good fortune.

*　　*　　*

"I can't hold my liquor," Emily moaned, rubbing her temples.

Jared slowed the car. "Should I pull over?"

"No, I mean I feel out of sorts and exhausted. I should be upset by the things Chase said to me, but I feel nothing. In fact, I feel..."

"Numb?"

Emily nodded, "Yeah, I guess." She cocked her head. "I feel a total lack of emotion."

"Marianna took over your body. I saw her jump out when I pulled you out of the street," Jared said softly and continued. "After a possession such as

295

this, you tend to be drained for a few days. The lack of emotions is a side-effect of the soul who took over your body. You'll be back to normal in a few hours since Marianna wasn't inside you for very long."

Emily shifted in the seat. "Does this mean Jenny is safe now?"

Jared shrugged. "Let's find out."

*   *   *

They arrived at Jenny's after midnight, but a light glowed in the living room.

Jared wrapped loudly on the front door. After a few minutes Jenny unlatched the front door.

She look disheveled and confused. "Jenny?" Emily asked softly.

Jenny shrugged, "I think so. What the hell is going on, Em?"

Lilly and Harold appeared behind Jenny. "Aw, Em! You look like hell," Lilly said sadly. Emily shrugged, indifferent.

Jenny's lips trembled. "I can see and hear them, Em."

Emily's eyes cut to her cousin. "You can see and hear who?"

"Them," Jenny turned and pointed to Lilly and Harold.

*   *   *

Gerald giggled deeply when the blonde vixen took him into her mouth. It'd been a long time since he experienced such pleasure.

He intended to appreciate the gift The Grey One gave him to the fullest.

*   *   *

When Jared walked Emily to her front door she sighed. The night didn't end the way she thought it would.

He gripped her hand. "I think you know by now my intentions are

296

honorable." She eyed him curiously as she unlocked the door and he continued. "Having said that, I don't think you should be alone tonight."

She shrugged, "Suit yourself, Jared. I mean Mitch. I'm going upstairs to change. Make yourself at home."

*   *   *

Emily came downstairs a short time later wearing a tank top and shorts. She glanced at Mitch on the couch. He'd taken off his gray jacket and unbuttoned the first three button on his shirt. "Wanna beer?" she asked.

He turned at the sound of her voice and quickly looked away. "Put some clothes on!" he admonished.

She rolled her eyes and went into the kitchen. Grabbing two beers from the fridge she headed back into the living room and took a long pull from her bottle. Tears formed in her eyes. She brushed them away and finished her beer in one gulp.

"Em?" Mitch said wearily.

Her bottom lip quivered and tears fell freely. "He called me a freak."

*   *   *

Cassie squealed, pulling Chase's head deeper between her thighs. "God Chase! It's like you haven't had sex in years!"

Gerald stopped licking and grinned against her soft black hairs, "Yeah, kind of how you haven't been a brunette in years."

*   *   *

As Emily slept in his arms, guilt tugged at Mitch's chest. He'd seen a spirit jump into Chase right before he said those horrible things to her. But yet, he let her cry herself to sleep.

He lifted his chin. He did what any good father would do. Emily could do so much better than Chase. Jared was perfect for her. He closed his eyes and drifted off to a fitful sleep.

Emily awoke gasping for air. She tried to sit up but her limbs wouldn't move. Her eyes darted up in a panic.

Grey stood behind the couch with his hands hovering above her head and Mitch's. He mumbled a low chant, feeling their life force drain from the shells they wore. A deep feeling of satisfaction overwhelmed him.

*   *   *

Gerald rested his head and body against the slick bedcovering. He'd never felt so worn out and exhilarated at the same time. The woman was insatiable! Didn't she realize a man needed to rest?

Cassie entered the bedroom with a bottle of wine. "Hey lover," she purred, crawling into bed.

He gaped at her. The woman didn't have a timid bone in her curvy body! Women in his time never walked around unclothed. His lips curved. It felt wonderful to be alive again! Maybe he'd just stay where he was.

*   *   *

Shekinah screeched, "Stop right there Grey!"

The sound of her voice broke his concentration, thus losing his grip of the two spirits so very nearly in his hands.

"Go to hell!" he bellowed.

"That's your job," Shekinah snapped. "When will you learn that good always conquers evil?"

Emily and Mitch gulped large amounts of air into their lungs, oblivious of the two behind them arguing.

Grey chuckled menacingly. "I've won this round Shekinah."

She lifted a defiant eyebrow, cast her palms above her and murmured a prayer. Ethereal light began to fill the room causing Grey to cower.

"She's mine!" he hissed. "I won't leave empty handed!"

"Take me!" Phyllis yelled, appearing from thin air. "You can have me."

"No!" Emily shouted, reaching for her.

Phyllis gripped her hand. "Em, it's time I face the music for what I did to my baby." Tears shimmered in her eyes and she swallowed hard. "It's *my* time to go, not *yours*."

"Take me, too!" Frankie bellowed materializing next to Phyllis. She cocked her head and he shot her a wink. "We're a team, baby."

Emily whimpered when Frankie wrapped his arm around Phyllis' shoulders.

Jared began to shake causing Emily to jump. She watched as Mitch's soul left Jared's body. His shook his shoulder length blonde hair. Then he palmed her cheek and shot her a wistful smile. "You can have me, too. Just leave Emily alone."

Grey brought a bony finger to his covered face, wiping an imaginary tear away. "How touching," he sneered. "Fine! Three rejects for her."

Emily gripped the billowy white sleeve from Shekinah's robe. "No! You can't let him take them!"

"My dear, it is their decision to go with him," Shekinah said softly. "They've traded their souls for yours."

*   *   *

Grey looked upon Gerald with a scowl and nudged him with his walking stick. "Time to go, Gerald."

Phyllis' eyes narrowed as a spirit departed from Chases' body. "Hey! Ain't that Chase?" Freddie mumbled.

"Yeah," Phyllis replied sadly. "Poor Emily will never know the truth."

*   *   *

Jared held Emily as she cried. Between sobs he was able to figure out the flapper and the greaser were her friends and now she had no one. Even Chase was out of the picture.

He wanted to console her, but felt no compassion; only numbness. He had all kinds of questions but all Emily could do was cry. So he held her until she finally drifted to sleep.

*   *   *

Chase stirred from a deep sleep. His arm was wrapped around Emily's waist, his nose nuzzled her hair.

He nuzzled his nose deeper, frowning. Her hair smelled of cigarette smoke.

He sat up on his elbow and looked down at her and gasped.

"What the fuck?" he growled, jumping from the bed.

His eyebrows lifted when he realized he was naked and still had a condom attached to his dick. His lips turned downward as he pulled it off and threw it on the bed.

He searched the room for his clothing and brought his foot down on something soft and gooey. Lifting his foot he scowled. Another used condom. His eyes scanned the floor and he counted five used condoms.

Six times? I fucked her six times?

He shook off the wave of nausea and quickly got dressed. He didn't bother putting his boxers on and shoved them in his coat pocket. He just wanted to get the fuck out of there before Cassie woke up.

He hoped the fucking chauffer was downstairs. If not, the guy's ass was grass and he was the goddamn lawnmower!

*   *   *

"Some night, huh, sir?" Randy asked with a smile.

Chases' stomach churned when he tried to remember the evening. The

300

last thing he remembered was Cassie making outlandish statements about Emily talking to ghosts.

"Um, Andy," Chase began.

"It's Randy, sir."

Chase rolled his eyes. *Like I give a fuck.* "Do you know why I didn't leave with Miss Waters?"

"I'm sorry, I don't understand your question," Randy replied, shifting in his seat.

Chase ran a hand through his greased hair. He cursed and wiped the shit on his pants. "I arrived at the theater with Miss Waters and not sure why I didn't leave with her. I thought you might know."

Randy shrugged, "I don't know sir."

Pinching the bridge of his nose, Chase rested the back of his head against the seat. His mouth was dry and tasted odd. His eyes grew large when he realized what the taste was.

He covered his mouth with his palm. "Stop the fucking car!" he screeched as his stomach convulsed.

*   *   *

Freddie walked into the house around noon and found Emily in Jared's arms on the couch. He nudged Jared's shoulder with a pointy index finger.

Jared's eyelids fluttered and opened wide when he saw Freddie standing in front of him with arms crossed over his chest and narrowed eyes.

"What the hell are you doing with my cousin?" he scowled.

"Um, sleeping?" Jared replied groggily.

"That better be all you're doing, pal," Freddie growled.

Emily awoke and pulled herself into a sitting position She brushed the

301

hair from her face and tucked it behind her ears. Warily she lifted her bloodshot and swollen eyes.

"Jesus Christ Emily! What happened to you?" Freddie sat on the coffee table and palmed her cheek.

She sniffled, "They're gone, Freddie and they're never coming back." Tears streamed down her face.

He cocked his head and murmured, "Who's gone, hon?"

"Phyllis and Frankie," she cried.

His eyebrows furrowed. "They went into the light? That's good, right?"

She stood and waved her hands. "No, it's not good! They didn't go into light! They traded their souls for mine!"

Freddie shot Jared a puzzled glance and returned his gaze to Emily.

She sighed sadly. "Coffee first then I'll explain everything."

*   *   *

Chase tore off his clothes the minute he entered his condo. He'd need to soap up five times to get the stench of Cassie off him and a bottle of acid to get the acrid taste of her from his mouth. The thought of him performing oral sex on her sent him running to the bathroom again to vomit.

Afterwards he pulled out a bottle of mouthwash and swirled the minty concoction around his mouth for several minutes. In fact, he used the whole damn bottle before brushing his teeth five times.

Cassie?

He shivered in disgust as he soaped himself. What the fuck lead him into her arms? Why the fuck couldn't he remember anything after running into her? And why the fuck was he so tired?

*   *   *

302

A smile formed on his lips as images of Emily flooded his dreams. Andrea stood alongside the bed, wringing her hands. Things didn't go the way she planned. Not only were Emily's friends taken from her, but Chase would never know the truth.

*   *   *

"So now what?" Freddie asked.

Emily stood and put her coffee mug into the sink. "Well, I have to pack for my trip tomorrow."

"You're still going?" Jenny asked.

Emily swallowed the lump in her throat. "Yeah, I gotta get away for a while. I might stay with my parents longer than a week. Just close the shop for a few weeks. We both need time to digest what's happened to us."

Freddie nodded to Jared. "What about you? What are you going to do?"

Jared pushed the chair under the table, shrugging. "Get on with my life."

Chapter Seventeen

The next day Emily arrived in West Palm Beach. The hired car barely stopped before her parents pulled her from the vehicle.

"Oh Emmy!" her dad crooned, pulling her into a hug.

Emily tried to smile, but tears fell freely and she broke out in uncontrollable sobs. Sam Waters shot a confused glance at his wife Martha.

*　　　*　　　*

Cassie Seton primped her hair as she walked down Michigan Avenue towards Storm Design Group's office. She gave him several days to recuperate from their sexcapade on Saturday night. No doubt Chase would be eager to see her.

A cunning grin slid across her face. Other than fucking him on a regular basis, she'd take him for everything she could, maybe even get pregnant. Not that she wanted kids. *Hell no!* But he'd be forced to pay through the nose for child support.

Deep in thought, she didn't heed the crossing signal and was killed instantly by a Chicago cabbie.

Grey grinned and took Cassie's hand as her soul left her body.

*　　　*　　　*

Emily smiled weakly when her mom handed her a glass of homemade lemonade. "Thanks mom," she sniffled.

"Emily, those weren't tears of joy," her father said softly as he rubbed her back. "What's wrong?"

Martha sat next to her daughter and brushed the hair from Emily's face. "Is it Chase?"

Emily sighed, "It's Chase, Phyllis and Frankie. They're gone."

*   *   *

Shekinah shrugged. Cassie Seton wasn't much of a loss. She looked heavenward, smiled and nodded. Grey didn't realize it yet, but he was now in check.

*   *   *

One minute Phyllis stood at the gates of hell, the smell of fire and brimstone burning her nose and the next minute she stood in darkness. The air felt cooler, calming even.

"Frankie?" she whispered.

A sudden burst of wind brushed past her and she heard rustling.

"Helloooo, baby," Frankie crooned, reaching out to her.

She clutched him tightly, burying her face into his chest. "Oh Frankie! I was scared I'd never see you again!"

Frankie held her tighter. "Me, too, doll." He caressed her cheek. "Hey, I never told ya, but as you'd say, I'm dizzy for ya."

Tears shimmered in her eyes. "Ah, don't be such a daisy," she replied hoarsely.

Frankie tilted her head back with his thumb and kissed her thoroughly.

"Okay you two, we've got work to do," Shekinah grinned.

*   *   *

"Why didn't you call us?" Sam Waters frowned.

Emily shrugged, "I didn't want you to worry, dad."

Her dad stood and paced the living room. "That's it! You're moving down here!"

Martha wrapped a reassuring arm around her daughter. "What your dad means is *if* you want to move in with us, you're more than welcome."

Sam's nostrils flared. "No, I meant she *is* moving down here!"

*   *   *

Chase woke up feeling rejuvenated. He hadn't slept that great since, well, *ever*. In fact, he didn't even need coffee. But, he noticed he *did* need a shower after getting a whiff of his underarms.

He showered quickly and barely dried himself off as he dashed to his pants laying by the door. Once he found his phone he checked the messages.

The first one was from Beth. She called him a string of obscenities then hung up.

The second was from Greg who wanted to know why Emily left with Buckley.

Buckley? Great! What the fuck?

He started to press a number into the phone when someone knocked on his door. Before pulling the door open he pulled the towel around his waist tighter.

"Hey Stormy," Jason murmured over his shoulder, walking in.

Chase waved his hand and sarcastically muttered, "Why don't you come in? Maybe make yourself at home while you're at it."

"I thought you might like to see this," Jason said snottily, handing Chase a newspaper.

Chase opened the paper and groaned, "Shit!"

"Nice picture of you with your hands on Cassie's ass." He looked over Chase's shoulder and amended, "My favorite is the one where it looks like your grinding your dick into her ass, very tasteful."

When Chase didn't respond derisively Jason moved in front of him. "Christ, Stormy, your face is almost as green as your towel."

"Fuck you," Chase growled, throwing the paper on the kitchen counter.

Jason laughed, "Hey, not here to cast judgment."

"Then why are you here?"

Jason sat on the leather couch and sighed, "To find out what the fuck got into you Saturday night."

Chase rolled his head back onto his shoulders. "I don't fucking know." He went into his bedroom and pulled out a pair of shorts and a t-shirt. "All I remember is Cassie accusing Emily of talking to ghosts. After that it's all a blank."

Jason lifted an eyebrow when Chase reentered the living room. "Is that it?"

"Yeah," Chase snorted, sitting on the couch. "Well, until I woke up this morning in Cassie's bed."

Jason blew out a hard breath. "You've been with her for three days?"

"Three days? It's only Sunday, dumbass!"

"It's Wednesday," Jason stated, crossing the room to retrieve the paper. He shoved it in Chase's face and pointed at the date. "See? Wednesday."

"What the fuck! I slept for three fucking days?" Chase growled, gripping the paper. "She must've put something in my drink!" His stomach roiled at the thought.

Jason rolled his eyes and sat down. "Saturday night you verbally attacked Emily, causing her to run outside. Beth and Neil ran after her and she nearly got ran over because she ran into the street."

308

Chase's eyes widened. "What the fuck did I say to her?"

"You told her she was a freak because she talked to ghosts," Jason replied sadly.

Chase leaned his head against the couch and closed his eyes. "Does she?"

"Talk to ghosts? Yeah," Jason mumbled.

He squeezed his eyes tighter and rubbed his temples with his forefingers. *Maybe she's only a little crazy,* he thought.

"She wanted to tell you, but was afraid you'd jet," Jason replied over his shoulder as he went to answer the knock at Chase's door.

"Dad?" Jason muttered.

Preston walked in with a file in his hand. "Hey Jason. What a surprise to see you here."

"Is everything okay?" Chase asked.

Preston glanced at the newspaper on the coffee table and lifted his grey eyebrows in displeasure. His gaze cut to Chase. "I thought you loved Emily."

Jason rocked back on his heels. "Um, yeah. I think I'm going to leave."

Chase and Preston dismissed him with a nod.

"Well?" Preston prompted after Jason left.

"I do," Chase muttered, ashamed. "Dad, I really don't know why I said those things to her." He stood and raked a hand through his hair. "It doesn't make sense. It's not like I had a lot to drink." His gaze drifted towards the photo in the newspaper. "Well, I mean before I said those things."

Preston sat on the couch and patted the seat next to him.

Chase eyed him warily before sitting. He lifted his chin to the folder in his dad's hand. "What's that?"

"Remember the night the four of us had dinner?" Preston began. Chase nodded and he continued, "Afterwards Emily pulled me aside and told me your mother communicated with her."

Chase's hands formed into fists and he tried to stand, but Preston pulled him down onto the couch.

"You're going to listen to what I have to say," he said sternly.

*   *   *

A wistful smile formed on Emily's lip as she dreamt of Phyllis and Frankie. They didn't seem to be in a bad place, in fact, they looked happy. The notion warmed her causing her to fall into a deeper, much needed rest.

*   *   *

"Well?" Preston asked after he told Chase what he learned from Emily.

"How do you know she didn't do some investigative work?" he hissed.

Preston waved the folder at him. "You're going to dismiss this? C'mon Chase! I searched the fucking internet for your mother for years and came up empty handed!"

Me, too, Chase thought glumly.

"Well, dad, love to stay and chat but I have to catch a plane to Paris in a few hours and need to pack."

"That's it then? You're going to walk away from the best thing that's ever happened to you?" Preston yelled.

Chase stood and turned abruptly. "I have a lot of shit to digest Preston. Get off my ass."

*   *   *

Passing the kitchen nook on his way out the door, Chase noticed the folder from his dad. He picked it up and threw it in his laptop case.

310

Downstairs a limo waited for him, but he stopped to see Rick first. He knocked gently.

A disheveled Rick pulled the door open. "Geez, Chase, you look like shit."

"Back at ya," Chase snipped. "I'm going to be gone for a while," he looked down at his feet, instead of his friends accusing eyes. "France."

"Taking Cassie with you?"

Chase's head jerked up. "What? No! What the fuck dude?"

Rick shrugged, "It's in all the papers, Chase. Hey, it's none of my business. I tell ya what though. If I had a girl as great as Emily I sure the hell wouldn't fuck it up."

"She thinks she talks to ghosts for fuck sakes!"

"How do you know she doesn't?"

Chase turned away and walked to the elevator. "Because ghosts don't fucking exist!" he spat over his shoulder.

*　　　*　　　*

Andrea giggled to herself. Her plan would work, it just had to!

*　　　*　　　*

The 10:00 p.m. departure for France was postponed temporarily due to mechanical problems. Since he had time to kill, Chase pulled out the manila folder and read the contents. His eyebrow lifted skeptically as he read the hospital documents. Then, when he lifted the final page in the folder and saw an envelope addressed to him, in his mother's hand, he picked up his carry-on bag and walked to the restroom.

Once the stall door was closed he opened the envelope and leaned against the door with his eyes closed.

When he was sure he was alone he slowly opened the letter. He glanced at the writing briefly, holding his breath. It was definitely his mom's

311

handwriting.

His throat became dry with each sentence he read and tears pooled in his eyes.

He read the letter several times, flushing the toilet to drown out his sobs.

A voice over the intercom announced that his flight was ready to board. Hastily, he wiped his eyes and blew his nose in toilet paper.

He took a cursory glance at himself in the mirror and lifted his chin. He had a flight to catch.

*   *   *

Emily awoke with the sun shining in her face. She sat up, stretched and tried to remember the last time she felt so rested. She glanced at the suitcase on the floor, then her purse. It was a silly notion, but she pulled out her cell phone and checked the messages.

She received several messages, but not one from Chase. Not that it'd matter. She saw the pictures of him in the paper. Her upper lip curled as she thought about the photo of him grinding his crotch into Cassie's backside.

Chase Storm could bite her ass!

*   *   *

Chase lifted his wrist from the bed and checked the time. He heaved a deep sigh and stumbled to the washroom for a quick shower. He had shit to do. A meeting so huge that it'd make him or break him.

*   *   *

Martha took her daughter downtown where she treated them to manicures and massages. Afterwards they had lunch and shopped.

"I have to admit, I wasn't looking forward to going out, but I'm really glad you pushed the issue," Emily smiled at her mom.

"Posh! Nothing makes a girl feel better than a manicure and a

312

massage!" her mom laughed, hoping a day on the town would cheer Emily up.

* * *

Once they returned home Emily threw on a pair of cut-off shorts and a bikini top. She grabbed her phone, a beach towel and headed out the sliding glass door to the beach.

She felt someone staring at her so she turned and saw her parents in the doorway. She laughed and shook her head. Some things never changed. When she was a child and walked to school they both stood on the sidewalk and watched her until she was out of sight.

* * *

Chase didn't know the area so he hired a driver to take him around. He glanced out the car window as the driver pulled to a stop. "Shall I wait for you sir?" the driver asked.

Wiping his hands on his khaki's, Chase muttered, "Yeah, that'd be great."

* * *

Chase had time to kill so he pulled his phone from his pocket and called Emily.

* * *

Emily placed her towel far enough away from the water. She had no desire to dip her toes in the Atlantic, but watched as others splashed around the blue water. A slight grin formed on her lips when she spotted a little boy building a sand castle with the help of his grandfather.

She wished she had her MP3 player, but couldn't find it before she left for Florida. She picked up her phone to listen to music when it rang.

Her breath caught when she saw Chase's name. She swallowed the lump in her throat and set the phone down on the towel.

* * *

313

"Fuck!" he muttered when she didn't answer.

He looked around and sat on a bench. Maybe she'd answer a text message.

Emily, please answer my call. I need to talk to you.

*   *   *

Her phone chimed, indicating a text message. She pushed a button and glanced at it from the corner of her eye.

Resolved, she responded.

What do you want, Chase?

He squared his shoulders.

The chance to talk to you and not by text messages.

She read the message and shook her head.

Fine!

*   *   *

His insides clenched as he dialed her number. He heard her pick-up, but she didn't say anything. "Emily?"

"Yes," she replied, pulling her legs to her chest.

"Emily, I'm so sorry."

Her shoulders sagged. "Okay."

He stared at his phone in disbelief. "Really?" He got to his feet and began to walk.

"Saying I forgive you means as much to me as you telling me you love me. *Absolutely nothing*," she snapped, with a caustic edge to her voice.

Abruptly, he stopped walking. "I deserve that," he replied softly. "But whether you believe it or not, I *do* love you."

Emily stood and paced. "Chase you once told me that you thought you were unlovable. I loved you but you looked for every opportunity to push me away. Well, congratulations because you finally did." Tears pooled in her eyes as she stared at the water.

She felt a hand on her shoulder and turned.

"God, Emily, I'm so sorry…" he choked out. He saw the pain in her eyes and felt it in his stomach.

A multitude of emotions ran through her. She wanted to believe him and throw herself into his arms but instead she backed away.

Her voice wavered. "Go home Chase. Go back to Cassie or whoever. I can't do this anymore." She picked up the beach towel and ran to the safety of her parents house.

*   *   *

Dejected, Chase knocked on the Water's door. Sam Water's gave him a thorough once-over. "I'm afraid she doesn't want to see you."

Chase fought to keep his voice from breaking. "I understand, Mr. Waters, but I need to see her."

Sam almost acquiesced until he heard his daughter's sobs from the bedroom. "I'm sorry Chase. Perhaps later…"

Tears stung the back of his eyes, but he lifted his chin and nodded. He took a card from his pocket and scribbled on it then handed it to Sam.

"Can you tell her I'm at the Marriott and leaving in the morning."

Sam nodded thoughtfully as Chase stepped away. "Chase? She's a headstrong woman, but worth the fight."

Chase turned, "Indeed she is."

*   *   *

Four hours later, and many bottles from the mini-bar, Chase gazed out the window into the city lights.

315

He pressed his forehead against the glass. He scoffed as tears fell from his eyes. "What the fuck?" he growled angrily, wiping them away.

Emily wasn't going to come and he didn't blame her. Even though he didn't remember saying those awful things to her, he said them nonetheless. He wanted to explain, but she wouldn't even give him a chance.

With that thought, he closed his suitcase, took a cursory glance of the room and left.

*   *   *

"Emmy, sweetheart, a man doesn't fly two thousand miles just for a *booty call* as you say," Sam Waters said softly. "I believe he loves you."

"He called me a *freak*, dad," she sobbed, blowing her nose into a tissue.

"Sometimes, when two people are in love, they say things they know will hurt the other person." Emily's eyes narrowed. Sam lifted his palm up. "It doesn't make it right, but it happens. Maybe he was jealous of this Brice fellow? Who knows why he said those things to you. If you give him a chance to explain himself…"

Emily pushed her chair away from the dining table. "I can't dad. I'm not ready to forgive him."

*   *   *

Chase trudged into his condo, throwing his suitcase on the floor. Even though he'd had enough to drink before his flight and during, he went to the wet bar and pulled out a bottle of Jameson. He peeled off his shirt and threw it on the floor on the way to the couch.

He sank into the plush sofa and felt something jabbing him in the ass. Scooting over he dug between the cushions and pulled out Emily's MP3 player with the ear buds attached. He carefully placed the buds in his ears and turned it on. Music filled his ears as tears filled his eyes.

After he took a healthy swig of whiskey he rested his head against the couch and closed his eyes.

Then, suddenly, he sat up and retrieved his laptop case from the kitchen nook. He sat on the stool and grabbed the notepad and pen next to the fruit bowl and began jotting down songs.

Songs that he hoped, in some small way, would show Emily just how much she meant to him.

*   *   *

Freddie tugged the front door open and pulled Emily into a hearty hug. "You should've let me pick you up from the airport!"

"I didn't want you to miss work," she murmured into his chest.

He pulled away and studied her face. "Ya better?"

"A little," she shrugged, walking towards the kitchen. She stopped when she spotted a package on the coffee table. "What's that?"

"Don't know. It came earlier."

She peered at the package and groaned. "It's from Chase."

"Yeah. I wasn't sure if I should throw it out..." he hedged.

She sat on the couch and held the small box in her hands. Slowly she peeled the brown shipping tape away from the seam. Inside was a note.

Emily,

Words can't begin to express how sorry I am. I hope the songs on your new I-Pod will. You once told me that I was out of your league. The truth is, you're out of mine. So I thought it only appropriate that the first song in the playlist be 'Out of My League' by Fitz and the Tantrums.

Yours,

Chase

p.s. I'm keeping your MP3 in exchange.

"Well?" Freddie prodded.

317

She waved him off and placed the buds in her ears and walked upstairs with her suitcase.

Once in her room she plugged the I-Pod into speakers and began to unpack.

She thought she'd cried herself out in Florida, but fresh tears fell as she listened to each song.

Several hours later she wiped her eyes and blew her nose.

Convinced she'd not shed another tear for Chase Storm.

*　　*　　*

Three weeks later

Chase tore open his door, hoping to see Emily. Instead Rick shot him a weak smile. "Bro, haven't seen you in a while. Wanted to make sure you're still alive."

"Barely," Chase shrugged. "Come in."

Rick eyed his friend warily. Chase's eyes looked shattered, tormented plus, he looked like hell and smelled funky. "Didja give up bathing?" he gently teased, walking into the living room.

Chase sighed. "Nah. Just got home. I've been working on the farmhouse."

"Why?" Rick snorted.

"Because I want Emily to have a nice home," he muttered, handing Rick a Corona.

"Have ya heard from her?"

Chase took a long swig of beer and shook his head. "She once told me she doesn't give second chances. Said that if it didn't work the first time, it wouldn't the second."

Rick shook his head, bewildered. "Then why the fuck are you wasting

318

time fixing that house? Why don't you raze it like you originally planned?"

Chase stared at him stonily. "Because I love her, man."

* * *

The shop wasn't the same without Phyllis and Frankie. Emily sighed when she passed the mortician table.

"Hi dear…feel up to company?" Lilly asked cautiously.

Emily smiled sadly. "Sure. How's things with Harold?"

Lilly smoothed her dress, frowning. "He thinks he's the reason Phyllis and Frankie are gone."

"Tell him he's not," Emily replied, emptying a box of depression glass.

The door chime rang. "Gotta go sell," Emily said half-heartedly.

She pasted a false smile on her lips. "Welcome to Play it again Sam."

"Hey Emily," Rick O'Shea grinned.

She cautiously walked towards him. "What's up?"

"My brother works for an interior decorator and wanted to check out your store. Blake, Max, come here. I'd like for you to meet someone."

Two handsome men strolled over. Emily couldn't tell who was related to Rick. They were both tall and looked to have rock solid bodies. Phyllis would've drooled at the sight of them.

Rick motioned with his hand, "Blake, this is Emily Waters, the owner of the shop."

Blake took her hand into his. "Very nice to meet you Emily. This is my boyfriend, Max."

She took Max's hand and shook it firmly with a friendly smile. "Hi Max, it's nice to meet both of you."

Rick expected Emily to be uneasy and was pleasantly surprised she wasn't.

"Are you two looking for something in particular?" she grinned.

"Not really, we're just browsing. You have wonderful items! I could go crazy decorating Ricky's condo, if he'd let me," frowned Blake.

Rick rolled his eyes and lifted the backs of his hands, waving them off. "Go and browse while I talk to Emily."

"If you find something you're interested in, I'm willing to barter," she called after them.

"Impressive," Rick stated, crossing his arms over his chest.

Emily cocked her head. "What's impressive?"

"It didn't freak you out that my brother's gay," he shrugged.

"Should it?" she laughed.

"I don't know. Some people can't accept it."

"I'm not one to judge. But enough of that. How've ya been?" she asked, moving towards the storage room.

"No complaints. You?" he nudged.

She removed newspaper from a plate and shrugged. "Not well, Rick."

"If it's any consolation, he's not great, either," he offered.

Emily placed her palms on the table. "You're not here to apologize for him again, are you?"

Rick lifted his hands. "Nope. *Honest*. Emily, just because you and Chase aren't together anymore doesn't mean you and I can't be friends. At least I hope it doesn't."

She crossed her arms over her chest. "Ground rules, then." He lifted a skeptical eyebrow and she continued. "One, no discussing *him* with me. Two, no discussing *me* with him. Three, I can see and talk to ghosts." She arched an eyebrow, expecting him to jet.

"Agree, Agree and I read the interview that Cassie did with the paper," he shrugged.

"Oh Emily? Honey, we found an armoire and Hoosier cabinet that we must have!" Blake exclaimed.

Her lips curved into a smile. "Duty calls," she mumbled, stepping by Rick.

*   *   *

Lilly and Harold beamed at their new owners when Emily handed them a receipt.

"Are you sure about this?" Emily asked softly. The new owners and the previous owners nodded their heads.

*   *   *

Chase pulled open the door to his condo. "Emily?" Unmistakable pain and wonder filled his voice. He reached out to her, but her form dissipated at his touch.

"Aw, look at him, Frankie! Even asleep he looks sad!" Phyllis mumbled.

"Whaddya doin'?" Frankie screeched when Phyllis sat on the edge of Chase's bed.

She brushed hair away from Chase's eyes. "Chase?"

Sleepily he lifted a hand to his face and rolled over.

"Chase?"

His eye shot open. Then, when he saw a figure sitting on his bed, the other eye shot open and he pushed himself to the other side of the bed.

"Who the fuck are you and how did you get into my house?" he shouted shakily.

Phyllis' mouth curved. "I'm Phyllis and that's Frankie. We're friends of Emily's."

Chase shook his head.

The flapper giggled and came closer.

*　　*　　*

"Ya wanna ride to the show tonight?" Freddie asked Emily the following week.

"Thanks, but Rick's picking me up," she replied, brushing away a wayward strand of hair.

He eyed her thoughtfully. "Is that why you're getting dolled up?"

"We're *just* friends," she snipped.

*　　*　　*

"For all that's holy! Call her for Pete's sake!" Phyllis whined.

"Look, you're her friends! Why the fuck are you haunting me?" Chase growled as he put the finishing touches on the jet tub.

"You missed a spot," Frankie muttered, pointing out an area that didn't have caulk.

"Oh, thanks," Chase mumbled, shaking his head. "Man, my tenuous grip on reality is quickly slipping away or…"

"Or what?" Phyllis pushed.

He sat on the floor and leaned against the wall. "Christ, I don't know."

Frankie motioned to Phyllis with his chin. "Tell him."

Phyllis yanked the ends of her boa. "About the hockey player?"

*　　*　　*

Rick blew out a whistle when Emily got into his Mustang. "I

322

should've brought my hockey stick to beat away the men tonight," he teased.

"I don't think that's necessary," she grinned, reaching into her purse for her ringing cell phone.

"Hello?" she answered.

When no one responded she disconnected the call and checked the caller ID, frowning. She called the number again, but no one answered.

"Um, Rick, I need to stop at the shop first."

He cocked his head. "Is something wrong?"

"There is when your shop calls you."

*   *   *

"Well, the thing is, Rick's taking Emily out tonight," Phyllis confessed.

"I'm gonna kick his ass! Fuckin' dick!" grumbled Chase.

Phyllis pursed her lips. "I thought Rick was a hockey player?"

Chase shot her an annoyed glance. "He is."

"But you just called him a dick. Ya know, a detective," she clarified.

Rolling his eyes he gestured to his nether region. "It means something completely different nowadays."

Phyllis' eyes widened at his gestures. Then she began to giggle. Loudly.

*   *   *

Later Chase sat at a small round white oak table in the newly refurbished kitchen as Alma placed her palms lovingly on the kitchen island.

Glancing up, his pen and notepad flew onto the floor. "Jesus Alma! Are you trying to give me a heart attack?"

"Nah. Not anymore. I kinda like you," she cooed, twirling in the kitchen. "I like what ya done to the place. Didn't think I would, but dammit! I

323

do!"

"I'm glad you approve," he replied dryly.

Her eyes narrowed. "Look sonny, I may be dead, but at least I ain't stupid."

Chase threw his pen on the table. "What the fuck is that supposed to mean?"

She sucked in an outraged breath. "I oughta give you a bar of soap to chew on!" She floated towards him. "Seems to me there's something missing in this house."

"Too bad it's not the ghosts," he muttered under his breath.

"Ya need to bring that lovely girl here. Make this place a home!"

"She doesn't want me," he replied sadly, standing. "Now, if you'll excuse me, I have a sunset to watch."

Alma watched him take a seat on the swing that he installed on the back porch and frowned.

Phyllis and Frankie appeared next to her. "Filly, it's time," Frankie said softly.

*   *   *

Rick opened the back door as quietly as he could. He pressed an index finger to his lips. Emily rolled her eyes.

Music wafted from the front of the store. Emily gasped, covering her lips with her fingers when she recognized Filly's favorite song, *Love Ain't Nothing But the Blues*.

Tears formed as she stumbled through the rooms. "Phyllis?"

"Hey doll."

Emily turned quickly in disbelief. "How?"

Phyllis shrugged, "Ya can't get rid of me that easy." She crossed the room to Emily and tried to wrap her arms around her.

"What's changed? Why can't I feel you anymore?" Emily asked with a catch in her voice.

"I think it's because you aren't close to the big sleep," Phyllis offered. "Em, we've gotta jaw."

*   *   *

Chase swayed on the swing when he really wanted to find Rick and beat the hell out of him. But instead, he waited for the sunset and ached for her.

*   *   *

Rick sat, transfixed, watching Emily converse with, well, air.

"I'm tellin' ya, I saw a ghoul rise out of Chase's body when creepy Grey took us that night," Phyllis stated firmly.

Emily rose slowly from the wrought iron bed and paced the small room. "So it wasn't really Chase saying those awful things?"

"Nope and that's why he doesn't remember what he said. Poor guy, he's been so sad."

Emily's eyebrows furrowed. "How would you know how sad he is?"

Phyllis' eyes darted as she slid the boa across her neck. "Applesauce!"

"Spill it!"

"I've been with Chase for a few weeks now," Phyllis said quickly.

"How could you? Don't you know how much I missed you and Frankie?" Emily gasped. "Is Frankie back too?"

Phyllis nodded sheepishly. "He and Chase are becoming pals." She bit her lip and continued, "Oh hell! It's not about me and Frankie! This is about you and Chase! He's been working day and night repairing that farmhouse. For

325

you!"

"Whoa! Wait! He can see you two?"

Phyllis nodded. "Yep! He's a very funny guy and I don't mind sayin' this...he has a *spectacular* ass!"

"You're impossible!" screeched Emily.

"No, you are. Go to him, Em."

*   *   *

On the ride to the concert venue Emily filled Rick in on what'd happened to her after the theater opening and the conversation she had with Phyllis.

Rick cleared his throat. "That's...surreal."

"You're tellin' me?" she snorted. "It happened to me and I still can't believe it."

He glanced at her. "So now that you know the truth, what are you going to do?"

"I don't know," she frowned.

*   *   *

After Phyllis told Chase where Emily and Rick were he jumped into his Porsche not sure what the outcome would be.

*   *   *

"Back by popular demand, my cousin, Emily Waters!" Freddie yelled into the microphone.

Emily crossed the stage, not feeling frightened anymore. She'd seen worse and survived. Singing was a snap now.

She grinned at Rick standing near the stage and belted out *Rescue Me*, one of the songs Chase put on her I-Pod.

326

Chase ground his teeth as he watched Emily gyrate on stage. *Her fucking dress is too short! And she's not wearing a bra!*

He crept closer to the stage, but hid in the crowd. Scanning the area he spotted Rick. His fists clenched at his sides.

Freddie asked for requests from the crowd. A few songs were yelled and Chase noticed Emily flinch at one of the titles. Then the crowd began to chant the song title. She looked at Freddie and shook her head sadly.

The crowd chanted the song louder and some began singing it. Emily breathed deeply and finally nodded.

She gripped the microphone stand and began singing softly.

Chase moved closer, in an effort to hear her, and his chest clenched when he heard the song. It was the song she sang for him on the fourth of July.

Her voice cracked several times as she sang. She tried to get the images of Chase out of her head as she sang, but dammit! She couldn't. The way he looked at her that night, how it was the first time she told him she loved him and the fabulous sex afterwards!

She ached for him and instead of listening to him, she dismissed him. Would he even want to talk to her now?

Tears fell down her cheeks as sobs racked her chest. She shook her head and ran away from the microphone.

Rick met her backstage and held her as she cried.

Now he knew what Chase meant when he said he felt helpless when she cried. Once he got her into his car he'd drive her to Chase's so the two of them could get their shit together. They belonged together and were too stubborn to realize it.

He felt a pointy finger jabbing his shoulder. He ignored it, focusing only on Emily's needs, until the jabbing got firmer, testier.

"Get your fucking hands off her!" Chase growled.

Emily lifted her cheek from Rick's chest and peered around him.

Chase's blue eyes smoldered and the veins in the backs of his hands protruded.

She hesitated, unsure what to do. Rick murmured, "Go on…"

She swallowed hard and walked unsteadily towards Chase.

His expression twisted with pained torment, knowing it'd kill him if she walked past him.

Instead she wrapped her arms around his waist and sobbed into his shirt. His breath caught in his chest as he ran his hand nervously over her hair.

Finally, he wrapped his arms around her and lifted her. His lips found hers and he kissed her with such intensity that it took her breath away.

He gently set her back on her feet, reluctant to break contact. "We're causing a scene," he mumbled huskily.

She straightened her shoulders and shot him a teary grin. "Then take me home."

Chapter Eighteen

Emily couldn't believe the transformation of the house, let alone the landscaping! Flowerbeds surrounding the front porch were filled with perennials along with little lights showcasing the front of the house.

She took a deep breath as she gripped the railing and walked up the steps.

"The rotted boards are gone," he said huskily.

She nodded. "So I see." She slowly turned to look at him. His hands were deep in his jean pockets and his hair was disheveled. "*You* were the person who made an offer on the house?"

"Guilty," he shrugged.

"But why? You hated this house."

"Because you said it was your house. Now, it really is," he murmured. He grasped her hand, linking their fingers. "Come on."

Emily's heart clenched. Even though the home was updated, Chase maintained it's old fashioned charm.

"Chase, it's beautiful."

He tugged her hand. "Wait 'til you see the upstairs."

He began showing her the guest rooms and the newly updated bathroom with a claw-footed tub when she breathily said, "I'm only interested in the master bedroom at the moment."

His nose wrinkled. "I probably smell like a barnyard. Phyllis told me where you'd be, so I raced over before showering."

Her lips curved when she sniffed his chest, then she knelt lower, brushing her nose against his crotch. "You smell mighty fine, Mr. Storm."

He pulled her up and cradled her head between his hands. "God, Emily, I thought I lost you."

"Kiss her, ya boob!" Phyllis hissed.

Chase lowered his lips to Emily's. "She never shuts up, does she?"

Emily giggled. "I think you'd better kiss me before she bursts."

After several minutes of kissing Phyllis broke in. "Okay, you two! We've got jawing to do!"

Frankie and Alma appeared, each tugging on one of Phyllis' arms.

*   *   *

He lifted her. "Wrap your legs around me," he rasped, between kisses.

She released a soft growl and gently grabbed a fistful of his hair. A moan escaped from his lips, causing her to smile.

Chase carried her to the bedroom, pushing the door closed with his foot. He walked past the antique sleigh bed, eliciting a whimper from her. He smiled beneath her lips and took her into the bathroom.

Her body slowly slid down his, breaking contact with his lips. He pulled away slightly, turning her around.

"Oh my!" she squeaked, with a hand over her mouth. The bathroom was larger than the one in his condo.

He dug his hands into his pockets and blushed when she glanced at him. "The house had more bedrooms than we'll ever need," he shrugged. "So I converted two into one bathroom."

330

"So I see," she grinned, grasping his hand. "I like the glass shower, by the way."

His cheek lifted. "What about the small pool?"

"Oh yeah, I like that, too. In fact, we might have to use both tonight," she leered.

His eyes smoldered at her expression. "Holy hell woman! I'm ready to burst now!"

She glanced at his waist, then lower. An expression of mirth covered her face. "I noticed," she teased. Turning, she murmured, "Can you unzip me?"

He swallowed hard and placed his palms on her bare shoulders. With her hair swept up into a clip he had easy access to her neck. He left a trail of kisses from shoulder to shoulder as he unzipped her dress. Deftly he palmed her throat, and ran his warm tongue along her ear and neck as he lowered her dress.

She leaned into him, moaning softly, when he tugged at her nipples until the rosy peaks grew to pebble hardness. Slowly his hands moved downward, pushing the light fabric away until it pooled at her feet.

He turned her so he could look at her. Emily's eyes hooded when he swept a long, lusty gaze over her.

She lifted his blue shirt up and over his head, casting it to the floor. Her eyes didn't leave his as she slid his jeans and briefs down. Kneeling at his feet, he held onto her shoulders as she removed the binding clothing.

Meeting his gaze, she ran her tongue over the length of him. He released a low hiss as her tongue circled him. "Em, I don't think..." he moaned.

She shot him a wicked grin and took him deeply into her mouth.

Chase removed the clip from her hair and fanned his fingers through her long tresses. She shot him a look so intense that he nearly lost it.

She gripped his backside and felt his muscles bunch beneath her touch. Chase let her set the pace even though he wanted nothing more than to pump faster. God, he was so close.

Sensing his need she made quicker, longer strokes sending him over the edge. He gripped her head tightly, trembling as the warmth from his seed spilled into her mouth. "Fuck!" he gasped.

Emily continued her ministrations until he pulled away from her. He cradled her head in his hands. He drew a long, slow breath. "That was…wow."

She stood and began to remove her high heels when he stopped her. "Uh-uh," he rasped, sweeping her into his arms.

He carried her to the sleigh bed and gently eased her down onto the antique quilt. His heated eyes raked over her slowly before he covered her body with his.

The prolonged anticipation of what was to come sent a tingling to the pit of her stomach.

His tongue gently circled her lips. She parted her lips greedily until she felt the warmth of his tongue against hers. Wanting more she twisted to straddle him. The corners of his mouth lifted against hers. "Someone's a wee bit aggressive tonight," he mumbled against her lips.

She shoved her tongue deeper into his mouth, exploring it fully. She'd never felt so wonton in her life! Her skin tingled as he ran his smooth hands over her back, her arms, her breasts.

He pulled himself up into a sitting position and ran kisses along her jaw then lower to her breasts. He cradled one in each hand, kissing and sucking in a heated frenzy. The gentle pressure of his mouth and tongue swirling over her nipples elicited a shudder that shook her body and she knew he felt it.

She sucked in a ragged breath when he took her by the shoulders and eased her down to the bed. His hands smoothed over her, leaving her skin sensitized everywhere. Slowly he removed her black lace panties and held them up to his nose, shooting a look so hot and intense, she thought she'd melt into the bedding.

Her back arched when he dipped a finger inside of her and brushed it against her clit. He loved the way her body responded to his touch. "God, Em, you're ready to burst, aren't you?" he teased.

She grabbed his hand and placed it against her, pushing down. A deep laugh bubbled from him. "Now where's the fun in that?" he asked as he lowered his head.

Sliding two fingers inside of her, he gently sucked and nibbled on her folds. A moan, low and deep, escaped from her lips when he ran his tongue softly over her bulging nub.

Her body squirmed under his stroking fingers. Every touch of his tongue sent pleasant jolts through her. She cried out, "Faster!"

His tongue slid up and down while his fingers moved in and out at a fast speed. When he felt she was near, he slowed his pace. "Chase!" she impatiently moaned.

He picked up the pace and when he felt her body become rigid, he went faster, pushing her over the edge.

She exploded in a downpour of fiery sensations. She lay panting, her chest heaving. He crawled beside her and rested his head onto his hand. "I crushed you, didn't I?" he grinned.

She playfully pushed his face away.

He ran his index finger from her neck down to her mound, causing her to quiver again. His cheek lifted. "Ready for round three?"

*   *   *

They showered and took their time exploring each other. Emily glanced at the fiberglass bench against the wall in the shower. "What's that for?" she asked.

Chase wiggled his brows. "What do you think?"

She blushed under his gaze and pulled him towards it. He grabbed her around the waist. "I'd rather make love to you in bed," he rasped into her ear.

"What are you waiting for then?" she grinned.

*   *   *

His voice was soft and seductive. "Get on your hands and knees."

She squeaked, "Huh?"

Chase's head cocked and a slow smile crept across his face as he kissed her hand. "Dog style?"

Emily blushed at her inexperience. "Okay…"

He palmed her cheek. "I thought we'd try something different, but if you're not up to it…"

She shot him a devastating grin and climbed on the bed. His breath caught in his chest at the sight. And then, when she wiggled her ass at him! *Gah!* He climbed hungrily over her and ran a trail of kisses down her spine. He planted warm kisses on each ass cheek and ran his tongue along the seam.

The feel of his tongue *there* shocked her. "Relax and rest on your elbows," he commanded.

He spread her thighs apart and licked the center of her. She thought she'd burst from the sensuality of his actions. The sensations she felt in this position were intense.

He slid in slowly until he filled her and gasped raggedly. Her breath hitched when he pulled out, then slammed deeply into her. "Did I hurt you?" he spluttered.

She turned her head, grinning. "No, I can feel more of you this way."

He nodded and gripped her hips tightly. He pushed in and out several times and withdrew. She started to protest until she felt his tongue covering her again. She was near the edge when he entered her again.

"Donnn't stop!" she groaned, arching into him.

"Give it to me, Emily!" he rasped, slamming into her.

Her insides clenched while her body shook from the most intense orgasm she ever had. He erupted inside her, calling out her name.

After their spasms subsided, he withdrew and fell onto the bed, pulling her against his body. He panted, "Sex with you is so intense."

She lazily ran her hand over his chest. "Why do you suppose that is?"

"Because I love you Emily."

*　　　*　　　*

Later, she threw on one of his t-shirts and he put on a pair of shorts and together they headed downstairs to the kitchen.

Her eyes lit up when he flipped on the lights. "It's just what I pictured!" she gasped.

He walked towards the fridge. "Ya like it then?"

She nuzzled her face into his shoulder blades. "I love it."

Chase turned and offered her a beer. Instead she opted for bottled water. "What about me?" he asked. She cocked her head and he frowned slightly. "Do you love me? I mean, you haven't said it at all tonight and I've told you twice," he mumbled.

She gently caressed his cheek. He closed his eyes and leaned into her hand. "Of course I love you, Chase."

He shrugged, "Sorry, I'm feeling needy nowadays." He hugged her tightly. "Em, I'm so sorry for those awful things I said to you. I don't even know why I said them."

She pulled away. "Yeah, about that. You didn't really say those things to me."

His eyebrows knitted together. "I don't understand."

"Now can we jaw?" Phyllis blurted, appearing in the kitchen doorway.

*　　　*　　　*

Together Emily and Phyllis gave Chase a brief summary of what happened that night at the Grandview. Afterwards Chase blew out a long breath.

"Christ Emily! You almost died twice that night!"

She gripped his hand. "If it wasn't for Jared, well I mean Mitch, I might've."

Chase lifted an eyebrow. "Have you seen Fuckley since?"

"No," she sighed sadly. "He said that he needed to get on with his life. I feel bad because he went through some heavy shit, too, and I'm not sure he has anyone to talk to it about like I have."

Chase's head fell back and he closed his eyes. "Em...you do know that I didn't mean to have sex with Cassie that night, right?"

She frowned. "Yeah. I hope you used protection!"

"I used six!" he grimaced.

"Damn!" Frankie laughed. Phyllis poked him in the ribs.

Emily gazed at Phyllis and cocked her head. "Filly, if you and Frankie came back a while ago, how did you end up at Chase's house and not mine?"

"Aw, doll," Phyllis replied sadly and motioned her head towards Chase. "I needed to be sure he really loved you." She walked towards Emily with her palms up. "Ya should've seen him, sweetie. He was cut up!"

Chase rolled his eyes. "I wasn't that bad."

Frankie crossed his arms over his chest and lifted his chin. "Yeah, you were. Especially when you put songs on that little record player for her. Even I misted up."

Chase scooted his chair from the table. "Well, she didn't call, didn't text. How the fuck was I supposed to feel?" He paced the large kitchen. "So, instead of cutting a wrist I threw my energy into rehabbing the house because the contractor's I hired would only work a day because Alma scared them shitless."

Phyllis grinned. "Yeah! But when she realized you weren't going to knock the house down she stopped scaring them."

Emily crossed the room to Chase and cupped his cheek. "What would've you done with the house if we didn't get back together?"

"I had my lawyer draw up papers giving you sole ownership of the house. I wanted you to have it even if you didn't want me," he shrugged sadly.

*   *   *

"I like the bed," she said softly.

Chase wrapped an arm around her, pulling her back against his chest. "Em? Can I ask you a question?"

She lazily ran her fingers along his arm. "Of course."

"Is there something...I mean..." he stammered.

Moonlight filtered through the gauzy curtains. She rolled over and searched his face in the sparse light. "What Chase?"

He released a puff of air. "Rick. Do I have a reason to kick his ass?"

She laughed gently and cupped his cheek. "No, silly. We're just friends." He shot an apprehensive look at her. "He wasn't trying to move in on me. Honest."

She rolled over, snuggling against his chest. "I love you, Chase."

Satisfied, he planted a kiss on her head and fell into a deep sleep.

*   *   *

"So...you're okay with my ghosts?" Emily questioned the next morning.

Chase took a sip of coffee and placed his mug on the table. "Kinda my ghosts, too." He whipped his head around when he felt a subtle ruffling of his hair. "Knock it off Phyllis," he huffed.

Emily cocked her head and smiled past him.

His eyebrows knitted together at her demeanor and he turned in his chair. "Mom?" he choked out.

She cupped his cheek. "Hi Chasey." Tears welled in his eyes. "There's no time for that," she gently scolded. "You've a wedding to plan and a nursery to prepare!"

"Huh?' Chase squeaked.

Andrea clapped her hands together in glee. "Well, not right away, of course, but soon! The baby I mean! Oh dear! I'm babbling!"

"I'll say," Phyllis snorted. "Tick tock, lady. You know the rules."

"You're right, flapper girl. Chase, you know I love you, right?"

His voice wavered, "Yeah. The letter you left helped. I just wish you would've stayed, mom. It was so hard for me."

Andrea's hands knotted in front of her. "I know and I'm sorry, but I was with you every step of the way. I'll always be with you."

When she began to fade away Chase blurted, "I love you mom!"

She grinned, "I love you, Chasey! Take care of him Emily!"

Chapter Nineteen

Six months later

Chase sidled up to the bar with two champagne glasses in his hands. "Hey sexy, how about a drink?"

Rick took a glass, smiling. "Ya did it, man! Never thought this day would come."

Chase grinned as he gazed at his bride on the dance floor with her dad Sam. "Yeah. I knew the minute I saw her that she'd change my life." He glanced at his friend. "It's your turn, bro."

"Kinda hard to find someone as great as Emily. All I get are puck bunnies."

"Puck bunnies?" Chase laughed and shook his head. "Never heard that term before."

Rick shrugged, "Yeah. No depth to them at all. Just a bunch of hollow chicks."

Chase eyed his friend thoughtfully and slapped him on the back. "You'll find her when you least expect it."

"Maybe. So ya headin' out tonight?" Rick asked.

"Nah. Tomorrow night." Chase took a sip of champagne. "My friends Greg and Tamara got us a room at a B&B on the east coast of Ireland. Their friends own the place and oddly enough, they're able to communicate with ghosts, too."

"No shit?" Rick asked incredulously.

Chase lifted his shoulders. "I think Emily is more excited about meeting them than the actual trip to Ireland."

Rick set his glass on the bar. "I better get my dance in with the bride. I got an early flight tomorrow."

"That's right! You're gonna kick Vancouver's ass right?"

"Damn straight!" Rick replied seriously. "You'll be back before the playoffs, right?"

Chase grinned, "Em would have my ass if we didn't. By the way, she really loves her O'Shea jersey. Especially since I used her Brice jersey for paintball practice."

*   *   *

Emily closed her suitcase and studied her friend. "What's up, Filly?"

"I'm gonna miss you," Phyllis sighed sadly plopping on the bed.

Chase entered the room with a towel wrapped around his waist. "Yeah, right," he snorted.

"I am!" Phyllis pouted. "You're going to be gone a whole month!"

"Look at it this way," Chase began. "You and Frankie can have all the wild sex you want and we won't have to hear you!"

"Oh no," Emily whispered.

Chase's eyebrows furrowed. "What? You hear them too! They're loud enough to wake the friggin' dead!"

When Emily and Phyllis didn't reply with sarcastic remarks he turned to look at them. The expressions on their faces made his stomach queasy. "What?" he rasped.

Emily pointed toward the doorway with dread etched on her face.

Chase wrapped a protective arm around Emily and pointed at the long blonde haired woman dressed in a white flowing robe. "Who the fuck is she?"

"My name is Shekinah," she replied softly. "Do not fear me, Chase."

Frankie quickly appeared next to Phyllis and mimicked Chase's actions. Phyllis wrapped her arms around his waist and shivered.

Shekinah glided towards the foursome with her hands outstretched. "I've come with news." When no one responded she sighed softly. "The Grey One will not bother you again, Emily. But…"

Chase squared his shoulders. "But what?" he snapped.

Shekinah cocked her head. "I need to take a soul with me."

Emily's eyes filled with tears. "Who?"

Alma appeared in the doorway, fixing her bun. "Me! I feel like a fifth wheel here. The four of you carrying on and such! Besides, I only stuck around to make sure my house was safe." She shot Chase an appreciative grin. "No need for me to stay."

"You're going into the light or whatever, right?" Chase asked softly.

"Don't know how much light there's gonna be with that jackass Lenny, but it's time for me to go," she shrugged.

Shekinah reached for Alma's hand. "Come along, Alma."

The two began to fade when Chase shouted, "Wait!" They turned and studied him curiously. He raked his hands through his damp hair. "Alma, I may not have told you, but you're a hell of a woman and I want to thank you."

The corner of Alma's mouth lifted. "For what?"

"For making me see what a great home you have," he replied hoarsely.

Alma nodded thoughtfully as she and Shekinah began to fade again.

Phyllis shouted, "Wait!"

"What now?" Alma frowned.

"Shekinah, are you sure the creepy guy isn't coming back?" Phyllis asked hurriedly.

"Yes, our game is over," Shekinah nodded.

"Game?" Chase snarled.

Shekinah shrugged, "It's something we do." She smiled slightly. "He tries to take all the souls he can and I stop him or take the good ones."

Emily's eyes widened. "You play a game with people's souls?"

Shekinah lifted her shoulders unapologetically, "Yes."

*   *   *

Four hours into their flight Chase glanced around first class at the passengers in various stages of sleep. He lifted Emily's hand to his lips and brushed a gentle kiss across the back of it. Her eyelids fluttered at his touch.

"Hello Mrs. Storm," he said softly.

She smiled lazily at him. "Hi Mr. Storm."

He ran his thumb along her thumb. "Thank you."

Her head tilted. "For?"

He shot her a mischievious grin. "The best airplane sex ever!"

"Huh?" she squeaked.

A corner of his mouth lifted as he slid from the seat. "Come," he murmured.

Emily's eyebrows knitted together. "Where?"

Chase wiggled his eyebrows. "To the washroom." She shot him a quizzical look and he grinned. "To be inducted into the mile high club."

About the Author

Kerrie DuBrock is an Office Manager by day and a romance writer by night. Her life-long interest in all things 'woo-woo' give her story's a unique twist. She is currently at work on her fourth book. She lives in the Chicago area with her husband, Roy and daughter Rachel along with Wolfie, a Doberman and two precocious cats, Twilight and Minnie.

To keep up with Kerrie and her ramblings check out these sites:

Face Book: Kerrie DuBrock Romance Writer

Twitter: @KerrieDuBrock

Website: kerriedubrock.wix.com/romancewriter

Blog: kerriegraydubrock.blogspot.com

www.ingramcontent.com/pod-product-compliance
Lightning Source LLC
Chambersburg PA
CBHW071041250626
47159CB00002B/331